Penguin Books
Captain James Cook

John Hooker was born in New Zealand in 1932. Educated in Auckland, he has lived in Australia since 1963. He worked in publishing before becoming a full-time writer. His books include *Jacob's Season*, *The Bush Season* and *Standing Orders*.

Peter Yeldham is one of Australia's leading screen and television writers. He has worked in England where he wrote and originated many top British television series. Since returning to Australia in 1976 he has written numerous mini-series including the multi-award winning *1915*, *All the Rivers Run*, and *The Far Country*.

CAPTAIN JAMES COOK

John Hooker
Based on the screenplay by Peter Yeldham

Penguin Books

PENGUIN BOOKS

Published by the Penguin Group
27 Wrights Lane, London W8 5TZ, England
Viking Penguin Inc., 40 West 23rd Street, New York, New York 10010, USA
Penguin Books Australia Ltd, Ringwood, Victoria, Australia
Penguin Books Canada Ltd, 2801 John Street, Markham, Ontario, Canada L3R 1B4
Penguin Books (NZ) Ltd, 182–190 Wairau Road, Auckland 10, New Zealand

Penguin Books Ltd, Registered Offices: Harmondsworth, Middlesex, England

First published 1987
Reprinted 1988

Copyright © John Hooker, 1987
All rights reserved

Based on the screenplay written by Peter Yeldham
for the Revcom/ABC Co-production of 'Captain James Cook'

Printed and bound in Great Britain by
Cox & Wyman Ltd, Reading

Contents

Featuring in the Revcom/ABC series

Keith Michell as Captain James Cook

John Gregg as Joseph Banks

Fernando Rey as Sir Edward Hawke, the First Lord of the Admiralty

Carol Drinkwater as Elizabeth Cook

Steven Grives as Marine Sergeant Gibson

Eric Hallhuber as Lieutenant John Gore

Jacques Penot as Lieutenant Charles Clerke

David Whitney as Mister William Bligh

Prologue

James and Elizabeth Cook sat close in the carriage as it rattled along the rutted country road. The Lincolnshire fields were green, the hedges high and the oaks spread their shadows across the turf where the prime cattle and sheep browsed. This was the heartland of England, Cook thought, here great estates spread as far as the eye could see. This was the place of the hunt, fine castles and stately manor houses, the domain of a society he did not belong to. He was the son of a day-labourer and had been apprenticed to a Whitby coal shipper.

Now he was going to Revesby Abbey, the home of the Banks family. Why had he been summoned there by Sir Edward Hawke, First Lord of the Admiralty? As he was a non commissioned officer he was somewhat surprised that Hawke would bother with him. Cook sat, straight and erect, watching the countryside roll by. Before long, he would have his answer.

'How far is it now?' Elizabeth asked.

Cook consulted the sketch map he had been given. 'Not far,' he said. 'Not far.'

Through the oaks, cypresses and elders, they saw the

1

towers of Revesby Abbey. Cook remembered his parents' house in the narrow street of his native Yorkshire village and smiled to himself. The estate was vast: the Banks family had done well, making their money from the law. The fourth son however, Joseph, was a botanist who also had been to Newfoundland and Labrador. And, Cook had heard, not only was young Banks a brilliant scientist, he was also a fashionable man-about-town. Banks was a man who did have friends at court, one of whom was Sir Edward Hawke. No matter about that, Cook thought, he would acquit himself well, whatever the purpose of this meeting. He took Elizabeth's hand and helped her from the carriage. Peacocks strutted on the lawn, pigeons warbled in the eaves and a young couple were walking toward a gazebo. Cook took all this in: this was how his betters lived.

Servants lined the steps of the main entrance.

'I am told that Mr Joseph Banks is expecting us,' Cook said as he and Elizabeth gave their capes and went into the vast, panelled hall. 'What a botanist wants with me, I cannot imagine.'

'I am sure, James, you will do your best,' she replied quietly. 'I have every faith in you.'

He was pleased and comforted as they followed the butler down the marbled corridor.

The reception room was crowded with handsome men and women whose talk and laughter rose above the faint strains of a string quartet. Servants moved discreetly among the guests with silver trays. Cook thought he recognised Banks at the centre of the group but waited for the butler to announce them. The talking ceased and Cook knew they were being inspected. He wished he were at sea: inspection was *his* prerogative there. A tall young man left the group and said:

2

'Welcome to Revesby Abbey. I, sir, am Joseph Banks.' His eyes were bright and smile broad.

'This,' Cook replied, 'is my wife, Elizabeth.'

The young man bowed. 'I'd begun to fear you were not coming. I trust the journey was not too tedious.'

'It was not,' Cook said, looking straight at Banks. 'I fear we've not come dressed for such a social occasion.'

'Social occasion? Just a few friends. Allow me to congratulate you.'

'On what, sir?'

'On your wife. She's uncommonly handsome.' The guests laughed as Banks smiled.

'You find that so unlikely,' Elizabeth said, 'that it requires comment?'

But Banks was quite unruffled. 'Madame, I was paying you a compliment.'

'At the expense of my husband. I don't find that complimentary.' Cook stood close at hand, he was proud of her.

'I am rebuked, madame,' Banks said. 'May I envy Surveyor Cook without risking more displeasure?' He smiled once more – without doubt, he was a charming young man. The guests began to drift away as Banks introduced the notables. 'Mr Cook,' Banks said at last, 'this is Sir Edward Hawke, the First Lord of the Admiralty.'

Hawke's eyes were as clear and blue as ice. 'Cook? Is that your name?'

'It is, sir.'

Hawke nodded to Elizabeth. 'Good. We should talk somewhere more private.'

The First Lord turned and strode off leaving Cook and Banks to follow him.

Leatherbound books lined the study wall and maps,

3

instruments and botanical specimens lay on the table. An inviting fire burned in the grate. Hawke chose the most comfortable chair, poured himself a generous glass of madeira and passed the decanter to Banks. He left Cook standing as he consulted a document.

'James Cook,' Hawke said, 'surveyor and ship's master of the *Grenville.* You navigated the St Lawrence River for General Wolfe and mapped the coast of Newfoundland?'

'I did, sir.'

Cook had served with the Royal Navy in the Seven Years' War, taken part in the capture of Quebec under General Wolfe and helped survey the coast of Newfoundland and Labrador. But there had been no recognition of his services: he had no friends at court. Nor did he want them – he was too proud for that.

'You were promised a commissioned rank and three times turned down by the Naval Board?'

'I was.'

'Did that not cool your enthusiasm for naval life?'

'Rather, it made me angry, sir.'

'You know,' Hawke said, 'that an expedition is planned for the South Seas?'

'I have heard so, sir. And I've heard that it will be commanded by a gentleman called Dalrymple.'

'Where did you hear that?'

'River talk, my Lord. I have no occasion to frequent the salons.'

'Alexander Dalrymple is infrequently mentioned there,' Banks broke in. 'But he has occupied the proceedings of the Royal Society – at some length.' He raised his eyebrows and went on. 'I am told there are no naval officers eager to volunteer for such a venture?'

'That hardly surprises me.' Cook was not completely

at a loss to understand where all this was heading and he was coming to realise that Joseph Banks was no mere fop. He recalled how this young man, at the age of twenty-three, had taken part in one of the most interesting voyages of natural history so far made. 'Why would no naval officer volunteer for a voyage to the South Seas?' Hawke asked as he put his glass on the table.

'There are no accurate maps,' Cook replied. 'The expedition will spend years at sea and risk being forgotten; there is no prospect to stir the ambitions of the upper deck.'

'Do you not think so?' Hawke and Banks considered this straightforward man.

'What ship would *you* send?' Hawke asked.

Another leading question, Cook thought, and he waited before giving his reply. 'A Whitby 'cat'.'

Hawke laughed. 'A collier? Are you suggesting the Navy recruits a North Sea coal ship.'

'I was asked for my opinion, sir.'

'You were, indeed. Indeed you were.' Hawke rose and stretched his legs. 'And I'm obliged to you, Surveyor Cook. Good day.' Once more the First Lord strode out leaving Cook puzzled as to what all this was about.

That evening, Hawke and Banks sat once more in the study. They drank port as the coals of the fire glowed.

'A Whitby coal cat?' the First Lord said. 'Why on earth would a man want to send a ship like that to the bottom of the world?'

'Is it such a ridiculous choice?' Banks' mind went back to the shoals of Newfoundland. And he thought again of Cook: a big man with honest answers and a steady gaze.

'A cat, my dear Banks, is an ugly ship. It has a fat, uncompromising bow, austere masts and rigging. It's a graceless cutwater, a lowly vessel, a draught horse when we have access to a fleet of thoroughbreds.'

'Then Cook made a poor impression on you?'

'I didn't say that: he comes recommended by Palliser. But there have been mistakes enough. This time, England wants the right man.'

'Not a labourer's son?'

'My job, sir, is to run the Admiralty, not to enquire into a man's antecedents.' Hawke sighed and shook his head. 'We shall see.'

Three weeks earlier, Joseph Banks had attended yet another discourse on the Great South Land this time given by Alexander Dalrymple. The Scottish geographer was a self-proclaimed expert on the 'problem'. Was there a great land mass in the South Seas to balance the weight of the continent of Europe in the north? Banks had read all the theories since that of the Egyptian geographer, Ptolemy, who believed that an unknown land in the south joined the southern coast of Africa, making the Indian Ocean a great inland sea. This had been disproved by the explorers, Diaz and da Gama, but now as late as 1768, the idea of a rich and enchanted continent persisted. And despite the voyages of Magellan and Tasman, the Pacific Ocean was still to be mapped. Was there a last great continent to be discovered? Despite his open mind, Banks doubted it. But he was a natural explorer, and after his voyage to Newfoundland, he longed to travel more – to discover unknown shores and to add to his burgeoning collection of exotic plants.

Now he was to have the chance he was to join an expedition the British Government was about to launch to explore the mysteries of the Pacific, the King had voted £4000 toward the project, and Dalrymple had been chosen by the Royal Society to command the voyage. The benches of the lecture room of the Royal Society were crowded with the leaders of science and the Enlightenment. Even though he had heard it all before Banks listened to Dalrymple carefully. Dalrymple was a zealot, he *believed* in the South Land. But Joseph Banks knew that geography was the science of facts – not unsupported theory.

The President of the Royal Society, the Earl of Morton, rose and rapped his gavel for silence. The first objective of the forthcoming voyage, he said, was to observe the transit of the planet Venus across the face of the sun at Otaheite. This event would not recur for another ninety-nine years and was important for the purposes of navigation. Then, the expedition would voyage south to seek the land that Tasman, Dampier and the other explorers had missed. The Earl introduced Mr Alexander Dalrymple.

'I have been chosen,' Dalrymple declaimed, 'to lead this expedition because I am the best qualified in the United Kingdom. My research has proved that the southern continent stretches from the equator through the tropics to the frigid zones at the very bottom of the world.' Dalrymple took up a brush and painted in the land mass in the southern ocean. 'There it is,' he said, 'there it is, awaiting a new Columbus. Have no doubt, learned colleagues, my hypotheses and calculations are correct and I shall discover it and claim it for England.'

Banks squirmed in his seat as he listened to Dalrymple's discourse on exploration from Ptolemy, Marco Polo and Magellan onwards. The audience was impressed and applauded, but Banks was confirmed in his opinion that the Scot was not only a conceited ass but he also ran the risk of being wrong. Banks hoped that Dalrymple would not lead the expedition – a brilliant seaman and navigator was needed for that. Whatever the outcome, this voyage to the Pacific would undoubtedly be the greatest event in his life. When he left the Royal Society, Banks hailed a carriage to take him to the Admiralty. He was to see Sir Edward Hawke to discuss a surveyor called James Cook.

Late that summer Plymouth Harbour was still crowded with vessels, even though the war with the French had ended five years earlier. There were frigates, sloops and men-o'-war, but in the middle of the confusion of craft lay the *Earl of Pembroke* – a bulky, unattractive ship with no figure-head or other decorations. She was a coastal trader, square-rigged and painted yellow. In the mid-afternoon beneath a dun coloured sky a longboat carrying Sir Edward Hawke, three officials from the Admiralty and James Cook was rowed towards the coalboat. The First Lord had been sufficiently impressed to take the matter of using a Whitby 'cat' further – and there still remained the question of a commander for the voyage to the South Seas. Hawke was a professional mariner with a profound distrust of theorists. At least he would see the vessel Cook had recommended and find out what the burly Yorkshire-man was about.

On board the ship the officials watched as Hawke and Cook walked about on the raised deck by the high stern. The decks were split, the pitch dry and cracked and the varnish flaked and peeling. They sniffed, the *Earl of Pembroke* was most unpromising.

'This is nothing but a common cargo carrier,' one of them said. 'If this hulk is chosen, what will the foreign potentates think? We do have the finest navy in the entire world.'

'And who is this man Cook?' asked another.

'No one of the slightest importance, he was once in the merchant service, I believe. His name does not appear in *The Gentleman's Magazine*. God alone knows why the First Lord should take up his valuable time with him, let alone consider this grimy coal tub.'

'Well, gentlemen,' Hawke said as he approached with Cook, 'what are your views?'

'This is hardly a speedy ship, my Lord. In fact, it's hardly a ship at all with its lack of square-rigging.' The officials dared not touch the rusted rails for fear of soiling their gloves.

'But Mr Cook insists on its suitability.' Sir Edward persisted in discussing Cook as though he were not there. The notables were an arrogant lot, Cook thought, and he remembered Banks' remarks about Elizabeth at Revesby Abbey. 'Mr Cook favours its shallow draught,' the First Lord went on, 'its light rigging and easy handling.'

'What rigging, sir?' One of them laughed. 'With respect, Admiral, Mr Cook is not even an officer. He has commanded nothing. I am sure that Mr Dalrymple would not put to sea in a vessel calculated to make us a laughing stock in foreign parts. I believe he favours a fifty gun man-o'-war.'

Hawke looked away at the shoreline and the grassy banks of Plymouth Hoe. 'I should think that Mr Dalrymple would favour any ship, provided we give him command.'

Cook stood silent and listened to all this. He thought it little wonder he had not been commissioned and God knows how they had ever won the Seven Years' War with administrators such as these. He looked at the officials as they shifted disdainfully about the deck. From the pallor of their faces, they had not been to sea for years, if ever. And what did Hawke mean about Dalrymple?

While Cook was listening to the naval bureaucrats, Joseph Banks and fellow botanist Daniel Solander were strolling in Kew Gardens past the strange plants and trees from the East Indies, Mexico and Brazil. Here, the afternoon was warm, and the air smelled of humus and tropical flowers. Solander was Swedish, and like his friend, was dressed to the point of perfection, his English like his clothes, was impeccable.

'What sort of a man is James Cook?' Solander asked.

Banks stopped and looked at the trees rising above the glass houses. The gardens were his favourite place.

'I have a great belief in first impressions,' he replied, 'and I've made some enquiries. He's plain, stubborn, self-taught and probably has a chip on his shoulder about people the likes of me.' Banks laughed. 'I don't think he cares for the aristocracy. But I have the feeling he's very strong of spirit. A man to be with at sea.'

'When will the choice of leader of the expedition be made?'

'It *has* been made, has it not – the unspeakable Dalrymple? But the First Lord has no love for prigs, and I have the strong feeling that an experienced mariner may be chosen in his stead. In any event, my dear Daniel, I'm delighted you're going to accompany me. Between the two of us, we'll set the scientific world afire.' Banks gazed over the lawns. 'Good Lord, to speak of the devil, whom do I see gracing the gardens? Why, I believe it's our esteemed colleague, Alexander Dalrymple. He's marching as if into battle. Keep your powder dry.'

The Scot did not bother to salute, nor did he acknowledge Solander. 'I am told, Banks,' he said, 'that you've offered a fortune to equip the expedition to the South Seas?'

'I have made a modest contribution, sir.'

'Ten thousand pounds, I am told. You may have the advantage of your family's fortune and your several great estates, but the expedition is to be mine.'

'And the Navy,' Banks said. 'Have *they* chosen you?'

Dalrymple stood his ground. 'I am in close accord with the Sea Lords. Of that, I assure you.'

'Then there seems to be little to discuss.'

'What I'm making quite clear,' Dalrymple insisted, 'is that if you wish to accompany my voyage, you may apply to *me*, and I shall give it consideration.'

Solander watched the geographer stride off. 'How extraordinary.'

'His ambition knows no bounds. That man is a self-server *par excellence*, but I think we shall need far more than a suspect academic, bemused by his own dogma for this enterprise.'

That evening, Cook sat by the window of their small room. Light rain was falling on the sprawling suburbs of

11

London and a watery moon shone through the smoke from ten thousand chimneys. Noises drifted up from the street below and their baby girl lay sleeping in her crib. 'Come back to bed, my love,' Elizabeth said. 'You'll do no good, sitting there.'

But Cook remained at the window, staring into the night. 'They treat us like animals,' he said. 'We have no feelings, we are the beasts of their pastures. I was a fool to have dreams.' He thought of the officials looking down their noses at the coal ship. He got up and looked at the baby sleeping and went to lie beside Elizabeth. She was warm and he stroked her hair. 'I should accept my good fortune,' he said, 'a beautiful wife and three fine children. Damn their arrogance, damn their politicking, damn them all. I shall not be part of it.' But James Cook remembered the waters of the St Lawrence, the shifting fog banks of Labrador, the icebergs grumbling and muttering and the anticipation of unfamiliar landfalls, waiting to be surveyed.

That was where he wanted to be.

To his surprise, Cook had been summoned to see the First Lord once again, and he had been waiting for Sir Edward Hawke for most of the day. Without holding too much hope, Cook had indicated his willingness to command the expedition, despite the reception given to his choice of vessel and the continuing belief that Alexander Dalrymple was to be confirmed as the leader. Although this would obviously be an act of folly, God moved in a mysterious way in the halls and chambers of the British Admiralty. Now, his legs were stiff and his patience stretched. The corridor was cold, airless and damp, and Cook wondered how ex-mariners could work in such surroundings. Suddenly in the evening gloom, the First Lord's door opened and Alexander Dalrymple strode out, his face black and his body shaking. Sir Edward Hawke was at the threshold.

'You may pull strings, Mr Dalrymple,' Hawke said, his voice raised, 'indeed you may haul on your ropes until your back breaks, but while I am First Sea Lord, no one but a naval man shall command a vessel under naval orders.'

'I shall go to the King, sir,' Dalrymple shouted.

'You may go to God in His heaven, but I command the Navy.'

Cook half rose as Dalrymple strode past, his shoes echoing on the marble tiles. 'My Lord.'

Hawke glared. 'And you, sir, will kindly wait.'

'I have waited all day, sir.'

But the door closed and Hawke was gone.

Late that evening when all was quiet and the corridor was empty, the door opened. It was Hawke once more.

'Well, Master Cook, a long day. But you have your coal ship and you have command of the expedition. I'm pleased to announce your promotion to First Lieutenant. You will raise a crew and prepare your ship for the voyage to Otaheite and beyond. Here are your orders. You have the best wishes of the Sea Lords.'

Cook took the sealed package, went to reply, but Hawke's door was already shut.

The colours of the Royal Britannic Navy flew from the

masthead, and the vessel had been renamed the *Endeavour*. The graceless coal ship was being transformed, the sound of hammering floated across the water. Cargo hatches were being fitted for better ventilation while wood stoves were fitted for warmth and to keep the mildew at bay. New sails were being cut and sewn and a false keel was installed to protect the hull from teredo worm. The decks were being freshly caulked and pitched and a new quarterdeck was being built. The specifications were exact and the work had to be of the highest standard for the voyage ahead. Lieutenant James Cook, RN, would see to that. He spent every waking hour on the ship. The shipwrights and new crew found him a hard taskmaster, but he knew that the expedition would take two years, if not more, and he could not afford to make mistakes. They were going to a distant part of the globe, where no other European had ever set foot before.

'Mr Hicks?' Cook was careful not to shout. His lieutenant was obviously hardworking and capable.

'Yes, sir?'

'I want that capstan and windlass overhauled and more space made for additional anchors. God knows what waters we shall be in.'

'Aye, aye, sir.'

'Mr Gore?'

'Yes, sir.'

'Where do you hail from?' Cook considered the other officer: he looked a likely fellow – slim, strong and thoughtful. At first blush, he seemed to have two good men beside him. Despite the brutal system, he thought, the British Navy could still produce officers of character.

'The American colonies, sir. From Boston.' In turn,

John Gore was impressed with his Captain – he had watched the preparations with approval.

'I'm told you've already sailed the Pacific and have some knowledge of those parts.'

'I was with Captain Wallis on the *Dolphin*, sir.'

'Otaheite, then?'

'That's correct.'

Cook was interested. 'Can you speak the language?'

'A little, sir.'

'I'm very glad to have you aboard.' Cook turned toward the ship's carpenter. 'I want ten new cabins up forward. And I want the galley and the sail lockers enlarged. Can you manage that?'

'Aye, aye, sir.'

Cook turned back to Gore, and they made their way down to the unconverted lower deck, where it was gloomy, damp and dark.

'Mr Gore,' Cook said, 'this will be no ordinary voyage. We will have many guests, most of whom have not been to sea for any length of time before. I'm afraid you and the other officers will have to occupy cabins down here. It will be hellish in the tropics and grim off the Horn, but I have no choice.' He handed Gore a signed order. 'I am commanded by the Admiralty to receive Mr Joseph Banks and his party, most of whom are important gentlemen and who will demand single cabins on the upper deck. You have heard of Mr Banks?'

'I have, sir. The botanist who sailed to Newfoundland.'

Cook was pleased at Gore's knowledge. 'We shall have more to put up with than is usual.'

'We'll manage, Captain.'

'I'm glad to know that. There will be other demands and debts to be collected before this voyage is over.'

'Aye, aye, sir.' Gore was puzzled; what did the Captain mean by that?

Several days later, Cook stood on the after deck in the warm summer sun. They were only six more weeks before they sailed, and next week Joseph Banks and his party would arrive. God knows what they would bring with them, and God knows what kind of men they would be. Quite a few provisions for the long voyage had already been brought aboard. Sitting on the deck were a number of barrels of salted pork. Cook lifted the lid of one, peered inside and angrily hurled it over the rail. 'Mr Hicks?'

'Sir?'

'Over the side with the others. Mr Gore and Surgeon Monkhouse, don't stand there. Lend a hand.'

'I must protest, sir,' Monkhouse said.

'*You* protest?' Cook considered the fat man in his civilian clothes, 'that salt pork is full of weevils and you passed it fit for human consumption.'

'Most salt pork is full of weevils.'

'Not on *my* ship, Mister Monkhouse. And you queried my order for barrels of sauerkraut. Is that correct?'

The Surgeon felt Cook's hard blue eyes upon him and turned away. 'I assumed it was a mistake, sir. No English sailors would eat German kraut.'

'I try to avoid mistakes, Surgeon Monkhouse, although there are some things beyond my control. My sailors will eat sauerkraut and they will take a portion of lemon juice every day. There will be no scurvy on my ship. Do I make myself clear?'

'Very, sir.'

In the evening, Cook sat in the great cabin. It had been refurbished and was now spacious and high-windowed, illuminated by candles in ornate brass holders. This was the heart of the *Endeavour*. It was chart room, recreation room, library and meeting place, but would however soon be used for other purposes. With Cook sat Charles Clerke, a bright, clear-eyed midshipman, who was carefully going through the ship's complement.

'How many are we still short, Charles?' Cook had instantly warmed to this straightforward young man.

'Fourteen, sir.'

Cook thought. 'Advise the press gang. I would have liked volunteers, if such a thing were possible.'

'There's a shortage of willing men sir.'

'Aye, there is. Inform the press gang to do their best. No rabble, if it can be avoided. Tell them that the Captain is a fair man.'

'Aye, aye, sir.'

Clerke rose to carry out the order. Cook knew that the midshipman would acquit himself well.

The following week, three longboats arrived along-side the *Endeavour*. Mr Joseph Banks and his group had arrived. The young man scaled the ladder easily and stood, cocky and resplendent, on the deck; he was dressed in the height of Mayfair fashion. The party seemed enormous, much too large for a bark of 368 tons which would circumnavigate the world. Banks was accompanied by Daniel Solander; Charles Green, an astronomer; Sydney Parkinson, an artist; Buchan, another botanist; Herman Sporing, a secretary; two footmen and two black servants. Banks was holding two greyounds by their leads as the chests of equipment were hoisted on the deck. The greyhounds barked and the ship's goats bleated. Gore stood rigid as he saw

Cook come up from below. Zachariah Hicks and Charles Clerke stood discreetly nearby. 'Welcome aboard, Mr Banks.' Cook put out his hand and showed no reaction to the chests piled up on the deck and the guests standing about.

'Thank you, Lieutenant.' Banks bowed low, then introduced the company.

When the formalities were completed Cook said, 'We'll have your baggage stored. You seem to have brought a great deal.'

'All more than necessary, I assure you, and there is more to come. This is, after all, a scientific expedition. Who knows what we shall find? Everything will have to be preserved, catalogued and recorded.'

'I agree, Mr Banks. Do the dogs have some scientific function?' Someone laughed, but Cook stood, impassive.

'They are pets, sir, of delicate disposition.'

'That being the case, they'd be better off ashore. But if they travel on my ship, they travel on deck.'

Cook and Banks regarded each other, the company was quiet, then Banks acquiesced. He moved off with Hicks.

Banks' inventory was vast: preserving bottles for small animals and fish; nets and trawls; chemicals for treating seeds and plants; drawing materials; a telescope for looking at the bottom of the sea; an extensive library; fine wines and delicate food; his personal supply of salted beef and even two electrical machines. Somehow, it was all stowed away and quarters found for his party. The work on the ship proceeded, the fourteen new seamen were inspected and all alterations and additions were completed to Cook's personal satisfaction.

THE
FIRST
V·O·Y·A·G·E

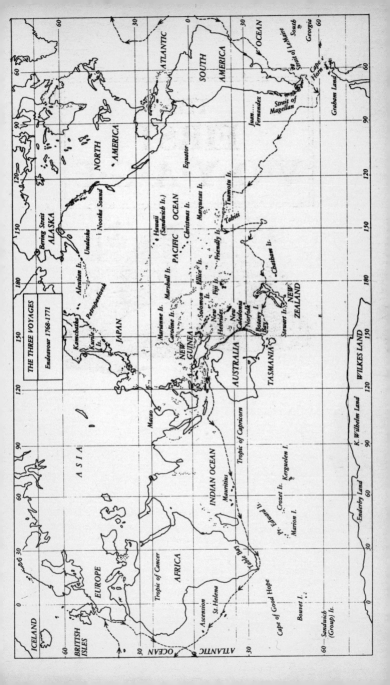

THE THREE VOYAGES

Endeavour 1768-1771

Chapter One

At last, on the 26th of August 1768, the wind blew nor' nor' west; the sails were unfurled and the braces and bowlines were hauled in and secured. The main topsail, the foresails and topgallant staysails were set. Cook stood on the quarter deck in the freshening breeze as the anchor was weighed. Banks, Solander, Green and the rest of his party watched all this from the forecastle. It was a good sailing breeze for a square-rigger and the heavily laden ship left Plymouth Harbour at four in the afternoon. The swell of the ocean grew. The *Endeavour* was at sea.

Alone in his cabin, Cook took down from the shelf the sealed package which contained his orders. He removed a signed document resealed the package and put it back on the shelf. That would have to wait until later, but he thought he knew what it contained. If his suspicions were correct, after measuring the transit of Venus, they would be ordered to search for the Great

South Land. The ship was running before the northwest wind and he stood easily as they sailed south. Their speed was five knots and that was satisfactory for a Whitby 'cat', laden as she was. He thought of his last night with Elizabeth, the warm August evening and her tenderness: she was getting big with their fourth child. He hoped it would be a boy; it would be born when they were far to the south, rounding the Horn. 'Don't lose your temper with Joseph Banks,' she had said. He would not, and he would be master on this voyage, no one else. *God speed, my darling, God speed*. He remembered.

Zachariah Hicks and John Gore entered the great cabin, all seemed to be confusion. Banks and Solander were unpacking books; Parkinson was setting up his easel and the servants were storing bottles of wine.

'Good day, gentlemen,' Banks said. 'We'll soon be ship-shape.' The officers had their reservations but they saluted and made their way through to knock on Cook's cabin door. He, too, saw the mess, but closed the door on it and said: 'Great forebearance will be required, gentlemen. The men of science deserve our understanding.'

Gore and Hicks exchanged glances.

Cook held up the orders. 'Our course is southwest to Biscay, then to Madeira, and west of Finistere to catch the trade winds. We call at Rio, round the Horn into the Pacific and should be at Otaheite by June to observe the transit of Venus. At Madeira, we will take on a quantity of onions.'

'Onions, sir?'

'That's what I said, Mr Hicks. I've told Surgeon Monkhouse and I'm telling you two now: I want no scurvy on my ship, and I want it clean. God help any man who doesn't partake of his fresh meat and lemon juice. Do you mark my words?'

'We do, sir.'

'Good. You may leave the organisation of the great cabin to me. All in good time.'

'With pleasure, sir.'

'Pleasure? We shall see about that. This is a navy vessel, Mr Gore, not a room in the British Museum. I have the feeling that in a day or two, our naturalist colleagues may be concerned more about their stomachs than their hypotheses.'

That afternoon, Cook stood with Hicks on the quarterdeck.

'Pray to God, Mr Hicks,' Cook said, 'bend your knee and pray to the Almighty.'

'For what, sir?'

'For bad weather. For a storm to put our men of learning on their backs and in their bunks.

But Hicks was not satisfied. 'They fill the Great Cabin – they have for the past several weeks – as if it's theirs alone.

'Patience, Mr Hicks'. Cook was smiling as he walked away. Over his shoulder he yelled, 'And prayer. A high wind and a rough sea can work miracles.'

Hicks wasn't sure if he had seen the Captain wink. He became aware of Gore standing nearby, near enough to have heard the Captain's words. 'That's all very well,' Hicks said to Gore, 'the truth is, the Captain's beholden to Joseph Banks.'

'Easy, Zachariah,' Gore replied. 'That's dockyard gossip.'

'Cook wasn't even an officer two months ago. He's

only a lieutenant – no higher rank than us.'

Gore cautioned his colleague. 'He's still the Captain.'

'That may be, but it takes more to run a ship than a knowledge of navigation.'

'I think you'll find,' Gore replied, 'that Master Cook knows far more than simply navigation.'

The Bay of Biscay did not let James Cook down. The wind shifted to the west and the seas became rough. White caps broke and the ship pitched as they tacked to windward. Amid the squalls and the flying spray Cook stood at the helm with Gore and Banks.

'Bracing weather, Mr Banks?' Cook looked at the botanist: he was not so chipper now.

'If you say so, sir.'

'I do, indeed. Are you not well?'

'It could be said that I'm not at my best.'

'I take it that you are not of a mind to open one of your jars of special potted beef?'

'I am not.' Banks' gorge rose.

'Try not to look at the horizon, sir.'

'There's nothing else to look at.'

'And brace your legs so. How are the greyhounds faring?'

'Damn the greyhounds.' Banks made a dash for the rail.

'Mr Gore,' Cook called, 'stand by to assist Mr Banks. We must on no account lose such an eminent man – it would bring great sorrow into the heart of many a young woman.'

Gore wanted to smile, but dared not. That Banks' companions were absent from the great cabin for several days was satisfaction enough for the officers.

It was the marines who were the filthiest although, Cook noted, a number of the crew were not far behind. He knew that no matter what he did, the ship would become foul with rats, mice and cockroaches. He made Monkhouse check for cold sores, swollen gums and dysentery, but his faith in the surgeon was limited. Cook knew the two enemies of a ship's master were scurvy and boredom; one lead to death and the other to mutiny. Cook was determined to avoid both. He looked among the men as they stood naked in the warm sun. Where was young Nick, the boy taken by the press gang? At last, Cook spied him, shivering and trying to hide his embarrassment. Cook felt a twinge at the methods of the press gang, Nick was barely twelve years old. Cook would make sure that he was well looked after.

The bosun, Wilkinson, supervised the sluicing. 'Right, you lot, dry out in the sun and line up for the surgeon. Let's see what you've got.'

Pushing and shoving they were dowsed and soaped ready for inspection by Monkhouse. The marines laughed, but not Webb, the Sergeant.

'His Majesty's marines,' Cook said as he watched, 'seem to have a particular aversion to soap and water. I want them attended to.' Cook pointed as one big man struggled. 'That fellow there,' he said. 'Give him the full treatment.'

The men shouted and laughed, until it came to their turn, but Cook and his officers made sure the bathing and cleaning was done. The decks were scrubbed and washed, but below the rats ran and it was beyond even Cook's power to do anything about it.

As the days rolled on the weather became calm and balmy, and curious porpoises splashed about in the wake of the *Endeavour* enjoying the sun as much as the men. Banks and his friends had by now gained their sea legs, and Banks began to collect plankton and jellyfish. Soon specimens of birds and fish were dissected and stored in jars and Parkinson began painting. On the morning of the 12th of September, the cry went out as the huge, jagged mass of Madeira was sighted on the horizon and later, that same evening, they anchored off the port of Funchal.

While the gentlemen went ashore botanising, Cook and his crew continued to work on the *Endeavour*, making it ready for the long haul to Rio and then south to Tierra del Fuego. They brought aboard the necessary vegetables, 3000 gallons of water, a live bullock, pigs and goats, and, as promised, the onions.

On the third evening of their stay in the harbour Cook was told that two men had refused to eat the fresh meat they had so laboriously taken aboard. The next day he summoned Gore to bring the men before him. For a moment he considered the seaman and the marine and had no hesitation, for he knew what would happen if he were lenient. 'I find you two guilty of mutiny,' Cook said, 'and I order twelve lashes.'

Even Gore was surprised: he thought the men deserved several days in the brig. 'Salted meat is their habit, sir.'

'I will break that habit, Mr Gore. Assemble the marines and get the bosun.'

The men were taken away and strapped to the grating on the forecastle; the sound of the rolling drums carried in the tranquility of beautiful Funchal Harbour and mingled with the men's screams as they were flogged with the cat. As their blood ran down the scrubbed decks Banks turned his head away, Solander and Buchan stood bowed. What kind of man, Solander wondered, would do this?

The horror of the flogging would not leave Solander – the sound of the men screaming and the sight of the blood running down their backs haunted him throughout the day. That night in the great cabin, when the meal was finished and the wine was being passed, Solander addressed Cook. 'Is not mutiny a serious matter, Captain?'

Cook considered the elegant Swede and knew what was coming. 'It is, indeed, Dr Solander. And it has to be dealt with.'

'The cat is a barbaric punishment, sir,' Parkinson said as he filled his glass.

'I'm inclined to agree, Mr Parkinson, but we are a small world of our own. Without discipline, you and I could be cast into the long boats – without your water colours, and perhaps without oars.'

'What was their crime?' Buchan asked.

'Their crime, sir, was not to eat fresh meat.'

All eyes turned to Cook, the cabin was silent except for the gentle lapping of the harbour waters against the hull of the ship.

'You mean they were flogged for that?' Banks said.

'They were, Mr Banks, and they will be again, if they refuse their ration.'

'Does that not seem rather extreme?'

Cook sat straight in his chair. 'I am going to take this crew to the Pacific and back again. Sailors die from storms and drowning – but most sailors die from the disease of scurvy. If they refuse sauerkraut, onions or lemon juice, they will be flogged. I intend to bring them home – bruised perhaps, but safe.' He paused. 'I should have thought that men of science and learning would know the beneficial properties of fresh fruit.'

'There are subjects of which we have less than perfect knowledge,' Banks said.

'There is another subject close to my heart,' Cook said, 'and that is tidiness and consideration for others. Usually, this cabin is reserved for the officers; here, we spread our charts and attend to the business of the ship. I would remind you gentlemen that you are here as guests. I am asking you to take up a little less space and make a little less noise. You may be concerned with higher learning, but my officers and I are at sea in one of His Majesty's ships.' He got up from the table. 'You will kindly excuse me.'

Gore and Hicks found themselves looking down at their glasses before them and held their tongues.

Cook stood alone by the rail looking over the moonlit water to nearby land. He heard Banks approaching and could feel his anger. 'Well, Mr Banks?'

'I must protest.'

'Of course you must.'

'What?'

'I would think little of you if you didn't. I am indebted for your company, sir, but there is one Captain

30

of this vessel, and I am he. Do I make myself clear? In a few weeks, we shall be at the Horn and only *I* will know what to do. Your library and electrical machines, your greyhounds and Mr Parkinson's water colours won't save us if Mother Nature has her way.'

For once Banks was speechless, what could he reply to this? He turned from Cook and went below.

On the 18th of September, in fine conditions, the *Endeavour* left Madeira for the two-month haul to Brazil. They would call at Rio de Janeiro, then sail south for Tierra del Fuego, one of the most inhospitable parts of the world.

Christmas day passed and the men celebrated with the usual festivities and general drunkenness. In the New Year, the temperatures fell as they weathered off the coast of Argentina. The latitudes were becoming high, the sea dark and the seaweed of a temperate hue. Lighter clothing was changed for Magellan jackets made of padded canvas. As gales blew up and rain swept the decks, whales and porpoises were seen cavorting around the ship. Despite the cold it seemed that all guests, officers and hands were enjoying themselves. The work was hard and varied and the warm blood pumped. The tropical heat of Rio seemed remote now.

Banks and Parkinson proposed a visit to the Falklands to send mail and botanise, but Cook would not alter his course and stayed well to the west. Once again he clashed with Banks, but Cook was immovable and had his way. He was anxious about rounding the Horn and making Otaheite on time to observe the transit of

Venus. However, the Captain knew he must make one last call before they faced the worst passage in the world. Before they could do this yet another gale sprang up. For two days it raged, books were swept off their shelves and the galley was filled with the sound of smashing crockery. Then, as dawn broke on the third day Cook discovered the land was not as formidable as it looked. There appeared to be an opening in the barren shore. After several attempts the *Endeavour* made it through and they finally dropped anchor in the Bay of Good Success, in Tierra del Fuego. The ship was in need of restocking with wood and water and Cook had agreed to allow Banks, Solander, Green and their servants to go ashore to collect specimens and explore. The weather was bitterly cold and the bleak country was covered in snow. It was latitude 55°.

The following morning in driving sleet, they launched a boat to take them ashore. The country was thickly wooded. They were unable to see much of the interior because of the sleet and mist. Cook didn't like the look of this weather, he knew the temperature could drop to freezing and he wondered if he had done the right thing in allowing Banks and his troop to have their way. There were a number of natives waiting for them on the beach. As the boat drew near they made signs of friendliness. Banks and Solander persuaded three of them to visit the ship. When they got on board, they were given clothes to cover their bodies. The crew wondered how men could go about almost naked in such cold climes. The Fuegans were tall and nomadic, with long straight hair to their shoulders, their faces covered with red pigment. They refused the food the men offered, they seemed to live on shell fish. Cook thought them the most miserable people he had yet seen on earth, but they were harmless and he was thankful for that. The worst thing that happened while they were on board was that the cover from a globe in the great cabin went missing.

It was on the second day ashore that Banks and his party set off. As Cook has predicted the southern weather did come down and Banks had never been so cold in his life. They had walked all that frigid day and were now heavily laden with plants and botanical specimens. Monkhouse looked bright enough, but Buchan, Green and Solander looked pinched and grey. The two sailors they had brought with them were drinking rum to keep the cold away. Banks was apprehensive, but not afraid until Solander suddenly slipped and fell, saying: 'I can go on no further.'

'Good God, man,' Banks said, 'you must. It's about to snow and we shall freeze to death if we stop.' Solander did not reply. Banks looked at the two black servants, Richmond and Dalton: they were shaking with fear and cold. Banks then saw the appalling risk he had taken and realised they would not make the ship that night. He cursed himself for being so foolhardy. There was no going on now, and to lose Solander was unthinkable. 'Buchan,' he said, 'I will stay with Mr Solander – you and the others will find a sheltered spot and make a fire.'

The snow was now driving into their faces and it seemed the wind was blowing right off the south pole. Dalton collapsed next to Solander – it was two down now – and Banks began to fear for all of them. Would they die and sleep forever under the snow and ice of Patagonia? He thought of Cook, Hicks and Gore on the *Endeavour* and imagined them safe below in the warmth of the great cabin, but he knew Cook would be on deck, waiting for them. Banks was fearful now, but tried not to show it. 'For God's sake,' he said to Buchan, Green and Monkhouse as they stood, immobile, 'be off and prepare a fire. I shall assist Mr Solander.'

The group, with the two sailors still swigging their rum, stumbled off and Banks remained with his friend. The snow was thick now and beginning to cover Solander and Dalton, should he pray? He hadn't done that for some time. After what seemed like an eternity with only the noise of the storm about them, Solander stirred.

'You stay here, Richmond,' Banks said to his black servant. I shall assist Mr Solander and send someone back for you and Dalton.' They had been his servants for some time now, but that was all he could do.

The blizzard blew all night; no one slept; the fire smoked and they spent all their time collecting wood to keep it going. It was too dangerous to go back to Dalton and Richmond. At daybreak, Solander had recovered a little and they went back up the track to find the two black men. The snow lay thick on the ground and one of the greyhounds discovered the frozen corpses. Black men, they may be, thought Banks, but they were part of my company and I have erred. It was a silent and forlorn party that moved through the bush to the beach.

Cook studied the land and water through his telescope and listened to the leadman as he called the soundings.

The barometer was rising, but it was a grey day with a low mist and biting wind. Tierra del Fuego was an inhospitable place and he could not understand how any human being could live there. Now they must prepare to round the Horn and he hoped there would be no further misadventures. As the *Endeavour* ran down the Le Maire Strait, Cook thought that Cape Horn would test all of them.

Below, Cook found Banks' cabin door ajar and let himself in. The young man was standing by the port-hole and turned to face the Captain.

'Whatever rebuke you wish to make is justified. It was crass stupidity and unforgivable of me.'

'It was unwise,' Cook said, 'to venture so far, but understandable after so long at sea.' Banks was surprised and studied Cook. 'I was afraid for you,' Cook said. 'I would have hardly been welcome back in England without Joseph Banks.'

'It is kind, sir, of you to say so.'

'And I'm sorry about your servants.'

Banks nodded. 'So, too, am I.'

'We are to be together a long time,' Cook said, 'you and I. We are different kinds of men from different backgrounds – nothing will change that. But without accord, this voyage will achieve nothing; our dreams will be wasted in empty squabbles. I think success and everything we crave depends upon us both.' There was a knock at the door and Cook opened it to admit a sailor carrying a tray with a bottle of wine and two glasses.

'I agree whole-heartedly,' Banks said as he stared at the sailor.

Cook poured out the wine. 'I took the liberty. Will you drink with me to my wife, Elizabeth, and our new child who must be born by now.'

'I'd be honoured,' Banks replied, 'most honoured.'

Cook smiled. 'Thank you.' They raised their glasses.

Cook and Elizabeth had decided, if the baby were a boy, it was to be named Joseph, in view of Banks' assistance toward the voyage. Cook was glad of his decision now. Should he tell Banks? He thought not – not at this stage. His mind now turned to the days that lay ahead. Next was Cape Horn, the stormiest and most treacherous passage in the world.

Chapter Two

Cook could round Cape Horn in several ways; and the most sheltered route lay through the Strait of Magellan to the north of Tierra del Fuego. But the strait was very narrow for a cumbersome square-rigger like the *Endeavour*. Because there were no reliable charts and soundings, and as the strait was infested with islands and reefs, previous voyagers had taken up to three months to get through this way. Furthermore, wind tunnels and down draughts blew from the mountains on either side. Cautious and careful to the last, Cook decided to sail to the east and then south of the Horn. The extra 1000 miles of easting did not concern him, as this way he had plenty of sea room.

As they sailed south, the weather lived up to its reputation of gale force winds and rough seas. The days became longer as they reached the high latitudes. By the end of the second week, they were at latitude 58° – further south than anyone had ever been before. There was no heat in the sun and the nights were very clear with a cold and angry sky. A few days later, the wind veered south and they were forced to sail close-hauled, meeting the seas head on. Heavy laden, the *Endeavour*

dropped into the huge troughs, the water crashing over her decks like a giant sledgehammer. Everything loose on the decks was carried away including the remaining livestock. The galley was swamped and gutted and drowned animals washed around the scuppers. A boom broke free, the sprit sail was shredded and a new one had to be bent on.

Cook continued to sail south – so far that even Gore began to have his doubts. Ragged black clouds had gathered so low they almost touched the mast heads. The rains came and tore off the top of the sea: it came in massive sheets so that they could not tell fresh water from salt. The days wore on and the passage seemed endless. Banks and his companions could do nothing but lie in their cabins, listening to the crash of the sea, the roar of the wind and the smashing of timbers. Again, Banks was prostrate with sea-sickness; the great cabin was a shambles and many of the specimens were lost. However, this time he was not afraid, he had no doubt that Cook and his officers would get them through. latitude 60° was reached on the 27th of January 1769, when Cook was able to alter the course northwest into the Pacific and warmer weather.

By early March, the sea had become bluer and the breeze carried a slight feel of the tropics. The sails were finally able to be repaired, and the galley refurbished. Birdlife abounded and Banks brought many down with his firearms.

One fine morning, Cook came on deck to find Banks lying in a chair with Solander beside him and Parkinson, sketching. Although the sky was clear, the wind was still cold.

'To think,' Banks said, 'I could be roistering in the salons of London. Can you not promise me fairer weather?'

'By my standards, Mr Banks, this weather *is* fair, but every day we sail northward and that will improve your disposition.'

'There is nothing wrong with my disposition: we are all grateful to be alive, and we owe it to you.'

Cook heard the sounds of shouting and a scuffle. The marines were fighting, several of them thrashing a quiet eighteen-year-old called Greenslade. 'If you don't stop that,' Cook roared, 'I'll have the lot of you flogged.'

'He's a thief, sir,' one of the marines said as he wiped the blood from his face.

'If he is, there are punishments laid down. Get up, Greenslade. They accuse you of theft – is it true?'

'A sealskin purse, sir,' the marine said, 'one that I bought in Rio.'

'Did you steal it?' Cook asked Greenslade.

The wretched boy could see no way out. 'Yes, sir.' He reached inside his shirt, took out the purse and handed it to Cook who heard the clink of money. Cook tossed it to the marine, 'You marines are not aboard this ship by my wish. Any more of this behaviour, and I'll have you in irons. Go below.' He turned to Greenslade. 'You know thieving is a crime?'

'Yes, sir.'

'It has to be punished. You will report to me at eight bells.'

Banks and Solander looked on and wondered what would befall the boy. Banks thanked God he was a botanist, not a naval captain.

Greenslade stood alone, unnoticed, his face still bleeding from the fight, his limbs shaking. The sun was high now, and the day clear and cold. Overhead kittyhawks flew and an albatross wheeled. He thought of the flogging of the two men in Funchal Harbour, the rattle of the kettledrums and the blood thick on the gratings. As the *Endeavour* sweetly rolled to the north and the isles of the tropics, he walked toward the taffrail, climbed the rungs and jumped into the Pacific rollers. A dolphin played, the birds screamed and no one saw him go. They searched for three hours, the long boats rocking in the swell, but there was no trace.

In his cabin, Cook began writing in his journal but pushed it aside. He was thinking of the marines who were now one short, one man who could not be replaced. More than that, they had lost a young man because of a system in which he had grave doubts. There seemed to be no answer. He heard a knock and the door opened immediately. It was Banks. 'May I?'

'I've recorded it in my journal,' Cook said. 'Punishments at sea are a part of naval life; they are essential for discipline and good order.'

Banks put his hand on Cook's shoulder. 'That, I know.'

'I am the arbiter,' Cook said. 'Sometimes, I do not wish to be, but there is nothing I can do about it.'

It was the first week of April, tropical breezes wafted and brightly plumaged birds flew around the ship. There was the smell of wood fires and sandalwood, it was the smell of land. The lookouts searched the horizon and all telescopes were out. The *Endeavour* continued her northwesterly course and on the 4th of April, an island was sighted. As they drew closer, they could make out the shape of the atoll, the lagoon and large clumps of palm trees. That night as they lay to

Banks and his companions were very excited, this was their first Pacific discovery. The next morning they saw outriggers in the waters of the lagoon, smoke rising and natives standing on the reefs and foreshore.

'Well, Captain?' Banks said, as they gazed from the rails.

'This, sir,' Cook said, smiling, 'is Otaheite.'

Dozens of canoes, ornately carved with high prows and flax sails, glided across the water. Their oars flashed, the men's backs glistened with salt spray and the women were calling in the warm air, moist with the sweet smell of the jungle.

The mountains climbed higher than the tallest church spires and the clouds wreathed the peaks. The crew laughed and shouted, pointing at the natives and their canoes and whooping at the sight of the women. Cook remembered the instructions of the Royal Society: they were to 'exercise the utmost patience and forebearance with respect to the natives, and restrain the wanton use of firearms.' Nevertheless, a four-pound cannon was run out and made ready for firing; the marines were assembled and the kettle drum rattled. The top gallants and top sails were lowered, the capstan turned, the chains rattled and the anchor was dropped. The canoes drew close, and the strange voices rose, each man stood at his station.

Cook was apprehensive: he wanted no more blood on his hands. 'What are they calling, Mr Gore?

'*Taio,* sir. It means friend, and the green boughs are a peace offering.'

The canoes circled the ship, the Tahitians waving and calling, the women bare-breasted, their long black hair down to their waists and flowers around their necks. My God, Banks thought, this is indeed the place of the noble savage. As he looked at their breasts and gleaming bodies, he could hear the marines shouting. They may have great trouble leaving this place he thought, the girls of the salons and gardens of London were nothing compared with this. His pulse beat, his blood pumped and his hands gripped the rails. Banks looked at Cook, but the Master showed no emotion. The natives were close around the ship now, their canoes thumping against the hull, the women standing and displaying themselves. The men were strong and powerful with broad shoulders and hard muscles; they, too grinned and shouted greetings.

'The maidens of Otaheite, gentlemen,' Gore said.

'An arcadia, Mr Gore,' Banks said, 'and we shall be the kings of it.'

'The price of love is a ship's nail,' Gore said.

Solander was scandalised. 'For shame, sir.' For all his elegance, he was a prude.

'From experience, sir?' Banks asked.

'Why do you think I came back?'

'I think it disgusting to take advantage of these simple folk,' Solander said.'

'I assure you, Doctor,' Gore replied, 'these "simple folk" are most co-operative and eager participants.'

'A nail?' Banks asked.

'A nail, sir. Believe me, for one nail, you will spend the most passionate and enchanting evening of your life.'

'I take it, Mr Banks,' Cook said as he looked down at the women, 'you have not forgotten the prime object of this visit?'

'I have not, Master Cook,' Banks grinned. 'But all work and no play makes Jack a dull boy.'

The smoke from the fires on the beach spiralled, the

sound of singing drifted as Cook turned away from the rail. The sun was low now, burning crimson behind the peaks where strange birds flew. Cook was uneasy – he knew there would be trouble.

In the brilliant sunlight as the marines watched from the skiff John Gore walked up the beach. The beach was crowded with men, women and children, their canoes lying on the sand. Because Gore had been here previously on the *Dolphin,* Cook had chosen him to go ashore first. He hoped to God he would be remembered. Gore recalled that despite their friendliness, the Tahitians were expert pilferers and nothing was safe in their sight. Native huts without walls stood under the palm trees and a space had been cleared for his arrival. He looked back at Gibson and the marines by the skiff, their muskets at the ready. The sand was hot through the soles of his boots and Gore sweated in the unaccustomed heat. As the children stared and the brown men stood with their spears and clubs, Gore tried to find a face he knew. At last, among the elders, he saw a familiar face. 'Owhaa,' he said, smiling, 'I am John Gore.' He waited and dared not to take his eyes off the old man. 'John Gore. Do you remember me?'

'Johngore,' the old man said, 'Johngore. Friend.'

The old Tahitian laughed, stepping forward to embrace the naval officer. The crowd laughed, talked and pointed, then cleared a path and Gore and Owhaa walked through the palms and hibiscus to the *marae,* the meeting place of the village. All looked prosperous and serene: breadfruit lay stacked in baskets; the native

43

gardens were well-kept and luxuriant and the people healthy and shining with coconut oil. Then he saw another person he knew: a tall, lithe girl called Parita who raised her hand to her lips. He was home.

On the *Endeavour,* the entire crew stood on the deck to hear Cook address them from the forecastle. Gore stood alongside thinking of what was to come. 'We will go ashore in orderly groups by longboat,' Cook said. 'Mr Gore assures me we will receive a friendly welcome.' He looked at his senior officer, but he was gazing at the shore. 'I'm aware,' Cook went on, 'that you've been eight months at sea and that it would be a vain and foolish commander who tried to prevent you from exercising the thought which is no doubt uppermost in all your minds at the moment.' The men laughed and Cook waited a moment for silence. 'However, I will permit no violence toward the people of Otaheite; there will be no cheating – no violation of their laws and customs. Remember, we are guests here. Any man who forgets that and who offends, will be severely punished.'

The men stood in lines. The boats were loaded and the pale-faced visitors – many of them press-ganged from the gorbals of Glasgow and the stews of London – rowed toward the shore. Cook watched them go: the lean, puritanical Solander, the perspiring Monkhouse, Parkinson with his water colours, Green with his telescope and Banks with his greyhounds. Cook usually did not pray, but this time he offered a silent prayer that all would go well. The last thing he wanted was trouble, he would not return home empty-handed.

Cook, Banks, Parkinson, Solander and Green decided to make an excursion into the country behind the village. They were accompanied by a large group of natives who seemed vastly amused by the white men in their three-cornered hats, brass-buttoned uniforms, wigs and knee-breeches. Banks ran ahead like a child, he had never seen foliage like this before. The air was heavy with the smell of tropical perfumes. The women were especially attentive, flowers in their hair, their limbs brown and gleaming. They made Solander uncomfortable but Banks bathed in every glance he could get. The salons of London were a far cry now with the surf booming on the reef and the palms bending and bowing on the blinding sand.

However, all was not as it seemed. There were signs of disturbance: a few of the huts were deserted and some of the natives seemed covetous, if not greedy for trinkets. Some of the gardens inland were in ruins, and as the crowd following them became bigger and more pressing, Cook started to wonder if this were such a paradise after all. He mentioned his concern to Banks who would have none of it. All Cook could do was hope to heaven that Hicks and Gore were keeping a close eye on the men, and that Sergeant Webb was doing likewise with the marines. Gore and Hicks he could trust, but Webb, he could not. Tomorrow they would start work on the fort and the observatory. That would keep them busy.

That afternoon, the *marae* was packed. The flutes and drums played and the men and women danced. The Europeans had never seen dancing like it. It seemed that the women and girls had hardly a bone in their bodies: they swayed and bent, their hips swivelling and heads thrown back. The feet thumped the ground in time with the chants of the men. Cook knew trouble and violence would occur sooner or later, and that when it came time to leave, there would be many a man disinclined to face the hardships of the sea and the monotony of the voyage. He doubted if the organisers of the expedition had any idea of the temptations present on the fair isles of Otaheite.

James Cook had been given the place of honour next to the Queen, Oberea; next to him sat Banks, Solander and the rest. In the crush, the pickpockets were already at work: snuff boxes, spectacle cases, buckles, kerchiefs – they all went faster and more expertly than they would have in the crowded streets of London. As the dancing continued the thieves melted into the tropical night.

The applause ended and Cook wondered what would come next. He saw the Queen beckon Owhaa and speak to him. Then the old Otahitian said in broken English that after the feast, the Queen and Cook would observe the local custom in her hut. He had heard of such native practices, he wondered how he could - - - without offending the Otaheitians hospitality.

'That is very gracious of the Queen, but show her this,' he said taking out a small locket containing a miniature painting of Elizabeth.

'Tell her,' Cook said, 'that is my wife, who is jealous and would be very angry. My wife is the mother of my children, and I could never deceive her. If I did, even so far away, she would know.'

Solander and Green were appalled by this heathen practice, but Banks was amused and his eyes gleamed as he watched the girls coming along with the food, their bodies shining in the light of the torches. He would have one soon – of that he had no doubt. Was he not to experience all aspects of Polynesian life to the full?

The feast seemed endless; pork baked in an oven in the ground, fish, oysters, fruit of all kinds and coconut milk. There was even fried vegetarian rat which to everyone's surprise, tasted delicious. They ate far into the night. With his belly full even Cook started to relax. He was relieved to see the men seemed to be behaving themselves. It was their fear of punishment, he thought, but how long could this last?

Then late in the night, Hicks came up and said: 'Excuse me, sir, I'm afraid they're a bunch of common thieves.'

'What's the trouble, Mr Hicks?'

'Dr Solander has lost a snuff box. Mr Parkinson, a spectacle case. Mr Green, a kerchief. And Surgeon Monkhouse has had a buckle taken from his shoe.'

Cook pointed to the Queen. 'I can't accuse this lady of her people's robbery while I'm eating her food.'

'We can't allow it to go unpunished, Captain.

'Nor can we provoke an incident while attending a ceremony of welcome.'

'But think, sir, of what else we may yet lose.'

'Thank you, Mr Hicks, I shall attend to it.' Cook got up. They would be here six weeks, a mixed bag of Europeans in a thieving paradise. Cook was determined that they would observe the transit of Venus, come hell or high water.

Chapter Three

There were men in the crew who quickly forgot Cook's orders about dealing fairly with the natives of Otaheite. Able seaman Jeffs was one such man. He had seen a woman carrying an axe and had decided he wanted it as a souvenir. He would take it home to impress his mates in Liverpool. He followed the woman down to the beach, so sure was he of his conquest that he did not even take the precaution of making sure she was alone. He demanded that she give him the axe but the woman did not understand. The seaman quickly flourished his knife with the expertise of one who was well experienced and snatched the axe. The woman's screams had brought her husband running across the sand and Jeffs knew he had a fight on his hands. The Tahitian was a thick-set and powerful man but Jeffs was sure he could make short work of him. The two men fought on the beach, they struggled and punched until the natives pulled them apart.

Cook's midshipman, Charles Clerke, saw this and ran down the slope. 'For God's sake, Jeffs, what's happening?' He thought of the Captain's instructions.

'This bastard tried to kill me.' The woman shouted and the big Tahitian waved his arms. To his relief,

Clerke saw Gore running up through the sand.

'Don't believe what these savages tell you, sir,' Jeffs said, 'I asked her if she could trade that stone axe, and the next thing I'm being attacked.'

Gore spoke to the man and his wife, then turned toward the sailor and stared. 'Are you carrying a knife?'

'Only a small one, sir.'

'This woman says you threatened to cut her throat unless she gave you the axe.'

'Lies, bloody lies.'

'They say,' Gore went on, 'these people are witnesses and that her hand was cut.'

'You can't believe that, sir.'

Gore spoke to the woman who opened her hand. It was cut and bleeding. 'Take this man back to the ship, Clerke,' he said.

'The Master will take care of this.'

Gore watched the man as he was pushed down the beach to the pinnace. He was glad Clerke was at the scene; the midshipman was reliable. By heaven, Gore thought, if any of these men attacked Parita . . .

The crew was assembled and Cook stood on the forecastle. He had made sure that the Tahitian, his wife and Owhaa were present to see that British justice was done. This would show them that he stood by his word. The instructions of the Royal Society would be enforced to the letter. 'Able seaman Jeffs,' Cook said, 'you have abused the hospitality of our hosts, disobeyed my strict instructions, and offered violence to a woman. Your punishment will be a lesson to us all, and I have brought those you offended here to witness that justice is done.' The sun was high in the sky now and the marine drummer sounded his kettle drum. 'Secure that man to the rigging,' Cook said, 'and give him two dozen lashes.'

The bosun raised the cat and began the punishment. After the first blow, the Tahitian woman cried out and as the cat bit into the seaman's back and the blood flowed, she began to scream. The bosun's mate stopped.

'Continue, man,' Cook said, 'continue.'

But the Tahitians were wailing and Gore said: 'I don't think they understand the punishment, sir.'

'Tell them this is the judgement for what this man did to them.'

'They say,' Owhaa said, 'it is cruel. Make it stop.'

'I cannot do that.'

The Tahitians sobbed and screamed as the man's back opened.

'Sir,' Gore said, 'it is beyond their comprehension.'

Cook raised his hands. 'Cease the flogging.' He motioned to Gore. 'Take our guests ashore and explain to them that this is British justice and that we are not barbarians.' He looked at Jeffs, manacled to the rigging; he would see this through. 'Resume,' he said to the bosun, 'after they've left the ship.'

That night as Cook sat alone in his cabin his thoughts were with his dear Eliza. He took up his quill and wrote:

My dearest Eliza, these weekly letters to you accumulate and I have no knowledge of whether I can ever despatch them. Otaheite is a beautiful place, but I do not know what to make of its people. They steal, they have no morals, and yet, like forgiving children, they weep when others are punished. I doubt if we shall ever understand them, or they us . . .

50

The Tahitians made love openly, on the beach and in the grass, even the young boys and girls with others looking on and shouting encouragement. The women looked at a man full in the face if they wanted him, this was a far cry from the dockside prostitutes, their bodies riddled with disease and reeking of gin.

Although even the basest men of the *Endeavour* were shocked by the open sexuality, their confidence grew as the dark-skinned women came to them during the tropical evenings. The more literate of them began keeping secret diaries where they recorded their liaisons. The nights were warm and long with dancing and feasting – who could resist these Polynesian *houris* as they laughed and whispered in the open huts as the sea beat on the beach? The lovemaking seemed to have no end and the men dared not contemplate the day when farewells would have to be made.

For Joseph Banks, the women of Otaheite seemed to promise more than the most expensive courtesans of the salons of London. Cook had made him the chief negotiator in trading business because of his charm and each evening, he watched the dancing, eating the roast meat and fruit and revelling in the life of the noble savage. For him, too, making love in the open was taboo, but he succumbed to the Queen herself – the forty-year-old Oberea who had once fancied Cook. She was a lusty woman with dark shining eyes. The young dandy from Mayfair became her favourite and many nights after his daily botanical rambles, Banks was obliged to 'seek lodgings' with the Queen. But he was a philanderer, and many of his colleagues were outraged by this, not the least his friend, Dr Solander. Surgeon Monkhouse was consumed with envy and frustration. He was obsessed by Banks' easy charm with the nubile

Tahitian women. Although they traded insults about Banks' lechery, victory had gone to Joseph who was seen to make a new conquest almost every day. Even the boy, Nicholas Young, had his girl and they all knew of Gore's love for the beautiful Parita, but Monkhouse had nothing. It would be hard to leave these isles when the time came – every man knew that.

Fort Venus was built on a headland, overlooking Matavai Bay. Earthworks were dug, ditches excavated, high palisades put up, a forge established and huts constructed. The men worked hard in the tropical heat, the sand blew in their faces and insects crawled inside their dirty uniforms. Each day, the curious natives watched the progress and waited for the chance to pilfer something made of metal. Two of the ship's four-pounder cannon were set up; a platform made for the heavy brass quadrant; swivel guns put in place; latrines dug and tents erected for the officers. Cook was well pleased with the effort: Fort Venus was an outpost of Albion in Polynesia – the Union Jack flew from a high pole, the marines stood guard and the place seemed impregnable.

One hot morning, Private Gibson stood with his guard of marines, cursing the heat and cursing the natives. As far as he was concerned they were thieving savages, cannibals, good for only one thing and for that matter it was the young girls only. A few girls had gathered by the edge of the clearing, chatting amongst themselves and smiling at Private Gibson. He put his musket down by the fence and went over. From the edge of the long grass, a native youth saw his chance, slipped over silently and grabbed the firearm. Too late; Gibson saw the young man and shouted to the marines. The bosun's mate, Wilkinson, seized his gun and fired. The crowd scattered and the girls screamed as the Tahitian fell on the path. Lieutenant Gore heard the fusillade and ran to the scene. The Tahitian was dead, his back open and his blood pumping on to the sand. Wilkinson was there, too.

'You've killed a man,' Gore said. 'You'll pay for this.'

'*Me* pay?' Wilkinson said. 'He stole a musket. What else could I do?'

The next day in his cabin, Cook gave his verdict. 'Gibson, for the neglect of your firearm in a manner that provoked theft, you are confined to the ship for fourteen days and your pay is suspended until further notice.' The marine was silent and Gore stood by. 'As for you, Wilkinson,' Cook said, 'you acted from a sense of duty, even if ill advised and hasty. No action will be taken. You may go.'

Gore waited for the men to leave the cabin then turned to the captain. 'That was a serious crime, sir,' he said.

'Are you suggesting that I'm derelict in my duty?' Cook asked.

'I was pointing out the gravity of the crime.'

'Even if we punished him, Mr Gore, our hosts would not necessarily consider it a virtue.'

'May I be excused, Captain.'

'No, sir, you may not. However stupid the bosun's act may have been, a musket was stolen. I want it explained to these people that their thieving has to stop. I want it known that we regret the killing. You're my emissary, Mr Gore, I depend on you.'

'We can't change their nature, Captain,' Gore said. It's their way to be generous with love and careless with possessions.'

'They are *our* possessions. I don't want to change their ways, just make them understand.'

Cook was left alone with his thoughts. He could not wait for the 3rd of June, when they would be gone from the confusions of this place.

That evening, John Gore sailed the skiff across the bay. The breeze was light and the scent of hibiscus wafted. He reached the shallow water, secured the boat and stepped onto the beach. The palms bent toward the water and the sea pounded on the coral reef. Gore walked up the sand toward the village. The *marae* was empty, not a dog stirred and the moon rose behind the huts. He stopped and stood uncertainly. 'Parita?' he called. 'Parita?' There was no reply.

As he walked on, birds scattered and insects shrilled in the twilight. There was the wooden bier and the body of the Tahitian laid out, Gore turned away. Then he saw a small girl coming across the *marae;* she was holding a small bouquet of flowers. He knelt, smiled and took them from her. As he did so, people came out from the shadows : there were Owhaa and Parita – they were smiling, and he, too, smiled with affection and love. It seemed they had been forgiven.

Despite the Queen and the other Tahitian women, Joseph Banks had been busy. He had brought down many excellent birds with his fowling piece and had taken long excursions into the hills and jungle to collect all manner of specimens. The great cabin was filled with plants and shrubs. The artist, Parkinson, who was spared the sins of the flesh by his religious convictions, had been observing and painting all he could see – a Tahitian war canoe, a priest figure, brilliant water and the colours of plants and trees. The cabin had a sense of purpose and order now, and James Cook was pleased. 'Don't let me interrupt you, Dr Solander,' he said. 'A naturalist's paradise?'

'Indeed, Captain. Can the ship accommodate all the new treasure this place has for us?'

'We'll do our best, sir, we'll do our best.'

The botanist smiled. 'That is good to know.'

Cook moved on and admired the paintings. 'Superb, Mr Parkinson. I wish I had the talent.'

'You, captain, can sail and navigate and I cannot.'

'But more than anyone,' Cook replied, 'you can show the people at home what the South Seas are really like.'

'But can I capture the light? Can I capture the innocence of these people?'

Cook exchanged a glance with Banks who was busy close by. 'You must try, sir. You must try.'

Astronomer Green was checking the quadrant and a Gregorian telescope. 'All is in first-class working order,' he said. 'I have to adjust the telescope, then we can take them to the Fort.'

'And pray for fine weather on the 3rd of June, Mr Green.' Pleased with what he saw, because it had a purpose, Cook left the naturalists. There would be much to show the Royal Society in London.

Outside his cabin, Lieutenant Hicks and Surgeon Monkhouse were waiting for him. 'Gentlemen,' Cook said, 'Pray, enter. What can I do for you?'

'Sir,' Monkhouse said, 'there has been an outbreak of venereal distemper.'

'If it is here,' Cook replied, 'we brought it.'

'No, Captain, all the men were examined a month before we reached Otaheite, and all were clear.'

'It *was* brought here, sir,' Hicks said. 'Captain Wallis' the *Dolphin*, and a French frigate under Bougainville.

Either one, we'll never know. But it's here, and increasing numbers are being infected.'

Cook fell silent and looked out at the peaceful island. 'In years to come,' he said, 'they will remember only the ravages we brought them.'

'But *we* didn't, Captain,' the surgeon said. 'I make that point.'

'Europe, Mr Monkhouse, the English, the French, the Spaniards. Does any of us really have the right to be here? In time, I expect, we'll bring our Christian doctrine to this place.'

'And a good thing, sir.'

'Is it?' Cook replied. 'Do you really believe it will be to the island's advantage, the day that priests come to make converts with a crucifix in one hand and a dagger in the other?' He came close to Monkhouse. 'Tell me in confidence, Master Surgeon, has any of our guests reported the disease to you?'

'No, sir.'

Cook turned to Hicks. 'The scientific instruments go ashore tomorrow. Work on the ship is to resume. Make her ready for sea.'

'Aye, aye, sir.'

'As soon as the sighting of the transit is done,' Cook said, 'I want to leave this paradise – leave it to its own people.'

The next day, the crates were taken shore, carried up the hill to Fort Venus and the quadrant was put in place. A guard was mounted and all was ready for the observation.

56

As usual, Banks was monopolising the table; he ate his fine food and drank his wine.

'I have had a remarkable day,' he announced, I attended a Polynesian funeral.' He sat with Cook, Solander, Hicks, Gore, Parkinson and the detestable Monkhouse. 'A truly unique experience: the deceased was laid to rest with his worldly goods in a tree, where the birds will pick him clean, and the bones will be discreetly scattered. All done with excellent taste, and the whole thing has given me a hearty appetite.'

'You will have much to tell the Royal Society back in England,' Solander said.

Banks knew he disapproved but persisted regardless, 'Yes, they'll be fascinated.'

'What other news from ashore, Mr Banks?' asked Hicks.

'Well, the market has changed for the worse. The price of love, they tell me, is no longer one ship's nail, but *three*.'

Someone chuckled, but Surgeon Monkhouse was not amused. 'The price of love may, one day, well be a most painful malady.'

'You can be a most tedious fellow,' Banks said. He turned to Gore. 'My knowledge of their tongue improves every day.'

'Close acquaintance is a good teacher, sir.'

Banks laughed and they exchanged a phrase in Tahitian, but Monkhouse pushed his chair back and said: 'Excuse me. This conversation is beyond my feeble wits.'

'Now gentlemen,' Cook said, 'this feud has gone on long enough.'

'I entirely agree,' Banks said. 'Surgeon Monkhouse should take himself ashore and be relieved of whatever irritates him.'

'You irritate me, sir, more than any distemper.'

'You provoke him, Mr Banks,' Cook said.

'I cannot help myself, sir.'

Just then, the door was pushed open and Green stood.

'Ah, Mr Green,' Cook said, 'come and join us.'

'Alas, sir, I cannot. The quadrant has been stolen, the thieving savages have taken it!'

The marines and the crew searched the village thoroughly, overturning mats, ransacking huts, combing the long grass and tramping over the *marae*. The children cried and the women stood with their heads bowed. Wilkinson was in charge of the search, shouting at his men and mopping his head with a filthy kerchief. He saw Cook striding up and said : 'No sign of it, sir.'

'Strip the place. Search every inch.'

'Right, you lads, did you hear what the Captain said? I want this place stripped.'

Midshipman Clerke was there. 'Sir, is this the best way?'

'You will not question me,' Cook said. 'I'll take whatever measures are necessary.'

Four marines stopped outside the Queen's hut with Gibson, dirty, unkempt and sweating. They beat the stocks of their muskets against the posts. Three Tahitians came out with Oberea.

'Take her, boys,' Gibson said. 'You're under arrest.'

The Queen did not understand. Gibson gave the order and a musket was fired into the air. Oberea shouted, her brown eyes wide and angry, her long hair drifting in the evening breeze. 'Banks,' she said. 'Banks.'

'Mr Banks?' Gibson snorted. 'That gentleman ain't here, and if he was, no good it would do you.' He pushed her. 'Come on, lads, take them to the Fort.'

When they reached Fort Venus Oberea was still shouting and the Tahitians putting up a mighty struggle. Gore was outraged. 'Who the devil ordered this?'

'I did, Mr Gore, I did.' It was Cook's voice.

'Sir, you must not.'

The Captain stood before him, large and forceful. 'Do not tell me what I must or must not do, sir.' He turned to Owhaa, who was standing near. The old man looked fearful. 'Tell the Queen I regret this, but her people leave me no choice. She is my hostage until the thief is found.'

When she understood, the Queen screamed.

Gore was white with rage, 'My God, sir,' he said.

Cook thundered. 'Don't shout at me. You will stay here until the quadrant is returned, and if you don't keep your peace, Mr Gore, I'll have you confined to your cabin.'

'Banks,' Oberea said, 'Banks.'

'Mr Banks, Madam,' Cook replied, 'is of no use to you now.'

Cook walked alone to the far end of the headland and saw the *Endeavour* at anchor in the bay, her lights gleaming. The sea rumbled on the reef and the sea breeze was stronger now. He fastened the top button of his jacket and cursed. Then he turned and gazed at the peaks, where the clouds clung. Someone was approaching, it was Gore. Cook waited until his officer was close. 'Do you realise,' he said, 'that if we don't get that quadrant back, we've come half-way around the world for nothing. It means failure. We'd be the joke of London, ridiculed in every coffee house and tavern.' This time, Gore knew not to speak. 'Some men,' Cook said, 'are allowed failures – they have family or

59

influence, but I was apprenticed in the coal trade. Thus I have only one chance and I am on my own. I must not fail, and I will not allow myself to do so.'

Cook had Parkinson draw a number of sketches of the quadrant and these were given to the men to show the natives. The search continued with Wilkinson in the vanguard. The bosun was a hard man; he enjoyed what he was doing and nothing was spared. He and his men marched from village to village, tossing out belongings and searching people physically, but without luck. Was the quadrant somewhere in the grassy flats by the bay or, worse still, up in the steep hills? Nobody knew.

At Fort Venus, Cook paced up and down powerlessly. He could not stop himself thinking of the consequences if he were unable to carry out his orders and observe the transit. Astronomers knew that Venus revolved around the sun inside the orbit of the earth, this transit could be used to measure the scale of the solar system. It had not been observed since the Astronomer Royal, Edmond Halley in 1679 and would not take place again for another ninety-nine years. Several different nations, apart from England, were preparing to observe it. France and Russia had already mounted expeditions, and there could well be more. Cook knew that the measurement of the transit had important implications for navigation and that was crucial to exploration and the building of England's Empire. The Royal Society held that the observation was important to the honour of the British nation. What if Cook failed because of some thieving native? He

60

would never be asked to command another voyage, and this prospect was too terrible to contemplate.

To add to Cook's troubles, the weather, which had been constant for weeks, was now becoming changeable. The winds were uncertain and clouds drifted across the sun. He was not a religious man, but he found himself praying constantly. Cook had a terrifying sense of foreboding. It seemed now, after a successful voyage to the South Seas, he was being pursued by the Furies.

Cook was pacing aimlessly outside the Fort when he saw Gore approaching.

'No news?'

'No, sir. But I think you should know that the marines are exceeding your orders, and antagonising the village people.'

'My orders,' Cook said in a hard voice, 'were to recover the stolen quadrant, and I don't care what means are used. Do you understand?'

'I do understand, sir,' Gore replied, 'how important it is.'

'I don't think you do, Mr Gore. Two days from now, we are to observe the planet Venus passing between the earth and the sun. The transit will, I'm told by our scientific colleagues, not be seen for another century. Am I to tell my marines not to offend the sensibilities of these people? Am I to return to England and say I could not play my part because the natives stole a vital piece of scientific equipment?' He took off his hat and wiped his head – the weather felt thundery now. 'I regret everything I'm being forced to do. And if you know a better way to find this thing, for God's sake tell me.'

Later that same day Cook summoned Banks and suggested they take a walk along the beach.

'I am told, Mr Banks,' Cook said, 'that you are on

somewhat intimate terms with the Queen.'?

Banks thought a moment of how to reply.

'Intimate, sir, but alas, our communications are limited to a rather narrow field.'

The botanist was not at all embarrassed, but this did not surprise Cook, he was getting to understand Banks well now. 'I take it, sir, that you have no objection to my taking the lady hostage?'

'Why should I? Whether it will work is another matter, but extreme situations call for extreme measures.'

'The Queen sometimes utters your name.'

'Does she? She may utter it all she likes, but I'm fully aware we have to get the damned quadrant back. If we do not, then it will go hard for all of us.'

'Myself, in particular, Mr Banks.'

Banks looked Cook straight in the eye. 'Yes, you in particular, sir. I shall do all I can to assist, you have my word on that.'

'I am grateful, Mr Banks.'

Banks managed to smile. 'As you doubtless know, I enjoy a certain popularity amongst these people, and perhaps that can be turned to our advantage. They are jackdaws who seem unable to help themselves, but even those black birds can often be persuaded to give up their treasures.' He stopped and looked at the hills of the interior. 'You will excuse me, I have a great deal to do.'

It seemed that the men of the hills were fiercer than those of the coast. Some were carrying clubs and sticks and others, stones. The hills were steep, the jungle hard going and Banks and Gore were tired. Green preferred to stay among the trees at the edge of the *marae* with Parita, but quite fearless, Banks marched up to the elder and proffered one of Parkinson's diagrams of the quadrant. Suddenly the people seemed good-natured. Banks and Gore were offered drinks in coconut shells and they waved to Green and Parita to come and partake. A Tahitian girl appeared from a hut and Banks' eyes grew wide. 'Good God,' he said. 'That's my waistcoat.'

'It is, indeed, Mr Banks,' Gore said, as he watched the girl approach with the waistcoat above her lap-lap. Gore knew they were on to something now and he listened as Parita talked to her kinfolk. Another girl came out from the huts, where the children played. 'Great heaven,' Green said, 'that's the stem of the quadrant.' The brass gleamed in the sun as the pieces appeared, one by one. When the offering was over, the astronomer knew all the pieces were there and he could re-assemble it.

The woman wearing the waistcoat took it off and went to give it back to Banks, but he would not take it. 'No, ma'am, for you,' he said.

Upon that, two men appeared, carrying a large bundle which they laid at the Europeans' feet. They opened it to reveal a musket, Solander's snuff box, Green's kerchief and Surgeon Monkhouse's silver shoe buckle.

Banks presented the buckle to the elder and saying: 'For you, sir, I only wish Mr Monkhouse were here to see my generosity.'

After a cloudy night, the day of the 3rd of June 1769 dawned hot and clear. The quadrant and all the instruments were set up in readiness. The transit of Venus would last from 9 in the morning until the mid-afternoon. Through their telescopes they could see an image of the planet crossing the disc of the sun and Green, Cook and Solander were delighted. The temperature climbed to 115° and conditions became very uncomfortable. But once again, it seemed that luck was not with them, they found they had been unable to mark the beginning and the end of the transit with any accuracy. Green and Solander sweated with disappointment. There seemed, to Cook, to be some shadow over everything he tried to achieve. At the end of the day Cook sat alone in his tent at Fort Venus. There was nothing he could do now except get on with the orders he'd been given – to find the Great South Land.

After the heat of the day, the night was clear and cool. The phosphorescence glowed in the water and the moon was full and high. From somewhere on the shore came the sound of the natives singing. Cook stood, alone once more, on the quarter deck, paying no attention to the beautiful night, or the canoes drifting around his ship. Banks taking a stroll along the deck saw him standing there and thought he looked a solitary figure. 'A penny for your thoughts, sir?'

'We were unable to measure the time of the transit properly and neither Green nor Solander could tell me why. It could have been the instruments, or it could have been those using them. We'll never know.'

'I sympathise,' Banks said. 'But one can only do one's best.' He hesitated. 'I regret that sounds most inadequate.'

'To have come so far,' Cook said, 'for a mistake and a failure.'

'There is a great deal yet to be done in the science of

astronomy,' Banks said. 'Our instruments are far from ideal. You're too gloomy, sir. There are other things to be taken home, new charts, plants and specimens, perhaps new territories for His Majesty and even the legendary great Southern Land.'

'As you say, Mr Banks.'

'My friend, Tupaia, wants to sail with us,' Banks said.

'Does he, indeed?' Cook turned and looked at Banks.

'He's a splendid specimen of his race, and would be a sensation in London.'

'Ah, sir, but would he survive there?'

'I will take full responsibility for him. Will you permit it?'

'If his mind is made up.' Who knew where they were going? Cook thought. It had already crossed his mind that an interpreter would be useful.

Chapter Four

There was a great deal to do before the *Endeavour* would be ready for the long voyage south. It was found that teredo worm had eaten away half the hull of the longboat. In the days that followed, the *Endeavour* was careened in Matavai Bay, cleaned of growth and given a fresh coat of pitch. Her deck was caulked, her rigging repaired and spars varnished. Cook oversaw it all and made sure the ship was fumigated for the long voyage ahead.

Banks persisted in his exploration of the mountains, Parkinson painted and Solander collected more specimens. Provisions had to be taken on board and everyone was kept busy. During all this activity the pilfering was rife, nails, tools and even firearms went missing. Cook was at a loss as to what action to take. As a desperate measure he retaliated by seizing a number of canoes. He regretted this unpleasantry but it did lead to some of the stolen goods being returned. All Cook wanted now was to be away from this place and at sea.

As for the men, they had lost their desire to return to the hard and dangerous life. They were happy with their women and Cook feared desertion was in the air despite the horrendous penalties. Even the puritanical Solander and Parkinson seemed at home in Otaheite now. Cook observed all this, and decided to make all haste to leave. As for Joseph Banks, Cook knew he would have no problems there. Banks' ambition was far too strong for him to be seduced into staying in these tropical isles.

At length, the day of departure came. As Gore said farewell to tearful Parita the thought of absconding passed through his mind. But, as she clung to him, Gore realised he could never abandon his post and could only hope to God he would see her again. A farewell feast was held. The flutes and drums sounded as the girls danced for the last time, the pilferering and the theft of the quadrant forgotten. The smoke from the fires spiralled to the heavens that evening and the singing and chanting echoed into the hills. For Cook it was an evening of relief, tomorrow, if the wind was right, they would be off.

But two marines, Sergeant Webb and Private Gibson had planned to stay: they both had 'wives' now and were convinced they could hide out and seek shelter in the mountainous hinterland. While the singing and dancing progressed, flight seemed very easy. They slipped away to their women, ran into the bush and climbed the slopes so high that, at last sweating and shaking, they could see the lights of the *Endeavour* as she lay at anchor on Matavai Bay. 'What time do they sail?' Webb asked. They were both tough men but had never run and climbed so hard in their life.

'On the tide, so they say.' Gibson stood up and tested the wind. 'The breeze is from the east, they'll sail at dawn.'

'Then we're safe?'

Gibson thought of the price of desertion. 'It looks like it.' Gone forever was the hard life in the marines.

At dawn on the *Endeavour,* Midshipman Clerke took the roll call. He went to Cook who was standing on the foredeck. 'There are two men missing, sir, marines Gibson and Webb.'

Cook remained silent. 'Do we sail, sir?' Hicks asked. 'The tide's full and the wind's in the east.'

'If we mount an expedition to recover them,' Gore said, 'it might take days.'

'Mr Gore, I'm well aware of that.' Cook still thought. 'Take Queen Oberea and six chiefs hostage. I want those men returned in exchange for her freedom.'

That day, Oberea and six of her chiefs were taken from the village. An angry crowd watched as they were put in the longboat and rowed out to the *Endeavour*. They raised their fists and shouted at the ship, anchored on the bay. The fires burnt and the news travelled over the group of islands.

Banks and Hicks watched the party come aboard. 'It's a mistake, I fear.' He thought of his nights with the Queen. Why had it come to this? He dared not go near her now.

'It worked last time with the quadrant,' Hicks said.

'My dear Hicks,' Banks replied, 'last time they *stole* the quadrant. They haven't abducted the marines – that's the difference and that's why they're angry.'

All through that day and the following night, a large crowed waited on the shore and drums beat. The moon was still big, Cook stood on the deck with Banks.

'I regret having to do this once again – especially to Oberea,' Cook said.

Banks was uncertain. 'How long can we hold them hostage?'

'For as long as it takes.'

'A week, a month?' Banks said. 'You'll have a rebellion on your hands.'

'Do you imagine, sir,' Cook replied, 'that I'm doing this just to get back two trouble-makers?'

'Then let the Queen go. It's wrong. It's a violation of her *tapu,* her sacred person. Why leave behind us bitter memories and anger?'

Even now, Cook could manage a smile. 'I do not seem to have your ablity for giving pleasure, Mr Banks.' Then he went on, 'What do you think will happen if those marines are allowed to desert? I'll tell you. We'll lose men every time we drop anchor. If I don't get them back, this is just the beginning.

The following day, Banks sat with his companions in the great cabin. Tupaia was there with Solander, Green and Parkinson. 'No matter how badly he wants those wretches back,' Banks said, 'It's wrong. One rash decision and all the good we achieved here is destroyed.'

Cook entered, but Banks showed no sign of embarrassment.'Tupaia,' Cook said, 'I need your help.' The Tahitian rose, nervous with all eyes upon him. 'You're to go ashore with Midshipman Clerke. I want you to make it quite clear to the people they are going to lose their Queen. I shall sail and take her with me if the runaways are not found by sunset.'

Banks rose, protesting. 'You can't do that.'

'I can and I will. Sit down, sir, and let me run my ship. Convince them, Tupaia, I mean what I say, be sure to make it clear.'

One hour later, Clerke and Tupaia stepped ashore from the longboat and the crowd was told the ultimatum.

Gibson and Webb were taken later that day in a small village, high in the mountains. Clerke and Tupaia were

69

there with a Tahitian guide. The marines were eating pork and fruit, Clerke's musket was cocked and pointed at them and they knew there was nowhere they could go.

'Come on lads,' the midshipman said, 'the ship's waiting. Don't make me shoot you.'

'What's the difference', Gibson said. 'You'll hang us soon enough.'

The wind kept to the east and the *Endeavour* left on the next high tide. The sails were set and the anchor raised. The bark moved slowly from the bay. Banks and his friends stood on the deck and gazed shorewards. 'No fond farewells for us, I fear. So much lost,' Banks said, 'through one foolish act.'

The ship made way as the sails filled and the flag was hoisted to flutter above the quarter deck. Banks could not believe his eyes as, around the headland, canoes filled with Tahitians came into view with others pushing out from the shore. It became a small armada and formed an escort on three sides of the *Endeavour*. In the middle of this fleet was the Queen's royal canoe. The Tahitians were singing and Oberea stood up, tears running down her face.

Cook stood and saluted formally. 'A forgiving people, Mr Gore. They cry that we are leaving. Perhaps they should have cried when we came.'

The crew shouted and cheered, and Banks sprang up the rigging and waved heartily. At last, the *Endeavour*, fully square-rigged made the open sea and the rollers of the Pacific, leaving the people of Otaheite behind her.

Gibson and Webb stood manacled in Cook's cabin. 'Have you anything to say?' the Captain said.

'No, sir,' Webb muttered.

But Gibson said: 'What's the use – we knew it was wrong. But I ain't ever known anything like that there.'

'Gibson,' Cook said, 'you've been nothing but trouble the entire voyage. Why did you join the marines?'

'I never joined, sir. I was press-ganged and made to fight in the French War.'

'How old were you then?'

'Thirteen, sir. Then I jumped ship, later on, but the gang got me again. They said it was my duty to serve England. Ten years of duty, I've had, sir.'

Cook studied them both, their rough faces – he could have been one of them, he had grown up among such lads in Yorkshire. The men waited without hope. 'Mr Hicks,' Cook said, 'I am reducing the charge from desertion to deliberate absence from the ship. Amend the log accordingly. They will each be given two dozen lashes.' He looked at the midshipman. 'Take them away.'

Later that evening the officers sat in the great cabin. 'He's astonishing' Banks said. 'It's hard to make the fellow out. They should have been hanged.'

'For once, Mr Banks,' Monkhouse said, 'you and I agree. The Master was far too lenient.'

'My good evening, gentlemen,' Cook said as he entered.

'The Surgeon and Mr Banks are reconciled,' Green said, as he drank his wine. 'They believe you should have hanged the wretches.'

'I'm gratified, gentlemen that you've reached accord on something. But it's easy to say hang when you are not the judge.' He bowed and went into his cabin.

That night, Cook opened his private locker, took out his secret orders and broke the seal. He sat and read:

Secret, from the Commissioners of the Lord High Admiral of Great Britain . . . It will add to the honour of this nation, if you observe the following instructions. There is reason to believe a continent or land of great extent exists, and you are to proceed southward to discover it. When this is achieved, you are to survey it, observe the nature of the soil, the beasts and fowls that inhabit it, its fishes and its trees and precious minerals. You are to report on the nature of its people, and with their consent, take possession of this land in the name of the King.

It was known that there were a number of islands to the west and Cook sailed for them. He surveyed Huahine, and at Raiatea, hoisted the flag and took possession of the island group which, as they lay close to one another, he called the Society Islands.

So far they had sighted seventeen islands and Tupaia told him there were many more. However Cook would delay no longer and on the 9th of August they sailed south. The weather became cloudy and the wind fresh. There were frequent light squalls which made observation very difficult. Day after day the lookouts studied the horizon, but there was no sign of land. Nor were there any indications – no seaweed and no birds. The monotony preyed upon them all. Cook made latitude 40° and the Pacific was empty.

In the great cabin, the men of science sat moodily. Green drained his glass of wine and said: 'We're either sailing in circles, or we just can't find it. What do you think, Banks?'

'I can see no reason why it shouldn't exist. I've always thought our friend Dalrymple was a conceited ass, but too many men of substance believe in it for us all to be wrong.

'It makes sense a southern land mass should balance the world,' Solander said.

'Exactly,' said Green. 'What would be the point of thousands of miles of empty ocean?'

The weather grew cold and stormy and still no land appeared – nor was there a swell coming from the south to indicate its existence. The horizon was thick and heavy with cloud and it all looked most umpromising. Cook called a meeting in the great cabin.

'Gentlemen,' Cook said, 'the joke seems to be on us. Our orders were to find, map and claim Mr Dalrymple's Great South Land. These many weeks of searching have proved but one thing, it does not exist.' Banks and his colleagues looked at each other. 'I know,' Cook continued, 'Dalrymple's theory has for long been supported by scholars and scientists – it is part of European mythology, and who am I to argue with such eminence?' He pointed to a map. 'But for the past weeks we have been sailing here, and last night, our position was here.' He pointed to Dalrymple's map and the centre of the 'continent'. 'In other words, according to Dalrymple's map we are standing on his Great South Land this very minute.' He waited a moment until he was sure they understood what he was saying. He knew he was countermanding strict orders but he had had enough.

'Mr Hicks,' Cook said, 'we've wasted time enough. Change the course to due northwest. We know New Zealand exists,' he said, 'and New Holland somewhere to the west of it. Let us stop looking for myths and mirages. Let us chart and survey the land there is.'

'Northwest it is, sir.'

It was young Nick who spotted land on the starboard bow. At first it looked like a cloud bank, but the birds and swell told otherwise. By sunset, they could see a bush-covered land with mountains thrusting high into the sky. Banks was delighted and Nick earned himself an extra gallon of rum, most of which was drunk later by the crew. The next morning they were in sight of a large bay. Smoke rose, indicating the country was inhabited, and they found a small river where they were able to anchor. Banks immediately went off to write in his journal that 'all hands seem to agree that this is certainly the continent we are all in search of.' But Cook was not quite so sure. That evening, he tried to go ashore in the yawl with Banks, Parkinson and Tupaia but they were attacked by natives brandishing spears. They were fearsome, tattooed warriors who looked like the Tahitians, but were far more aggressive. They were huge and muscular men, their faces twisted with fury, tongues hanging out and eyes rolling. Their spears were strongly crafted and their axes made of an unusual green stone. Shouting and chanting, they tried to encircle the longboat. Tall, proud and utterly without fear, they looked most formidable adversaries. Cook and his men crouched behind their boat in fear of their lives.

'My God,' Banks said, as they knelt in the wet, cold sand, 'this is not quite like the reception in Matavai Bay.'

The natives were getting much too close for comfort and Cook told the marines to fire their muskets. It was touch and go, and to his regret one of the warriors fell, mortally wounded. They made it back to the *Endeavour,* shaking and cold. This was the North Island of New Zealand.

The Maoris shouted and danced all through the night. Cook realised that they would not be able to go ashore here and so he ordered that they weigh anchor and sail west in the search for wood and water. But the savages seemed to be everywhere. When the crew went ashore again the Maoris broke into a fearsome war dance hurling their spears. Once again Cook ordered the marines to fire and two more natives were killed. Cook had had enough of this bloodshed, but another pitched battle arose when two war canoes with ornate prows came out to the ship and surrounded the pinnace and the longboat. Finally, the Maoris withdrew and the marines took three of them from the water. As the natives crouched in the bow of the *Endeavour,* reconciled to death, Banks had Parkinson make some drawings. Tupaia found that he could make himself understood quite easily, and for that, everyone was thankful. The captured warriors became quite amiable when they were fed with salted pork and ship's biscuits; and the next day, Cook let them go. He knew the situation was fraught. Banks and Solander had managed to collect a few specimens and they had replenished their wood and water supply. It was time to sail further north. Here they found the country and the people more attractive. This time, when they went ashore, the natives were more friendly, the men even learnt to rub noses in greeting. The country was green and lush. The men welcomed the variation to their diet as the native women dived for the biggest lobsters they had ever seen, the oysters were excellent and Banks was able to bring down many birds. The weather was cold and clear in the mornings, and temperate by noon. This was a well-organised and vigorous people, certainly not of the same temperament as the Tahitians. As Tasman's map was incomplete, it was still a possibility that New Zealand was part of a larger continent and Cook decided to circumnavigate the land.

It was the start of the southern spring and as they sailed north along the east coast, the land became lush with grey-green mountain ranges close to the shore. They saw many native settlements and gardens where sweet potatoes grew. The fishing was good and with parties going ashore from time to time to gather wild celery they all ate well. Although Cook was still concerned with his men's diet, their eating habits had improved. Hicks, however, had developed a trouble-some cough, and it seemed to Cook he could remember it back in Otaheite.

Officers and crew alike were puzzled at the behav-iour of the Maoris which was most erratic. Sometimes they were generous and friendly, and at others, menac-ing and warlike. It was nerve-wracking going ashore for provisions and it meant always having two or three marines with firearms at the ready. The country in the north was subtropical with forests of huge straight trees which, as Parkinson noted, would make fine spars and masts.

. All this time, Cook was at his happiest, surveying, charting and navigating. In the New Year of 1770, they rounded Cape Maria Van Diemen in the north and battled down the dangerous west coast off a lee shore. The *Endeavour* was getting foul again – inside and out and fresh water was becoming short as day after day, they searched for a suitable place to shelter. At last on 14 January, they anchored in a wide, sheltered bay. There were native forts on the headlands and a stream flowing down rocks into the sea. It looked an idyllic place and everybody, especially Banks, was anxious to stretch his legs after weeks at sea.

Mussels and oysters lay thick on the rocks. Banks, Green and Parkinson clambered ashore and disappeared into the bush. Here they found the air was heavy and moist and thousands of birds singing with bell-like tones. Amongst the tangled clematis, they stopped and listened, none of them had heard such a beautiful sound before. It was then that they stumbled on the bones.

'Good God, sir, what's this,' Parkinson said as he stopped to examine. There, in the moss and humus, lay piles of skulls and bones in old, rotting baskets.

'We are, gentlemen,' Banks said, 'in the presence of cannibals.' The trees dripped and all was silent. 'I would assume they eat their enemies and not their friends,' Green said.

'I very much fear we fall into the first category,' Banks muttered.

'After this incident the men of learning lost some of their zest for discovery. They kept close to the shore, the marines and the longboat. When they heard of it the crew quickly lost their sexual appetite, only one went ashore with this object in mind and returned unsatisfied – he was offered a boy.

It was a week or two later when Cook and a few of his men climbed the highest hill. There he saw the ocean to the east joined by a strait and this convinced him he was sailing round a large island. The myth of the Great South Land looked almost dead and buried. In a way he was relieved. He resolved to sail through the strait and go south.

The further south they went the higher the mountains became. Banks thought the alps were equal to those in Switzerland; the peaks rose to the heavens and snow gleamed in the summer sun. The rivers were broad and stony blue, but it was the fiords on the southern west coast of that great island that excited Banks most. The cliffs were high, the entrances narrow and the bush grew down to the water's edge. He knew the treasures these mighty inlets would contain.

'Those fiords are ideal for research,' Banks said as he and Cook gazed from the taffrail one autumn morning.

Cook studied the currents and felt the wind. Again, they were on a lee shore and the mountains climbed high. 'That's impossible, I'm afraid.'

'I don't think you understand, James. Solander and I want to go ashore.'

'I understand perfectly,' Cook replied. They were on first names now, but Banks had lost none of his arrogance. 'I have no intention of jeopardising my ship for more foliage with Latin names. Excuse me.'

Banks was angry as Cook moved off to talk to Clerke. Damn these Yorkshiremen, damn them.

'Are we going ashore, sir?' Clerke asked.

'No, Mr Clerke, we are not.'

'There was talk among the gentry in the great cabin yesterday.'

'The "gentry" as you call them, have nothing to do with the running of the ship. The "gentry" are aboard as privileged passengers, and will behave accordingly. I want the great cabin cleared of "gentry", and a private meeting of my officers in one hour. One hour, do you hear?' He turned to see Banks approaching once more.

78

'I think we have discussed the subject Mr Banks.'

'Not to my satisfaction.'

'Do you think so?'

'Are you denying us the right to land and collect plants?'

'You've collected plants,' Cook replied, 'you've pressed them and catalogued them. The ship is weighed down with plants – we've got more vegetables on board than Covent Market. I sometimes think this is a floating greenhouse and not one of His Majesty's ships.'

'I need to know,' Banks said, 'for my journal and my report to the Royal Society. Are you denying me the opportunity for further study ashore?'

Cook studied the botanist with his expensively cut clothes and powdered wig. How did the man keep so clean? 'Yes, I am. Write it in your report, for I shall certainly note it in the log. "To secure the safety of the vessel, the Captain refused to enter what he considered highly dangerous waters".'

'And, sir, lost a great opportunity. There could be precious minerals among those glaciers.'

'The whole of this coast, Mr Banks, is a lee shore – I hope by now you know what that means. Inside the fiord will be deep water, too deep for anchorage. It's a foolish place to sail into, a stupid and unnecessary risk, and I will not take it. Put that in your journal. If those glaciers were made of gold, I would not hazard this ship.'

On the 24th of March, the *Endeavour* rounded the northwest point of the South Island. The circumnavigation of the two islands was complete and the myth of the continent in these parts totally demolished. Once more wood and water were needed and Cook put into

Queen Charlotte's Sound. This was their last port of call. Cook kept himself to the great cabin, where he completed his maps and charts of the entire coastline. He was more than satisified with himself and thought his map of New Zealand a masterpiece of navigation. The Maoris, although warlike, were a highly skilled and intelligent people and the country was rich in natural resources and blessed by a temperate climate. It would, Cook thought, make a desirable colony for industrious people, and it now numbered as a possession of His Britannic Majesty.

This time, Cook allowed Banks and Solander to go ashore on their last botanical hunt. Altogether they had collected over 360 species of local flora. This ship was cleaned and provisioned, wood and water taken on and the sails and rigging repaired for the voyage home. What, Cook wondered, would be the route?

Once again, Cook and his officers met privately in the great cabin. There was scarcely room for them in the abundance of specimens, diagrams and paintings. A map of New Zealand was set up, together with an early chart of the South Seas, showing the South American and African continents and their southern capes. Most of the ocean was shown as empty of any land mass. 'Our position,' Cook said, 'is here, on latitude 41° south. We have now mapped and circled both islands. We have fulfilled our orders, as far as we are able. It is time for us to decide which way to go home.' He studied their reactions for a moment and then gave them the alternatives. 'Do we return east along the roaring forties, back to the Americas and Cape Horn? That way might at least prove or disprove the existence of Dalrymple's Great South Land.'

'Is that your choice, sir?' John Gore asked.

'What is yours, Mr Gore?'

'We'd be running into winter. Our sails are threadbare, the rigging's taken a beating. If there's no land between here and the Horn. I doubt the ship would make it.'

Hicks spoke up, 'The hull's foul with growth, sir, we're fothering leaks and we need to make repairs.'

'If we go west,' Cook said, 'we should find the coast of New Holland. It must be here, somewhere. If we find it, we can chart it northwards, sail around the top of it, and home via the Cape of Good Hope.'

'I favour that,' Hicks said'.

'And young Charles Clerke,' Cook questioned, 'what do you favour?'

'If we find and map New Holland, sir, that would make up for . . .'

'What?'

'For failing to discover the mythical Southland, sir.' Clerke hesitated. 'What I mean is . . . *we* know it doesn't exist, but people at home will be disappointed.'

'That it doesn't exist, and that we didn't discover it?'

'Yes, sir.'

'You're quite right,' Cook said. 'They've believed in it for so long. There'll be red-faced scholars and angry armchair Admirals. No one is going to love us for demolishing their long-held dream. I'm glad we're in accord, gentlemen. We continue to sail west.'

Chapter Five

 The east coast of New Holland was uncharted and the Dutch interest in it had waned after Tasman. As usual, they were sailing into unknown waters and Cook was eager to survey whatever they might discover. He did not let the condition of the *Endeavour* deter him, and for a week and a half they were favoured by a good breeze and fine weather. Then it became calm, so much so that Banks was able to get into his small boat and shoot seabirds. When he brought down a wandering albatross some of the crew were apprehensive; killing that bird meant bad luck. Cook, however, was not impressed by such superstition, he also knew that this was the calm before the inevitable storm: it came two days later – a shrieking gale from the south whipping up huge seas almost as big as those at the Horn. Only the crew could go up on deck and, as usual, Banks and his friends lay in their cots with seasickness. Banks retched and cursed: it seemed he would never get used to rough seas and he wondered how Cook and his men adapted to it. It must have something to do with a sense of balance – he would get his physician friends in London to work on

the phenomenon. When the storm abated the weather turned gusty, angry and cold. They were at latitude 38°.

One morning while Cook and Hicks were navigating with the sextant, Hicks was stricken with a dreadful fit of coughing. He doubled up in the cold wind and seemed quite powerless as he shook. Cook was worried. His first thought was that Hicks may have contracted consumption, he remembered Hicks coughing even in the heat of Tahiti. He ordered his officer to see the Surgeon immediately. To lose an officer would be a disaster, but to lose Hicks would be the greatest tragedy and he dared not contemplate it.

As they continued west, the antipodean weather was infuriating: it rained with great violence; the sea was sloppy with fogs; but at last it became fine once more, with a biting wind and a pale sun. Even the Captain's spirits became low as the wind veered to the south and the ship began to roll. Hicks' coughing continued and Cook confined him to his bunk. The lieutenant was bringing up phlegm and blood, and Cook was little cheered by Surgeon Monkhouse's diagnosis of a mere chill. He had seen consumption before. Cook cursed this misfortune; if it wasn't scurvy, it was something else. Hicks' cabin was too small to take a wood stove, and the entire ship seemed dank and mildewed. To add to Cook's worries, Charles Green had taken to drinking and Cook feared the effect this would have on morale. That night, yet another storm blew up with lightning and booming peals of thunder. This passage, Cook thought, was worse than that south of Tierra del Fuego and this weather was perverse, uncertain and only adding to the already low spirits.

In the great cabin, the candles flickered, the timbers creaked and the spray beat against the high stern windows. A desultory mood hung over the room. Cook played cribbage with Clerke; Banks was trying to read a scientific journal and Parkinson was showing some painting to Tupaia. Green was drinking and the smell of the grog made Banks feel worse.

'Would you like a glass?' Green said. There was a trace of spittle on his chin and Cook noticed he had neglected to shave.

They had been unable to wash for over a week now and their clothes were grimy.

'Good God, no,' Banks answered, looking at the half-empty bottle.

Green burped. 'It takes your mind off this endless, damned sea.' It was obvious he wanted to talk but everyone seemed preoccupied. 'How long, Captain, how many months till we see England?'

Cook fiddled with the pegs on the board. 'It's difficult to say.' It could be some months before they got to Batavia and the West Indies.

'Try to say. After all, who else can tell us?'

'A year, perhaps.' Cook returned to the game.

'A year,' Green said as he rocked on his chair. 'Hear that, Banks?'

'I heard.'

Green knocked the bottle, but saved it. 'A stinking year – twelve wretched months, and all we do is sail on and on. No famous south land. No rich continent we were promised, bigger than Asia, more abundant than Europe. Nothing of value. Wasted time, Banks, precious time out of our lives, and the whole thing's a damned failure.'

Green rose swaying and trying to find his feet. Cook pushed the board aside the shrugged at Clerke. 'I believe you've won, Charlie, you're much too good for me. Help the gentleman to his bunk.'

'Aye, aye, sir.'

But Green rejected the midshipman's arm and protested. 'I can manage. A year. Dear God, we'll be old men before we see dear old England again. What I would do for roast beef and Yorkshire pudding.'

Banks swallowed. 'Be quiet, Mr Green.'

When Clerke had helped the astronomer out, Cook looked at Hicks, he was pale and sweating. 'Come with me, Mr Hicks,' Cook said.

In his cabin Cook closed the door and turned to study Hicks, 'The Surgeon reports you have a slight chill. Do you think he's right? Is it a chill?'

'No, sir, I think it's more than that.'

'Young Charlie Clerke can take over some of your duties.'

'I can manage, Captain.'

'We both know you can't,' Cook said. 'I want you to rest and get well. We can't afford to lose you.'

The storm damage was being repaired and the carpenter and the sailmaker worked with their mates. Gore inspected the work as the calm sea ran. The *Endeavour* sailed before a mild easterly and Cook and Clerke stood on the quarter deck. 'As Mr Hicks is so severely indisposed, Lieutenant Gore will be acting first officer,' the Captain said, 'and you'll take over as second.'

The young man was proud. 'Thank you, sir.' He hesitated. 'May I say something?'

'You usually do.'

'It's about the astronomer, sir, he drinks too much, because he didn't get it right – the transit of Venus.'

'I know why he drinks,' Cook answered.

Clerke plunged on. 'Only I think someone ought to tell him – if he can't talk sense, he ought to stop getting drunk so often.'

'Never mind him.'

'But I do, sir,' Clerke said, 'I mind what he says, we all do. It ain't wasted time. Or a failure. You're making charts of this sea that other men will sail by – probably long after we're all dead.'

Cook was moved: at least someone knew what he was at. 'All righ, the wind's rising and you're officer of the watch. What do you do, mister?

'The mizzen, sir. Hoist the jib.'

'Then do it.'

'Aye, aye, sir.' Clerke ran forward and began bellowing commands. Cook was proud of him.

Then the weather became foggy, and this time it was Hicks, up from his cabin, who saw the land first. Cook found to his regret that they had sailed too far north to ascertain whether Van Diemen's Land was an island or not. But it was too late for that now and they continued on their course. The country they saw looked flat and wooded and had none of the steep mountains of New Zealand.

Banks spent a great deal of time studying it through his telescope. They were hard put to find a suitable place to land but on the 27th of April they made one attempt and stood to, with the wind offshore. Cook, Banks and Tupaia crewed the longboat, but the surf was far too high and they were obliged to turn back. However, they did see some dark figures near the shore and some rough huts. Even though they got the longboat quite close in, the natives appeared not to notice them, and this puzzled Banks greatly. 'They must have seen us,' he said more than once. 'They must have seen us.'

At latitude 34° on the 28th of April, they came on a broad bay in an otherwise barren coastline. The entrance was wide and deep and they could sail out on a westerly wind. The *Endeavour* moved through this channel and passed several natives spearing fish near the beach. Once again, they appeared not to notice the ship and did not even look up. It was as though the ship and the Europeans aboard were invisible. Banks was greatly intrigued. Why did they not look at the big square-rigger and the pale-faced men hanging from the rigging?

After an hour, they anchored in front of a tiny settlement of half-a-dozen huts: this time an old woman did look at the ship, but expressed no interest whatsoever. Some of the crew thought this might be like Otaheite, but Cook thought they would be disappointed. Beyond the bay, the land stretched, flat and featureless to the west. This looked an unpromising country.

When they landed, a group of natives appeared, carrying spears and curved pieces of wood. The day was silent and windless and the smoke from the fires rose straight to the sky. All was silent and unearthly as the blacks stood watching the longboat. Tupaia shouted, but there was no response. Cook, Banks, Gore and the marines stood on the beach, Tupaia shouted once more; it was as though they were all in some kind of dream. Suddenly, two black men threw spears. Gibson raised his musket. Cook's mind went back to Poverty Bay in New Zealand, the war-canoes, the shouts and the dances. He stood, hot and sticky in his uniform; he told the marine to put his firearm down. More spears were thrown, one of them narrowly missing Parkinson; but then it was a stand-off, the intruders and the inhabitants contemplating each other. Banks was the first to lose patience, 'I'll give them some beads,' he said.

'Go with Mr Banks, Gibson,' said Cook. 'I don't want anybody injured.'

Banks walked apprehensively up the beach and threw the trinkets into the sand. The natives came forward picked up the trinkets and examined them and pitched them back without interest. Birds screeched from the stunted trees and the blacks disappeared. It was a strange landing indeed.

The bay abounded with giant stingrays and mangroves flourished in the muddy shallows. There were plenty of oysters and mussels and this fresh food was welcome. The blacks were rarely seen, and then only as shadows in the dun-grey bush, they seemed as timid as deer. Birds were everywhere – some as black as ravens, and others were brightly coloured parrots which they shot, the gunfire echoing across the dry, sandy hills. Cook had never before encountered such a vastly silent place.

Banks, Solander and Parkinson did not share Cook's misgivings. They went into the bush as if it were a paradise. Not since Tierra del Fuego had they been able to hunt for speciments without being harassed. They worked day in and day out collecting, classifying and painting. As the men took fresh water, wood and food to the ship, Cook surveyed the bay and did some sketches of his own.

A few days late, several of the men caught a huge haul of fish, enough to feed the entire company. In the late afternoon they rowed toward the shore to clean and gut the catch. Cook watched from the beach with Banks, Tupaia, Solander and Parkinson. The catch was large and varied and Cook was pleased. The men were now keen on fresh food and had given up their old habits. The catch was dumped on the sand and the cleaning began. Then the Aborigines appeared, silent and menacing. Gibson was anxious but Cook appeared to be relaxed. 'All right, Gibson,' he said, 'there's no need for alarm. They've been perfectly friendly so far.'

'Not this time, sir, step back – you too Mr Banks, and the rest of you gents.'

'Don't be ridiculous,' Banks said. 'They're a timid race – Parkinson and I should know.'

'Begging your pardon, sir,' the marine said. 'But don't be a bloody fool – get in the boat – they're going to attack. Hurry.'

The Europeans were tense and apprehensive now as the blacks came closer, their bodies painted with white stripes and their long spears raised. The flies crawled over the fish and the birds called from the trees. Gibson moved in front of Cook, his musket at the ready.

'Do as he says,' Cook said. 'Get into the longboat.'

As they stepped into the boat, the first spear landed at Gibson's feet. 'For Christ's sake,' he said.

'Shoot him.' Banks' voice was steady.

'If I do,' Gibson replied, 'they can rush us before I can reload.'

'God in heaven, Mr Banks,' Cook barked 'get into the boat.'

'What about the fish?'

'Leave it.' Gibson ground his teeth.

'Dammit, that's a pity.'

'It's what this is all about, don't you see? Leave it. For God's sake, hurry up.'

When they had all got into the longboat only Gibson was left on the beach. The next spear narrowly missed him. He fired and the black fell. The other natives halted, staring at the dead man and then at Gibson as he climbed into the boat. They came forward to examine the body and watched as the longboat was rowed out on the bay.

Cook sent Clerke to fetch Gibson and after the young officer had gone they stood alone in the cabin. 'Congratulations,' Cook said.

'I beg your pardon, sir?'

'It makes a change, Gibson, to commend you instead of punishing you.'

'I thought, sir, you had me up for being rude to the gentry.'

'Whatever you may have said, I didn't hear it.'

'No, sir,' the marine said. 'Thank you, sir.'

'What did you mean,' Cook asked, 'When you said the incident was about the fish?'

'I think that's why they were angry.'

'Because we caught their fish?'

'Because we caught so much. They're not like us. They don't care about our beads, or our coins – or even us. I think they only take enough fish to feed their women and kids.

'And they thought, by catching so many fish and turtles, we were being greedy?' Cook was thoughtful, he seemed very interested.

'Maybe, sir.'

'If you're right, Gibson, they won't attack us, provided we don't threaten them or their supply of food.'

'I'm not sure if I'm right, sir.'

'Well, we shall see.'

After the episode on the beach, they harvested their food more carefully. All dined well on stingray cutlets, oysters, mussels and wild spinach. The May sunshine was warm and their stay pleasant. Such was the abundance of flora that Banks and Solander went their separate ways through the dry, silent forests. The blacks were hardly ever seen, and when they were, they seemed to be mere shadows, ghosting between the eucalyptus trees. Cook carefully surveyed the bay, and when that task was completed, he determined to sail north. It was decided to leave a simple memento of their sojourn at Botany Bay; and one hot morning as the blacks watched from a distance a sapling was cut.

As the work proceeded, Gibson and the marines stood tense with their muskets at the ready. A sign was carved and the Union Jack hoisted. The ceremony was brief and the party saluted the flag. The carved sign left standing on the beach read: BOTANY BAY. LT JAMES COOK, ENDEAVOUR BARK, 28TH APRIL, 1770.

The proceedings were completed, they looked around for the blacks but found they had disappeared.

It seemed a long, silent row back to the *Endeavour*. For some strange reason Cook was relieved to leave the bay with its silent, aloof inhabitants.

By the last week of May, they had reached the tropics. The weather was warm and humid, and birds and fish were plentiful.

It had been calm for several days, and the *Endeavour* failed to make headway in the glassy sea. Banks spent his time shooting seabirds and Parkinson sketched the rugged shore, Cook worked on his map of the coast of New Holland, Point Hicks, Cape Howe, Mount Dromedary, Bateman Bay, Port Jackson, New South Wales. The going was slow and the currents swift and uncertain. At Bustard Bay, Banks and his colleagues went ashore, but were driven back by hordes of ants and mosquitoes. The leadsman kept reporting variable depths and Cook was aware of treacherous shoals. Water became short, the country unfertile and the ship's bottom foul. The bark was becoming unresponsive and started to wallow as they groped northward. One brilliant June evening, a coral shoal was sighted and Cook laid off all night to avoid it. But, by keeping the land in sight they seemed to have been entrapped by a great reef.

A sounding boat was put out for the leadsmen. He worked by day and by night, under a huge moon, the sea glowing with phosphorescence. Solander and Parkinson found it hard to sleep, They wandered up and down the decks and listened to the leadsman's melancholy call. They were forced to keep on putting about, but whatever course they took, they were baulked and progress became nerve-racking and painful. Every league became an effort and on 1 June a quick storm blew up. Cook was stretched to his limit. Although it was gone in an hour to two, even Banks lost his enthusiasm and kept looking at the land, the shoals and the waves breaking. They had encountered nothing quite like this on the entire voyage. What was happening to them?

That night, Clerke and Gore were on watch, with Wilkinson helping the leadsman in the sounding boat. Cook made his way on to the quarter deck and Gore noticed that the Captain was tense, his face drawn and lined. Clerke saw this too, and became worried. 'Three leagues off shore, sir,' Gore said, 'and twelve fathoms of water.'

Cook peered in the moonlight. 'No more of those coral reefs?'

'Not since mid-watch.'

'It's a magnificent coastline,' Cook said, 'but I won't be sorry when we map it to its northernmost point.'

'And then?' Gore asked.

'Batavia, then home. Next week will be my daughter's birthday. She'll be five.'

'We'll drink to her, sir.'

'Thank you, Mr Gore. I've a mind to be home before her sixth. Both my sons will be growing out of recognition; I think it time we all went home.' Cook was weary and, for the first time on the voyage, fear was enveloping him. He turned away from Gore, his face in the shadows.

Clerke went foward and stood with Wilkinson, as the lead was swung. 'Twenty-one fathoms.' he went to the port side. 'Ten fathoms.'

'That's not possible.' Clerke watched with great care.

'It's ten, sir,'

'Seven fathoms,' Wilkinson called.

'Lord God,' the young man said.

Cook and Gore took all this in. 'Another coral reef, sir?'

'Shorten all sail, Mr Gore.'

'Aye, aye, sir.'

'Seventeen fathoms.'

Clerke breathed and went back to his colleagues. 'Seventeen fathoms, sir. Wind, east southeast.'

'Mainland north,' Gore said, 'bearing west, half west.'

'All's well, Captain,' Clerke said. 'Get some rest.'

'I will. Call me in one hour.'

They all heard it – Banks in his cot, Cook in his cabin, Hicks as he coughed and sweated and the sailors in their quarters below. The shock was violent. Everyone tumbled out into the clear, hot night, Cook dragging on his trousers. He ordered the sails clewed and lines run out for boats to pull the *Endeavour* off. The sea was calm and the wind light. I must be grateful for small mercies, Cook thought. Then the ship lurched, the timbers crunched and he saw timber in the sea. Furthermore, he knew it was high water and they had no hope of getting free until the next high tide.

Gore went below and made his way through casks and provisions. Holding the candle lantern, he paused and heard the water slapping against the hull. He listened to the creak of the timbers and then the ugly sound of the keel on the coral: it was as sharp as any knife and the ship as soft as a piece of cheese. As he scrambled and struggled through the gloom he could hear the rats scampering. He hit his head and feeling the water up to his knees, he cursed. He was standing in more than three feet of water and the hold was filling rapidly.

In the morning, the sea was calm and the breeze as light as a zephyr. The tide had receded and they found that the *Endeavour* was firmly stuck on a reef of coral. The ship lurched on to her side and more water poured into the hold.

Chapter Six

The pumps went continuously, the men sweating and straining in the dark, their arms breaking and the water up to their thighs. Gore went down every so often to encourage them, but found them cheerful: not one oath was heard. Seabirds wheeled around the stricken ship, screeching and diving as the men started to jettison cargo to lighten the weight. The sun was hot and the day was tranquil. As he worked, Cook kept glancing at the sky, but to his relief, there was no sign of rain or a storm. Land was seven leagues away and smoke climbed high. He was thinking if the ship sank, there were not enough boats to get the men ashore. Plus they would lose all the specimens and scientific data they had collected with no chance of their being rescued from this unknown and hostile coast.

'I want you to know, James,' Banks said as they watched the barrels of salted pork being thrown over the side, 'I and my colleagues will do all we can to assist.'

'It means manual work,' Cook answered. 'It means getting your clothes dirty; it means working like any other man.'

'Are you implying that we are incapable of that?'

'I'm not implying anything – I'm simply telling you what the work will be like.' Cook thought back to his first meeting with Banks, his patronising and elegantly coiffured women of Revesby Abbey.

'Dammit, sir, I shall work my heart out, and so will the rest of us. We shall get the *Endeavour* off this reef and sailing again, if it breaks our backs.'

'Right, Joseph, kindly report to Mr Clerke, and he will instruct you.'

'I shall do that, James.' Banks ran to the companion way and bellowed to Solander and the rest, then hurried to the forecastle, where he spoke to Clerke. Cook watched as the young botanist start pitching gear overboard and was gratified.

By the end of the day, over forty tons of ballast, wet and unusable food, stores and spare gear had been pitched into the sea. The four-pound cannon went and the pumps were worked continuously. Banks worked below alongside the men and, in between sessions, collected his specimens in case the boat went down. Not one man lagged and Cook knew he had the finest crew in the British navy.

The tide rose again, and the pumps could not keep the water level at bay. Cook knew he had to heave the ship off, whatever risk was involved. As the tide got higher, the *Endeavour* lurched and groaned, the knife-edged coral carving into her very entrails. Five anchors were put out, and linked to the capstan and the windlass, ready to pull her off. Despite his fair-dealing, Cook knew that mutiny was not uncommon in times of shipwreck, and he was well aware that there were some desperate characters in his crew: men from the Gorbals of Glasgow, fugitives from the London prisons and labourers from the ravaged villages of Ireland. These men would often try to take command and pillage the ship, then return to such places as Otaheite. He kept his eye open for such disaffection and disloyalty, and to his great relief, found none. His men were steadfast, and this meant as much to him as any of the discoveries, the surveying and the work of the botanists.

By dawn next day, the *Endeavour* looked like a half-abandoned hulk – her masts stripped and the sails stored on the cluttered deck. The time had come to winch her off, the capstan was manned and the men stood ready. Wilkinson was supervising the leadsmen in the chains. He came up to Cook, dirty, sweating and his clothes torn. 'What's the depth, bosun?'

'Port astern, four fathoms, Midships, three fathoms. Starboard bow feet, sir.' He paused when Cook said nothing, 'I said 'feet' sir.'

'I heard you, mister.' Cook turned to Gore. 'What time to high water?'

'Mid-morning, sir. Three hours from now.'

'The anchors are set, sir,' Hicks said, 'ready for heaving off.'

Cook thought for a moment, 'We could rip the hull open. See if you can find a man able to get underwater and observe it. I'm going below.'

In the hold, all hatches were open, lanterns were burning for extra light and the sailors worked the hand pumps. Clerke stood waist-deep in the water and the air was foul. The shift ended and the men staggered past to rest. Banks and Parkinson struggled through the debris. 'We need more pumps,' Banks said.

'We've only three: there are no more.'

The young man was far from being a Mayfair dandy now. 'Well, we'll have to pump twice as fast, won't we?'

The sailor came up from inspecting the hull and gave

Cook his report. The damage was worse than anyone had thought and Cook decided to delay the operation until the high tide of the following day. He was now of the opinion that heaving off would tear the ship to pieces, but there was no other option.

In the great cabin, Cook told Parkinson to start packing his paintings and sketches. The artist wanted to go back to the pumps but the Captain insisted he stay. He collected his logs, journals and charts, stored them in a watertight bag and prepared himself for the worst. Although the pumping continued, the level of the water was rising and they were being forced to use buckets, or anything that would hold water. They worked all through the day, the debris floated around the ship, the seagulls swooped and the pelicans dipped and dived in the glassy water. As each group of men finished their shift they collapsed on the deck and fell into the deep sleep of the exhausted.

The sunrise was brilliant, and the lanterns gleamed as he addressed the crew. 'The pumps,' he said, 'cannot stop the water for much longer. We are almost at high water, and the risk of delaying for another twenty-four hours is too great. The time has come to heave her off. Can you hear me there, out in the boats?' The longboat, the pinnace and the yawl bobbed in the moonlight as the men called back. 'I want you to heave,' Cook went on, 'you men on the capstan and the windlass – when the moment comes, heave your hearts out. But first, I want to say something. I'm proud of this ship and I'm proud of you. I never saw or heard the sound of fear these two days, yet we were all afraid – only a fool would be otherwise. No ship's company I've served with has ever behaved better than you. Take up your positions, and thank you all.'

The tide was full after nine. The men heaved and

strained, the capstan and the windlass turned notch by notch, the cables tightened and the timbers creaked and ground against the coral. The *Endeavour* gave a mighty lurch and floated free. The men below pumped and anxiously watched the water level. It rose no further.

By noon, the wind had swung to the east, the foretop mast was set up and they made way slowly toward two islands and the shore. Cook had decided to 'fother' the ship. Oakum and wool were sewn on to a sail, it was covered with dirt and sheep's dung, lowered over the bow and dragged under the hull. This was sucked into the hole and the rush of water abated. Gore took the helm and the ship was steered in search of a likely place for repairs. They were out of danger.

They put in at a nearby river. The ship was careened and the damage inspected. It was almost as bad as Cook had feared. The false keel had all but been torn away, the timbers cut as if by a saw and the protective timbers to ward off the teredo worm were virtually gone. However it appeared that, Providence had been with them, a piece of coral had broken off the reef and lodged in the hole it had punched in the timber. Wooden scaffolding was built around the hull, a forge set up, trees felled for timber and the repairing commenced. Once more, smoke from the natives' signal fires rose. Among the tropical mangroves of the river, they settled down to work and wait in this strange, silent country.

Cook was able to continue to carry out his surveys

and Banks and Solander set out for the interior to see what they could find and collect.

This coast was not hospitable. The mudflats of the estuary stank and the sandy hills stretched all around, yet the sea teemed with fish and the air was thick with birds. Banks soon realised that the place was fecund with wildlife and he rejoiced. He could not let an opportunity such as this go by and was shooting pigeons when he saw a strange animal disappearing in to the bush. His greyhound bailed up another of these animals the next day, but it, too, eluded them. This time, Banks got a better sight of it and thought it hopped – or bounded – rather than ran. What did they have here? they wondered. It was John Gore shot the first one: it was a strange animal with two powerful hind feet, two smaller ones and a very long tail. The meat was excellent eating and it was skinned carefully to take back to London. Banks was determined to have it stuffed, and he would ask his friend, George Stubbs, to paint it. Alligators were seen in the river and they caught large turtles in the sea. The food was good and the entire company ate like kings.

Although they knew the blacks were about, they were the least of the Europeans' worries. None was seen for about a fortnight, when four men in an outrigger came into view. They were as shy as the animals and only after the sailors threw them trinkets and beads were they persuaded to come close. The Aborigines showed little curiosity: the ship on its side, the tents or the forge did not interest them, but they were pleased with a gift of fish. Then they paddled away quietly without looking back. Banks, Cook and Solander were still intrigued by this indifference. It was

101

a kind of self-sufficient loneliness, Banks thought – it was as though they had no need of the Europeans' knowledge and inventions. He told Cook that he had entered in his diary that they were but one degree removed from the brutes. They possessed no substantial dwellings and they ran around the countryside as naked as animals. However, Cook disagreed, he thought them well adapted to this strange country and indeed far happier than the white men. The two men enjoyed long conversations on the subject and Banks recalled the taciturn Yorkshireman he had first met. Things had changed – not only was James Cook an excellent seaman and navigator, he had an acute, enquiring mind and would have made a more than passable man of science. Banks thought of Dalrymple and his cronies in the Royal Society, and laughed to himself. How would they have coped with this Robinson Crusoe-like existence?

For the men, the stay at Endeavour River did not have the interest it had for Banks and his friends. Cook knew they were anxious to be on their way home. Not one day passed when he did not think about his dear Elizabeth and the children. What were they doing, and were they all well? Would they recognise him on his return? When this voyage was over, he told himself, he would apply for a shore job. But he knew he never would.

The myth of the Great South Land was not completely demolished and who knew what lay in the South Pacific east of New Zealand? There was also the unsolved riddle of the Northwest Passage. So much to do, and he had been given but one chance.

It took six weeks of hard work and the men cheered as the *Endeavour* was refloated. The masts were struck and she lay at anchor in the bay. That afternoon, Cook and Banks climbed the highest hill in sight and regarded the scene.

'Soon, you say?' Banks asked. His greyhound tugged at its lead and Cook marvelled how the animal had survived.

'As soon as we can. The men are homeswick, as I must confess, am I.' Cook pulled out his telescope and studied the reef below. 'The hull is as sound as we can make it, and with favourable weather we can reach Dutch Batavia and make proper repairs.'

Banks watched him, studying the view. 'Are you satisfied we can safely negotiate the channel?'

'My dear Joseph, there is no channel.' Cook gazed at the shoals stretching to the horizon; he knew the passage north would take every ounce of skill and determination he had. 'The prevailing wind,' he said, 'is from the southeast, we cannot go out the way we came. There's nothing for it but to venture north.'

Cook spent hour after hour in the pinnace with Gore, trying to find a way through the shoals and their hopes of leaving grew bleaker. The sun beat on their backs as the sailors rowed and sounded the depth with chain and lead.

'Three fathoms, sir.'

'Try the starboard side.'

'Two *feet*, sir.'

Cook wiped the sweat from his eyes. 'There's no pattern to this reef, it's the work of the devil.'

'We're eight leagues off shore,' Gore said.

'It extends a hundred miles south,' Cook replied. 'We know that – God knows how far to the north.'

Gore leaned over the gunwale and admired the coral. 'I have to admit it's beautiful, Captain.'

Cook nodded. 'Beautiful and lethal. A botanist's joy,

Mr Gore, but a navigator's nightmare. There's only one way to get out of here – and that's by inches.'

By the end of July a light land breeze had sprung up and Cook knew it was time. The ship was put under tight sail and Clerke and Green manned the pinnace to take the soundings. They swung the lead and reported the depths hour after hour – back-breaking, boring work. Cook sat atop the main mast, listening intently to the calls as the shadows of the reefs glided by in the clear water. He spied the hazards and called down: 'Extensive coral reef to starboard, shallow reef to starboard ahead, hard to port, helmsman.'

The voices sounded in the hot, moist air: 'Three fathoms, six fathoms, four fathoms, shoal water. . .' The day seemed endless and when they anchored that night with the heavy chains down, they had made little progress.

In his cabin Cook lay on his bunk fully dressed. It was useless, he couldn't sleep. Apart from his other worries he knew that morale was dangerously low. Perhaps a walk topside in the cool evening air would cure his insomnia. The night was still and silent and huge moths fluttered around the lanterns. Banks saw him walking there and said: 'You should be resting.'

'Once we're out of this place.'

'When? The reef seems to go on forever. The shoal water and the coral – how many more weeks?'

'Not many, please God. The men are getting tired.'

'You've inspired them,' Banks said. 'No other sailor could have got us through.'

'I had to – it was my fault.'

'Nonsense.'

'I mean it,' Cook said. 'I blame myself. It was vanity – the prize of being the first to chart this eastern coast, the honour of claiming it for England. I could have sailed off it, far out to sea.'

'And be accused of timidity.'

'Aye. There'll be some at home to accuse – and to cast doubt on our accomplishments.'

'Confound it,' Banks said, 'you're in a gloomy mood tonight.'

Cook leant against the rail, his back aching from the hours in the topmast. 'Believe me, there'll be dissent, and complaints. Our sighting of the transit of Venus was a failure and we can't please Mr Dalrymple's many supporters by finding his South Land. So in fact, what have we achieved?'

'A great voyage, James. New territories, vast information for the mapmakers, the scientists, and the botanists. Hardly a man has perished in this long journey. England will sing your praises – and mine – you'll see.'

Cook still favoured a north-east passage out of this labyrinth. The days ground by with constant sounding, tacking and putting about. When a gale blew up during the morning of 6 August, more cable was paid out and the top gallant yards were taken in. Once again Cook climbed the masthead to see only an endless line of surf pounding. A larger anchor was put out, and after discussions with Gore, Clerke and Hicks, it was agreed they should try and break out of the trap by following the coast. The weather had become diabolical with sea mists, gales and heat haze. Several days later, Banks and Cook manned the pinnace and spent an uncomfortable night on a small, barren island, where they were plagued by sandflies. After an exhausting climb, they reached the top of the hill only to find the haze made observation impossible. Both men were silent now, their clothing torn, their bodies sweating, the flies crawling and the insects biting. Just when it seemed there was no way out. Gore, who had been over to the mainland, reported clear water to the east, although it appeared to him that the channel was rather narrow for a ship such as the *Endeavour*. Cook had no such hesitation, and as a strong wind blew up, they sailed east. This was their only chance. The gale steadied and they approached the channel. After half an hour they were in the open sea, they had made it through and the next morning were out of sight of land.

As they made their way slowly north more shoals and islands appeared. These were surveyed and they were forced to anchor each night as a passage in the dark was far too perilous. A few days later they seemed to be clear of the islands and they headed for the northern-most tip of the continent. With this achieved, Cook with Banks and Solander went ashore in the longboat. They saw no further land so took possession of the entire eastern seaboard in the name of His Majesty King George III. The exploration and charting of this part of New Holland was completed.

The ocean they were in now had been charted before by Dampier and Torres, and some of Cook's crew had even been here with Wallis on the *Dolphin*. Compared with the past months the sailing was easy. The entire company could relax a little and Cook spent many hours writing up his journals. The Aborigines continued to be a source of wonder to him and he was very worried about Hicks whose condition he knew was worsening. On top of that, Tupaia had contracted scurvy and Cook had his doubts that Banks would be able to show the Tahitian off in London. Either way, Cook thought, the poor fellow was doomed.

On 29 August, the coast of New Guinea came into view and a landing was made for water. The natives there had none of the timidity of the Aborigines, but the attack was fended off easily. Cook and Banks could find no reason to linger as the *Endeavour* was now badly in need of repairs. Half her rigging was rotten, she was still taking water, the sails tore at the slightest of breezes and God only knew what was happening to her timbers. On 17 September, they made the island of Savu and three weeks later they anchored in the harbour of Batavia in the Dutch East Indies. But the season was bad there: malaria and dysentery were raging.

They learnt from a British East Indiaman that the Russians had attacked the Turks and that the American colonists had refused to pay their taxes: it looked as though war was likely. There was rioting at home against the King, but this news did not deter any of them from wishing he were at home. The crew of the East Indiaman were skeletal and Cook compared them with his own healthy men. It looked as though these waters were just as perilous as those from whence they had come.

Chapter Seven

Once a fine and elegant colonial city, Batavia had fallen into disrepair. Earlier an earthquake had devastated the city, the system of canals had been ruined and now countless mosquitoes bred, bringing the inevitable malaria. The sea roads were crowded with cargo ships, three of which were British. Again their crews were ghost-like and feeble and Cook wondered if he should let his men near them. He looked out at the crumbling wharves and warehouses, the emaciated natives and the filth of the quayside as a steamy rain fell on the stained buildings and decrepit huts. He did not like this place, its dirt and disease offended him. He had sent Hicks ashore to berth and get assistance from the Governor and Hicks had returned with fresh fruit and the Governor's welcome – repairs could be made, but at a price. That afternoon, Cook was invited to be received at the official residence.

The Governor's wife was fat and pockmarked, her teeth rotting. She lay her be-jeweled hands on her ample lap. The rain was still falling and Cook sweated.

'The *Endeavour*' she said with her eyebrows raised. 'Surely we heard it was sunk?'

'It was not ma'am.'

The Governor was a most unimpressive chap. He did not inspire great confidence or respect in Cook. In appearance he was like his wife – they could have been brother and sister. 'We were told so. Each ship that called here said it was known you were lost.'

'Not so, Sir.'

'How disturbing for your wife,' the Dutch woman said. 'Are you married, Lieutenant?'

'Yes, Ma'am.' Cook was getting impatient and wanted to get down to business.

'Children?'

'Four, one of whom I have never seen. We've been at sea two and a half years.'

'Your poor wife.'

The Governor, too, was impatient. 'Quite so. Your papers, Mr Cook, have been lodged at the port office, I understand?'

'Yes your Excellency. I must apologise for not saluting when we entered the harbour, but I have no guns in working order.'

'Extraordinary. No guns.'

'I have guns, sir, but none in working order,' Cook would give as little away as possible. 'My ship's leaking, sir. The hull is patched and beginning to split. Our rigging and sails are in bad shape. We need to careen her and make urgent repairs to get us home.'

'You are fortunate,' the Governor said. 'We have the best dry dock facilities outside Europe.'

'Which is why we came to Batavia, sir.' Cook was suspicious he did not trust this man. He wondered what was to come next.

'A charge must be made, of course, on your government. These are Dutch regulations.'

Cook considered. 'Of course. My men are fit, they can do the work.'

'Unfortunately that is not possible. Netherlands regulations insist that our own contractors carry out the repairs, and that you are obliged to stand guarantor for moneys to them.'

'I see.' Cook new he was back in the rapacious world of the Europeans now.

'I am merely the servant of my government, Mr Cook. I hope that is understood.'

'Quite.' He rose and saluted the Governor's wife.

She looked at her husband. 'Don't you think you should tell him?'

The Dutchman was disconcerted. 'I don't think so.'

'He should be informed.'

The Governor and his wife spoke in Dutch. 'It is of no importance, Lieutenant. We need not delay you.'

Cook bowed and left, he was most puzzled.

The *Endeavour* was moved to nearby Kuyper Island and stripped of all moveable stores; then she was drydocked for inspection. The hull needed extensive repairs if the passage to England were to be made. Tents were put up for the crew who found the site badly drained, muddy and infested with mosquitoes. Banks stayed one night in a government hotel but found it appalling and rented a house nearby. He then hired a horse and carriage and set about showing the ailing Tupaia the sights. Parkinson was very impressed with the wide boulevards and ornamental gardens, but the canals were stagnant. They were told about malaria and the flux and put the diseases down to personal uncleanliness. Although they found Batavia equal in grandeur to any European city, the warm rain fell ceaselessly and the insects crawled and bit.

110

With nothing much to occupy them in the oppressive heat, the men sat around and watched the Dutch workmen. They found the cooked food strange, highly spiced and not to their liking. As the days dragged on, the crew idled their time in the streets of Batavia, where the rich merchants and their wives promenaded – elegantly dressed and pomaded, but pale and sickly in appearance. This was strange town and the days were counted until they could set sail for the Cape.

Cook saw the Governor again and learnt that the cost of repairs was to be 5000 Rix dollars – it was to be loaned by the Dutch Executive Council and encumbered on the Lords of the Admiralty. The charge was exorbitant, but he was powerless to do anything about it.

As Cook left the Governor's residence he found the Governor's wife was waiting for him in the tangled, neglected garden. The rain had stopped but the dark green trees dripped. 'Lieutenant Cook?'

He stopped. 'Yes, ma'am?'

'Take your ship and leave.'

'I beg your pardon.'

'My husband should have told you, you have a right to know. This place is a graveyard.' Cook stared at her, not understanding. 'Last year,' she said, 'fifty thousand people died of fever and dysentery. Few ships call here any more. I beseech you to leave, before your men become ill.'

'But I can't leave,' Cook replied.

'You must.'

'Ma'am, without repairs, we wouldn't reach Java Head. I accept what you say and I'm grateful, but we have no alternative – we have to stay.'

The woman stepped towards him, Cook thought she

111

may say more but she quickly turned and went inside. Once again Cook left the Governor's residence deeply puzzled.

The drenching monsoon rain fell on the encampment. Cook and Gore sat in the marquee as the water dripped. The *Endeavour* sat, deserted in the dock, surrounded with scaffolding.

'The Port Officer,' Gore said, 'says the rain is holding up work on the ship. The truth is that the dockyard is short of skilled men. Something's wrong with this place.'

'Yes, their wretched insanitary drains for one thing.'

Cook thought of the Governor's wife and slapped at the mosquitoes. 'At least no one has reported sick.'

'No, sir,' Gore replied as he smiled. 'The Surgeon reports all men are well – except for himself. He declares *he's* feeling poorly.'

Cook inspected the work on the ship to find as he had expected that progress was indeed slow. A big section of the hull had been stripped and was open to the weather. The foreman spoke rapidly in Dutch and the port official translated.

'He says the work cannot be hurried. A whole new keel is needed. The timbers are worn and infested. It is a miracle you sailed so far.'

But Cook would not be put off. 'How soon can we leave?'

'I know you are anxious,' the official said, 'but do not believe all you hear about Batavia. If we do have malarial fever here, so do all the other ports in the world. Do not form hasty opinions about us.'

'Sir,' Cook replied, 'I have no opinion about Batavia, except that I am here by necessity and not from choice. My men are homesick, and there is only one cure for that.' He picked up his oilskin. 'Speed up the work, and let me take them home.

John Gore ran through the rain to the tent, ducking his head at the entrance. Clerke and the Surgeon's mate, William Perry knelt by the stretcher where Monkhouse lay sweating.

'How is he?' Gore asked.

'We need quinine, and they have none. I don't give him long.' He got up. 'You'll have to excuse me, I have other patients.'

The fever had struck and over twenty men were down. The contagion was spreading and the young mate found himself running from one patient to another. The Surgeon died that night. The sickness had struck like a hammer and nothing could stop it.

Perry found Banks pacing up and down on the verandah of his bungalow. The mate threw down his oilskins and tipped the water out of his hat. He said nothing, went inside and Banks followed. Solander lay, feverish and sweating, on a settee.

'Young William,' Banks said, 'I sent for Surgeon Monkhouse – not, with respect, the Surgeon's mate.'

Perry looked up from the prostrate Solander. 'Be thankful, sir, you've got anyone. Keep him warm wrapped. I have no medicines.'

'I have quinine.'

'Then give it to him,' Perry said, 'and take a dose as well, and count yourself fortunate.'

Banks was affronted. 'Now look here, young man.''

'I have no time to listen.'

'I don't care for your attitude, Master Perry. It offends me. Why didn't the Surgeon come?'

'The Surgeon is dead,' Perry said flatly.

Banks saw the tears in Perry's eyes. 'Monkhouse?'

'He was the first to die.'

Banks sat down. 'Dear God.'

'Now is there anyone else here who needs my attention?'

Banks covered his face with his hands. 'I can't believe it.'

'There'll be more, Mr Banks. This place is a cesspit of disease. If you need me . . . '

'Tupaia, in the next room, he had dysentery last night. I told him to rest.' They went into a small adjoining room, where Tupaia lay on a narrow bed. 'He slept the whole day,' Banks went on, 'he said to wake him before dark.'

Perry knelt for a moment over the Tahitian, he looked up at Banks, 'He's dead.'

Tupaia was buried on the island of Edam in the cemetery for convicted European felons. Banks was heartbroken, but Cook was less touched. He had never been sure about giving a berth to Banks' noble savage and had never liked the man. Despite Tupaia's use as an interpreter, Cook had always thought he was overly proud, obstinate and disagreeable. And he also thought the idea of Banks' taking a Polynesian savage to the salons of London was an absurd indulgence.

Banks set about doing something about this wretched disease. He got hold of a local surgeon who prescribed blood-letting and mustard plasters for Solander. The Swede came close to death one night and Banks sat with him through it all. By the morning, he had improved and the two moved out to a house by a stream, open to the breezes.

By the time they were ready to leave Batavia, seven men were dead, more than forty were sick and hardly a dozen could be mustered for duty. The *Endeavour* was like a hospital ship. Hicks was still alive, but obviously sinking and the draughtsman, Sydney Parkinson, was also very ill. However the Dutch captains that Cook talked to said they had been lucky not to lose a lot more. Cook took on nineteen extra seamen; the ship was refurbished and they sailed the day after Christmas Day, 1770. A British Indiaman gave them the honour of a fourteen-gun salute.

But sickness and death pursued them, even in the fresh breezes of the open sea. There were more deaths, Sporing, Banks' secretary, and Sydney Parkinson. Hicks hung grimly on to life, but on the 29th of January, the astronomer, Charles Green, died terribly. By this time, the ship's company was so ravaged, Cook could hardly run the ship. Mosquitoes continued to plague them and it was found they were breeding in the drinking water. Cook recorded the last death on the 27th of February. The sick men were taken on deck, out of the foul-smelling hold and as they sailed on through the Indian Ocean, many began to recover. Strangely, Cook made one appalling error of navigation and almost drove them ashore on Southern Africa. This mistake plagued him, was he losing his grip? But on the 10th of March the Cape of Good Hope reached out to meet them. They stayed a month at Capetown while the surviving crew was restored to good health.

In the warmth of the Southern African summer, Cook looked back on the voyage. It was now nearing an end.

He was fearful of criticism of the loss of thirty-eight men, all this after he had taken such pains to combat scurvy. What would the Sea Lords say? And the Royal Society? And worst of all, the London press? As he worked steadily on his voluminous report, he knew the Admiralty would have seen nothing like it before. Although he thought privately that the voyage of the *Endeavour* could be one of the greatest in recent history, Cook was careful to be modest in detailing the achievements. He had charted over 5000 miles of coastline, often under difficult conditions. He was sure his calculations were generally accurate and on top of that he included descriptions of the seas, winds, rivers, uncharted rocks and the native races they had encountered. As far as he knew, no seaman had done this before. He had, however, secret misgivings. It was not he who had discovered Otaheite, New Zealand or New Holland and most of all he had failed to find any trace of the Great South Land. What would the scholars and geographers think? More than that, the Pacific still harboured its mysteries, and despite his weariness he found himself already thinking of how he might solve them.

On the 1st of May, they reached the island of St Helena. In the harbour lay a convoy of twelve Indiamen on their way to England. Despite the trouble he would have keeping up with this fleet, Cook decided to sail with them. He thought it was about time they had some company. They set sail on the 14th of May. Despite her condition – her growth, barnacles, rotten rigging and threadbare sails, the *Endeavour* was able to keep up, much to the delight of the crew. The sailing was plain now and it was comforting to see other ships day after day. Then as Cook had been dreading and much to all their grief, Zachary Hicks died. At last the victim of the consumption that had gnawed at his lungs since Tahiti. Hicks was buried at sea with great ceremony, he would be sadly missed. Soon after Cook announced that Charlie Clerke was to be promoted to Lieutenant. That night, the Indiamen disappeared and once again they were alone on the sea.

July was the best sailing period for a square-rigger and they made good progress as the sealanes became busy with trading ships making for the channel ports. They were near to home now and spirits lifted. The ship was cleaned from stem to stern, the masts and spars varnished, the tackle overhauled and the sails repaired. Banks was in great form and his friend Solander fully recovered. The only shadow was the death of the remaining greyhound which expired in the great cabin. Cook did not share in Banks' sorrow. Again, it was young Nick at the masthead who sighted Land's End. The crew cheered as the familiar coastline of southern England appeared. On the 12th of July they cast anchor in the Downs and the next day, Cook, Banks and Solander mounted the coach for London.

Joseph Banks and Daniel Solander both gave dissertations at the Royal Society under the chairmanship of the Earl of Morton. They were received with acclaim wherever they went. In the two years and eleven months they had been away from England, they had collected the most comprehensive and amazing specimens of flora and fauna ever seen. Added to these were the comprehensive paintings and drawings of Sydney

117

Parkinson. As Joseph Banks said, the world was their oyster.

For James Cook there was no joyous public reception and his family news was tragic. The baby, Joseph, born while he was in the southern fastness of Tierra del Fuego, had survived only one week, and his daughter, Elizabeth, had also died. In a south London churchyard, he rose from a tiny gravestone. *IN MEMORIAM Elizabeth Cook, Beloved Daughter of James and Elizabeth. Aged 4 Years. RIP.* He was stricken with guilt. Why was he not like other men? Why was he now obsessed with the vastness of the Pacific and the puzzle of the mythical continent? The mystery of it all; the winds, the tides, currents and the navigation of unknown shores had reached into his soul. He could do nothing about it. As much as he wanted to stay in England with Elizabeth and his children, he knew already that given the chance he would put to sea once more.

That night as they sat quietly in the living room of their house in Stepney, Elizabeth passed a news journal to Cook. 'Have you seen this?' she asked.

'Yes.'

' "Joseph Banks' triumphant voyage",' she read. ' "Mr Banks returns from the unknown. Mr Banks and Dr Solander to meet the King".'

'Yes, I've seen it.'

'And you are not angry at being overlooked?'

'My dear,' James Cook replied, 'I'm happy to be home with you. We'll go back to Yorkshire and the moors, and I shall put my mind to thinking whether I wish to go to sea again.'

Elizabeth took his hand. 'I'll settle for Yorkshire. The other is more than I could ever hope for.'

He thought before he answered. 'Retirement? We'll

see.' But Cook was only forty-three years old and his thoughts were of reefs and shoals and the coasts uncharted.

Chapter Eight

 A brisk north wind blew as they walked over the uneven ground of the moors. The air was filled with the cries of curlews, lapwings, gulls and golden plovers. James and Elizabeth Cook strolled arm in arm and the boys ran ahead along the limestone path where the barns and cottages huddled. This was the place of his childhood but Cook still found himself unsatisfied. His childhood joys seemed distant now and he missed the movement of the sea, the wind and the smell of the salt. He still thought of the reception given to Banks and Solander by the King, the accolades bestowed upon them by the press and the Royal Society. No matter, the voyage of the *Endeavour* belonged to him, and no one else. He was proud of all he had done and nobody could take that away from him. The two boys, laughing and shouting, disappeared behind a stone wall, their cries carrying on the breeze. The cotton grass gleamed and the sun was high, but his thoughts kept turning to the south and the ramparts of the Antarctic. What lay in that forbidden region? Would he be promoted to lead another expedition to solve the mystery?

They saw the rider as he topped the ridge and

watched him approach. What was a rider doing out here? Elizabeth wondered, though in her heart, she thought she knew. He was an official. He saluted and handed Cook a despatch. Cook opened the envelope quickly and scanned the letter. 'My promotion has been gazetted,' he said and Elizabeth had to strain to hear him.

'To Post-Captain?'

'No, to Commander.'

'Commander? That's hardly a promotion at all. That's almost an insult.'

Cook frowned. 'Do you think so?'

'James,' his wife said, 'it's not what you expected.'

'No, it's not: promoted to Commander and required to return to London immediately.'

Elizabeth felt sorely for him. Although he would never express it she knew he was deeply and bitterly disappointed.

The meeting was held in the First Lord's room in the Admiralty. Sir Edward Hawke had retired and now the rakish Earl of Sandwich sat behind his desk facing Captain Palliser and James Cook. The Earl looked at Cook. 'You know Captain Palliser, I believe?'

'Indeed, my Lord. Quebec and Newfoundland.'

Palliser smiled. 'Mr Cook was ship's master under my command.' Sandwich got down to business. 'Gentlemen, we are considering a new voyage to the South Seas. The King desires it, the Royal Society desires it and the Secretary of State has granted the funds. Furthermore, there are the French – our old friends

121

Marion and Kerguelen and, of course, the Spaniards. The Iberians have annexed Easter Island and they have fears we are everywhere in that part of the globe.' He laughed. 'And we will be; it is imperative that this country lay claim to new territories. There is also the question of Mr Dalrymple's great south land to be resolved.'

Cook interrupted. 'My Lord, it does not exist.'

'Do you think so, sir? That has not yet been proved to my satisfaction. Banks still believes it is a possibility, and that somehow you missed it. Dalrymple claims you didn't bother to look; he insists you sailed right past it.'

Dear God, Cook thought and checked himself from raising his eyes heavenward. This is what he had dreaded. 'Then your Lordship must decide whether to believe Mr Dalrymple in his London club, or me.'

'There's a weighty body of scientific opinion against you.'

Cook thought of what he should say. The Earl of Sandwich was a powerful man – a politician now rather than a sailor; he was said by some to be slippery and his estate in Lincolnshire adjoined that of Joseph Banks. 'With respect, sir, most of them couldn't find their way out of the Thames estuary.'

The Earl grunted. 'Then I take it, if we offer you command, you would be inflexible about a renewed search for the south land?'

'Not necessarily, if you offer me command, I would map the entire hemisphere from the tropics to the polar regions. Whatever is in those seas, it would be my task to find it.' Cook rose, pointing to the large wall map of the Pacific. 'I would sail by Africa and the Cape of Good Hope, using the westerly winds. I'd base here at Queen Charlotte Sound and replenish at Otaheite and the Society Islands. And I would request two ships this time.' His mind went back to the *Endeavour* grinding on the coral reef.

Sandwich leant forward. 'Would you, by God?'

'That is, my Lord, if you offered *me* command.'

Sandwich cleared his throat but said nothing.

'Two ships would be far safer,' Palliser said. Although he was now in the Navy Board, Palliser had not forgotten the danger of the sand bars and shoals of Newfoundland.

'What type of ship?' Sandwich asked.

'Whitby merchantmen,' Cook replied. 'Converted coal carriers such as the *Endeavour*. She proved her worth, my Lord.'

'There are two available, sir.'

'Don't rush the matter, Palliser. There is much to be decided.' He eyed Cook. 'If indeed we were to offer you this, what about Joseph Banks?'

'My Lord?' Cook knew what was coming.

'He is to go. He wishes it, so does the King and so do I.'

'Mr Banks and I are firm friends,' Cook said. 'I would welcome him.'

'Good.'

Cook pressed the advantage home. 'Provided it is made clear that *I* have command. If that is to be so?'

The Earl leant back in his chair. 'You may take it, Mr Cook, it is to be so.'

Commander James Cook has his way: he was appointed leader of the second expedition and the British navy purchased two North Country-built ships – the *Resolution,* 462 tons, and the *Adventure*, 340 tons. The Admiralty recognised their good fortune in having such an explorer and navigator. Cook was also given some excellent officers, some of whom had sailed with him before and those who had not, he held in high esteem. Cook took command of the *Resolution* and command of the *Adventure* was given to Tobias Furneaux, who had sailed previously on the *Dolphin* with Wallis.

While he understood why he was not appointed commander, Joseph Banks was progressing with his ambitious plans. He was going to take a staff of fifteen, including musicians to fill in the idle hours, and he had put aside £7000 for the refurbishment of the ships, to be chosen by him. The crowded conditions of the *Endeavour* were a thing of the past. The Earl of Sandwich was on his side. Did he not call with his mistress frequently at Banks' town house in New Burlington Street? There would be no more converted coal carriers for Joseph Banks.

Cook stood on the quarter deck as the carpenters and sailmakers worked. The *Resolution* was a larger ship, but the *Endeavour* would always remain his first love. Again, Cook supervised everything with great care, he was determined that no detail would be overlooked. Across the way he saw a skiff approaching. It was Joseph Banks. 'Welcome,' he said as his friend mounted the ladder and came aboard.

'My congratulations on your appointment,' the botanist said.

'Thank you.'

'But *not* on your choice of ship.'

'I beg your pardon?'

'I can't think what possessed you. This is quite unsuitable.'

Just then, Charles Clerke came up. 'Mr Banks, sir. Delighted to have you aboard HMS *Resolution*.'

'Clerke has been promoted', Cook said, 'he sails with us as Second Lieutenant'.

Banks was not impressed. 'It remains, sir, to be seen if anyone sails. This vessel is not satisfactory. It simply will not do.'

Cook and Clerke exchanged glances. 'I suggest, Mr Banks, that we continue this conversation in the privacy of the great cabin.'

Banks waited until they were below and Cook had shut the door. 'It's hopeless,' Banks said. 'It's a coal barge, quite unfit for any gentleman to sail in.'

'Unfit?' Cook remembered Banks working the pumps when the *Endeavour* was tearing itself to pieces. When would he understand this man?

'Totally.'

'No more than the *Endeavour* was.'

'Which, indeed, it was. Perhaps not to your standards, but those of us used to better things found it cramped, unstable in a bad sea, and falling to pieces on the way home. I have no intention of putting to sea in the discomfort of a coal tub again.'

'I see.'

Banks went on. 'I sincerely hope so. The vessel is not spacious enough for my requirements, and therefore it must be changed.'

'Then you had better petition the Admiralty, because I intend to sail in this ship, with the *Adventure* as escort.'

'You, Sir,' Banks intoned, 'will do what your masters tell you. And I expect them to remind you that I am the whole purpose of this voyage. I provide finance, equip and choose the scientists, the artists and the naturalists. In all of England I am the only man who devotes his time and fortune to such enterprises. I think you will find that when *I* petition the Navy, *you* may not be sailing anywhere.'

Cook remained seated as Banks left the cabin. Was this the same man?

That week, Banks invited the Earl of Sandwich to dinner in his town house. The finest wines were served and the female company was exciting. It was here that the First Sea Lord learned of Banks' plans for the voyage, his choice of the artists, the naturalists, the musicians and the delightful young woman who was to be the botanist's personal assistant, it seemed he was impressed. Breeding and money, Banks believed, could assure anything.

Two other Sea Lords accompanied the Earl of Sandwich that morning as well as Cook's old colleague and mentor Captain Hugh Palliser. Cook, outranked, sat apart and listened to Joseph Banks.

'Commander Cook and I are friends, let no one be in doubt about that. We could not have spent three years circumnavigating the globe if this were not so.' He glanced at his friend, but Cook was impassive. 'But friends differ. I want a ship with space to it, with extra cabins and storage, a ship of the line, or an East Indiaman, or even a frigate. Something worthy, and this time with a modicum of comfort. After all, I am prepared to hazard my fortune and devote my life to

126

exploits that benefit this country. In fairness, I should not be asked to do this aboard such an inadequate vessel.'

Sandwich looked at his colleagues and tried to gauge the reaction. 'Are there any questions?' This, he thought, was a damned awkward affair.

Palliser spoke up. 'Do you mean inadequate or uncomfortable?'

'I mean, sir, unfitting, unsuitable, unwise, too small, too slow, too limited in every possible way.'

Palliser thought Banks was a bloody fool, but it was Cook's turn now. 'My Lords,' the Yorkshire man said, 'I know the argument for larger ships, for East Indiamen or frigates. I know they are more spacious, they sail better, and they certainly *look* better. But I cannot map new coasts unless I am given a strong ship with a shallow draught to sail in close. I cannot discover new lands unless you give me a ship that will hold a year's stores and take the force of any wind known to man. Ships of this sort are colliers, built in the North – there are no others. Let me remind you we lagged behind the French and Spanish for years in oceanic exploration. You and I both know it was unfit ships, not necessarily unfit men that was the cause.'

Banks jumped to his feet, aware of the force of Cook's reply. 'Sir, I will not go to sea in that vessel. I will not sail unless another ship is chosen. Nor will my artists, or my scientists and nor will my £7000 be available to equip the voyage.'

'My Lord,' Hugh Palliser said, 'no civilian can come here and threaten the Navy Board and the Sea Lords in this manner.'

'Quite,' the Earl said. 'Mr Banks, you are out of order, sir.'

The Sea Lords looked at each other, they had had enough of this. One of them spoke, 'I suggest the whole proceedings are out of order and most irregular.'

But Sandwich was a diplomat. 'It is an attempt, my Lord, to settle a difference of opinion.'

'Whose opinion? I prefer the opinion of our finest seaman on matters of the sea.'

Sandwich raised his hands. 'No one is doubting Commander Cook's worth, my Lord.'

But the Earl's colleague was not convinced. 'This whole enquiry is doubting his worth. I shall take the matter to the Parliament if this continues.'

'There is no cause for that,' Sandwich replied. 'We are agreed that Cook's choice of vessel must stand.'

Banks protested. 'Then these proceedings are a farce.'

Palliser lost his patience. 'You, sir have made it so.'

'Now, gentlemen,' Sandwich said, let us have some order. I am sure this can be resolved.' He turned to Cook. 'Commander?'

'Sir?' Cook wondered what was in the mind of the First Sea Lord.

The Earl spread his hands on the desk. 'Mr Banks, what if the *Resolution* were modified to suit your needs. Would you object, Commander?'

Cook was suspicious now. 'If your Lordship means reasonable modifications.'

'Would you reconsider, Banks?' the Earl of Sandwich asked.

'Alterations? Improvements in the accommodation? That would seem a sensible solution.' Banks warmed to the proposition. 'Thank you, my Lord, for reminding us of the fine English art of compromise. I shall draw up plans and solve this minor contretemps.' He rose to his feet.. 'An adaptation of the vessel. Splendid. We both achieve what we want. Mr Cook shall have his shallow draught, and I shall arrange the superstructure. The ugly duckling will become a handsome ship, a most elegant vessel. You'll see.'

As the meeting rose, Cook and Palliser looked at one another; they were both wondering exactly what sort of plans Banks had in mind.

The *Resolution* was docked and the masts were taken down. The decks were removed and the carpenters began building a large round house with additional cabins. The London journals were filled with stories of the reconstruction and Banks' plans; the French Ambassador was entertained on the fore deck and Banks' friends picnicked there while a string quartet played. The alterations were the occasion of the season. Sir Edward Hawke, Hugh Palliser, Charlie Clerke, and Elizabeth were appalled, but Cook merely watched the proceedings, bided his time and appeared not to worry at all. When the conversion was finished, Banks arranged for a large party of friends to be present at the seagoing trials.

The day was fine, and when Banks arrived at the dock he found Clerke waiting for him. 'Lieutenant Clerke,' Banks said, surprised, 'where's my ship?'

'If you mean the *Resolution*, sir, she won't be coming.'

'Nonsense.' Banks looked at his friends. 'I've arranged to board her for the sea trials.'

'They've been cancelled, sir.'

'Cancelled? On whose order?'

'The Captain, sir, James Cook. He's ordered the ship back to Greenwich. All new housing and decks are to be removed.'

'What?' Banks threw back his head in disbelief.

Charlie Clerke was enjoying this encounter. 'Everything, Mr Banks, is to be put back the way it was. That's the message I was asked to bring to you.' He moved toward his horse and mounted. 'That's the message.'

'Cook? Cook thinks he can do that?'

'Indeed, sir. Not only can do it – *is* doing it.'

Banks squinted as he looked up into the morning sun. 'I'll see to you, Lieutenant. I don't care for your tone. As for Cook, he's insane. I'll have him replaced.'

'You do that sir, and good luck.' Clerke dug in his heels and rode down the dock, his horse's hooves clattering on the timbers.

'God damn you, sir!' Banks shouted after him.

At Greenwich dock, the shipwrights worked. Banks, Cook, Palliser and the pilot moved away from the noise. 'What do you mean she won't sail?' Banks said, his voice raised.

The pilot stood his ground. 'She won't.'

'And who the devil are you?'

'This man is the pilot,' Cook said.

The big fellow raised his arm. 'I wouldn't take her down river let alone to sea, and you can forget the other end of the world.'

'What, sir,' Banks asked, 'are you talking about?'

130

'She useless, a floundering death trap. She's top heavy.'

'The extra superstructure,' Cook explained, 'all those improvements of yours weighed too much.'

'What?'

'The ship was overburdened, drawing too much water. We had to lighten her by taking out ballast.'

'Which, if you knew ships,' Palliser said, 'compounded the problem. Made her even heavier up top. A crank. Totally unstable.'

'She could hardly carry sail without capsizing.' Cook was enjoying himself.

The pilot cracked his knuckles. 'Like I said, top heavy. First decent wind and she'd fall over.'

'What?'

'Fall over. The most unsafe ship I've ever set foot on in all my years as pilot. I never seen such rubbish.'

'And I'm afraid,' Cook put in, 'my officers have declared they'll not go to sea in such a ship.'

Banks stared. 'You did this.'

'I beg your pardon?'

'You planned it. You allowed me to modify the ship, knowing this would happen.'

'I don't recall your being of a mood to take advice from me, Mr Banks, or anyone else for that matter.'

'You set out to humiliate me, Cook. Well, we shall see who is to be humiliated.'

Lord Sandwich looked up from his desk. 'Pray, sit down, Joseph.'

'You know what is being done to that ship?'

'What ship?'

'Damn it, sir. The *Resolution.*'

'Reports have come to me that it was unseaworthy. And we cannot have that.'

'I will not tolerate it. I now request a more suitable vessel. And I want Cook replaced.'

Sandwich leant forward. 'My dear fellow . . .'

'Or else, by God, I withdraw from the voyage. And you can't allow that. The whole of England is aware I'm to journey to the Antipodes. But there are other sailors quite capable. It boils down to this: Cook can be replaced, but I cannot.'

The Earl cleared his throat. 'I find myself in the most extraordinarily difficult position.'

'It can be made quite simple. Dismiss Cook.'

'No.'

'Then advise him he sails under my orders.'

'No.'

Banks spoke quietly now. 'I assure you, my friend, I am quite determined on this. I will withdraw.'

'I think you must.'

'What?'

'Withdraw,' the Earl of Sandwich replied, 'since you force me to choose between you and Commander James Cook. I choose Cook.'

'You cannot mean it.'

'Of course I mean it. If I were to reject the finest sailor in the realm, there would be an uproar in the Parliament. With great regret, I accept your offer not to go on the voyage.'

'Political expediency. You damned hypocrite.'

The Earl had looked after himself. 'If I lose your friendship, it would be a pity. If I lose Cook, it would be a calamity. Good day to you.'

THE
SECOND
V·O·Y·A·G·E

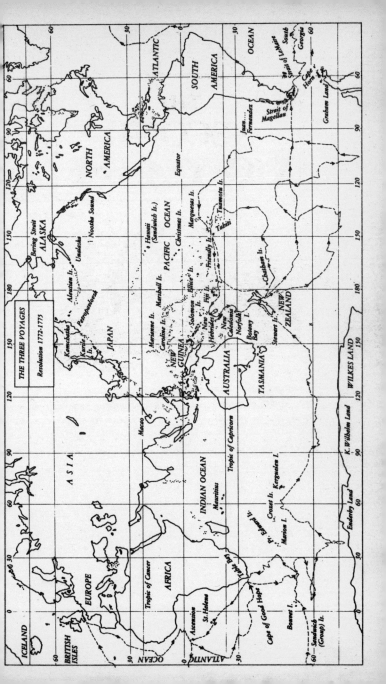

Chapter Nine

On the 13th of July, 1772, the *Resolution* and the *Adventure* were ready to sail from Plymouth Harbour. Cook's instructions closely followed the route he had proposed to the Earl of Sandwich. He was to leave Capetown at the start of the southern summer then sail south to latitude 54° south to Cape Circumcision to see if this formed part of a southern continent. Upon this landfall, he would survey, chart and establish contact with the local inhabitants. After that he would progress east and then as far south as possible, keeping to the high latitudes. It was a journey that would circumnavigate the globe and return to England via the Cape of Good Hope. There was a second plan, he could sail north, find a suitable place to refit and discover new islands and territories in the South Pacific. Strictest secrecy prevailed, England must outdo the French and Spanish in their voyages of discovery.

The pennants were raised and the pipers played. The officers of the *Resolution* looked a likely bunch. In addition to the faithful Charles Clerke, there were Lieutenants Cooper and Pickersgill and James Patten, the Surgeon. Because Banks had withdrawn and gone to Iceland in a great huff, the botanist was one John Reinhold Forster, of German descent who had with him as assistant his son, George. William Wales was the astronomer.

Cook surveyed the crew, looking for familiar faces: there with the marines he saw Gibson, he was a corporal now. The Captain of the *Adventure,* Tobias Furneaux, was also aboard: he and Cook chatted on the quarterdeck as the sails were rigged and the crew prepared to man the capstan. Cook became aware that someone was speaking to him.

'I am John Reinhold Forster, the botanist. This is my son, George, and this is Mr Wales.'

Furneaux bowed. 'Welcome gentlemen.'

'This,' Cook said, 'is Lieutenant Furneaux who commands our escort ship, HMS *Adventure.*'

Furneaux bowed again. 'I shall be astern of you – all the way, I trust.' He saluted Cook and took his leave.

Forster touched Cook's sleeve. 'A word with you about our accommodation, sir.'

But the Captain was not to be distracted. 'Not now,' he said and went forward to inspect the marines. '*Corporal* Gibson?'

'Yes sir. Your report got me promoted. You put in the good bits and left out the bad.'

'I understand you volunteered?'

'Yes sir.'

'I'm glad to have you aboard.'

'Thank you sir. The marines will be first class this voyage. And clean – I'll see to that.'

Cook watched him march off and was heartened.

A brisk south wind blew, the anchor chain was hauled and the lines taken in. The ship was under way.

Cook stood next to the helmsman and watched the *Adventure* following astern. The new voyage had begun and he could feel Clerke's excitement. 'Full sail, Mr Clerke.'

'Full sail, Captain.'

'Course due south – Madeira, Capetown, and after that, well, we shall see.'

As before, they had taken animals on board; chickens, sheep and cattle. This time, however, there were no greyhounds. Cook wondered how Banks was faring in Iceland. As he paced the quarter deck, he heard voices raised in argument and turned to Clerke. 'Trouble?'

'Our new botanist, sir, is not an easy man to please.'

Neither, Cook thought, was our last. He saw Patten arguing with Forster. 'What's the matter, Mr Forster?'

'Reinhold Forster, if you don't mind.'

Cook ignored the botanist. 'What's the matter, Surgeon Patten?'

'The gentleman doesn't like his cabin, sir.'

'It has insufficient fresh air,' Forster said. 'It is damp and mouldy and I wish to acquire the sick bay instead.'

'I'm sorry, that request is refused.'

'I shall pay you. I can afford it.'

'Thank you. No.'

'Then,' Forster said, 'I will advise the Admiralty and King George on my return that you were rude and uncooperative.'

'You must most assuredly do so.'

'You may depend on it.'

Cook watched Forster as he strode off along the deck and turned to Patten. 'You never met Mr Banks, did you?'

'I heard lots, sir.'

'A difficult man was Mr Joseph Banks – irascible at

times, selfish and domineering. But he had one redeeming feature: he had charm. I think, in time, we are going to miss him.'

Late in July, they reached Madeira and Cook again picked up large quantities of onions. He also acquired goats, pigs, more chickens and fresh water. He would apply the regimen that he knew to be successful. There was no scurvy on the *Endeavour*. And this time he thought to himself, they would avoid Batavia, whatever happened. When it rained, he had the ship fumigated and the hold dried out with stoves. He hoped Furneaux was taking the same precautions on his ship. At the Cape he learned that Marion and Kerguelen had called earlier, it seemed the French were abroad. No matter, but this made his own voyage all the important.

As they sailed south, the air became colder and the crew donned their Fearnoughts. Gales blew up and they were obliged to reduce sail; the chickens froze and the cattle staggered in their pens. One morning they found it had snowed and the rigging was stiff with ice. The cold pierced the men to the heart and it seemed nothing could keep it out. Surgeon Patten had none of poor Monkhouse's prejudices and kept the lemons and oranges in steady supply. The men were all in good shape and Cook determined to sail as far south as possible. They were entering uncharted seas.

The first ice was seen in latitude 50°, stretching far to the south. Search as he might, Cook could see no passage through it. Much to his chagrin he was forced

140

to sail north and then, when the ice field was gone, turn south once more. He would not give up. The icebergs became enormous – as high as churches, carved by the wind into fantastic shapes and awesome to behold. Some were two or three miles in circumference and several hundred feet high. They moved like some prehistoric colossus, rising and sinking in the water, the waves breaking upon their blinding white cliffs. Huge pieces would break off with a thunderous sound and fall like an avalanche into the turbulence. The ships stayed off these monsters as Cook searched for the mysterious Cape Circumcision, but land eluded him. Wales took a fix of their position and they were in latitude 60°. The two ships then worked east and then once more to the south.

John Reinhold Forster and his son, George, stood with Wales at the rail and surveyed the icy scene. They dared not touch any metal for fear of losing the skin off their fingers. 'My God,' Forster said, 'this is a bitter place. If I had but known . . .'

'You forget, father', George said, 'that we're making history: no man on earth has been this far south before.'

'Yes, indeed,' the astonomer said, 'by my calculations, we are at latitude 66° and the temperature is minus 34°.'

'We should have been warned,' Forster went on. 'If I'd realised it, not even the £4000 salary voted to me would have been enough.'

Wales was surprised. 'That was supposed to be confidential,' George said, he was annoyed at his father.

'If I were you,' said Wales, I would keep it so. My own stipend for the voyage is £800. The Captain is paid six shillings a day. He'll be lucky to see £300 at journey's end. Four thousand? I would not complain so much if I were you.'

Son looked at father as Wales walked off. 'You said that deliberately.'

'Let them know what I'm worth. They may treat me better.'

A few days later, the Antarctic Circle was crossed and they were blocked by a huge field of ice. They had to retreat, enveloped by a thick fog. Icicles hung from the rigging and the cold ate into their hearts. Visibility became impossible and they hove to. Try as they might, the could see no sign of the *Adventure*. On board his ship, shrouded in fog, Furneaux could hear the muffled sound of cannon fire. Cook, Clerke, and the officers stood together, anxiously waiting for a return of fire from the *Adventure* to fix their position. Another cannon sounded.

'Losing him, sir.'

'We are, we're drifting apart.'

'He's shifted northeast, I think, sir,' Pickersgill said.

As they stood by in the unearthly silence, another voice was heard.

'What's happening? Are we lost?' It was Forster.

Cook turned. 'Off the deck if you please, Mr Reinhold Forster. Fire signal to HMS *Adventure* on your order, Lieutenant Cooper.'

'Aye, aye, sir.'

'What the devil is going on?' Forster was still with them.

'We're trying to run this ship, Mister,' Clerke growled. 'Get to hell of the quarter deck.'

'Who said that?'

'One of my officers,' Cook said, 'with my approval. Now get below before you fall overboard, or get pushed.'

'How dare you, sir.'

Another cannon sounded, then one more, but the *Adventure* was lost.

The candles flickered in the gloom of the great cabin as Clerke, Forster, George and Wales sat at dinner. Several places were unoccupied and the food was cold.

'So on top of everything else,' Forster complained, 'we have lost the other ship.'

Clerke looked up. 'Temporarily.'

'How can we find her in this?'

'We can't and we shan't try.'

'Then we're alone down here in this God forsaken, frozen place?'

The lieutenant pushed at his food. 'Yes, sir. Alone.'

'There's no help if trouble strikes. Suppose we hit an iceberg?'

Wales dropped his knife on to his plate. 'I swear, sir, if you are not better company, I shall eat in my cabin.'

'Eat where you wish. I'm concerned for our safety. Where is the Captain?'

'Resting,' Clerke replied. 'He's been on watch for eighteen hours.'

'He should never have taken us this far south.'

'Father,' George said, 'you are not an expert on seafaring matters.'

'It doesn't need an expert to know we are in fog surrounded by pack ice. And that we have lost our escort. If the ship struck, what hope would we have?'

Wales threw down his knife and fork, got up and angrily walked out.

'What hope, Lieutenant?'

'Very little. Excuse me.' and Clerke also got up and left.

Now they were alone, his son said: 'We are here as botanists. Can we not just do our work. Must you make us so disliked?'

'It's the truth they dislike. And the truth is we could be in danger, our lives jeopardised by Cook's recklessness. And what is there to observe? Nothing.'

The fog persisted, the anchor chains were run out and they drifted. Cook joined Clerke and Pickersgill in the great cabin. Earlier that day he had been stricken by sudden pains, but now he was warmly wrapped and felt somewhat recovered. He was sure the distemper would pass – he was a strong man and looked after himself.

'A very slow drift, sir,' Pickersgill said. 'South sou'west.'

'Have you taken soundings?'

'Still too deep, sir. We can't find bottom.'

'I think,' Cook said, 'the fog is lifting.'

'Yes, sir.'

'We won't find Furneaux, but he has my charts and orders. We'll meet him in Queen Charlotte's Sound three months from now.'

Then suddenly the pain struck taking Cook's breath away.

Clerke turned. 'What's the matter, sir?'

'A slight colic pain. It's nothing.'

'I'll call the Surgeon.'

'It's nothing, Mr Clerke. Let me sleep. I'll have him examine it tomorrow.'

It was the first time Clerke had seen his master so white and obviously shaken. He would make sure the Captain kept his word and saw Surgeon Patten.

'You can get dressed now,' Patten said. 'Can you keep food down?'

'Not easily.'

'I'd prescribe rest, but how do I make *you* rest, Commander Cook? It's the digestive system. Too many years of sea diets, too much salt meat and nitrate and greasy pork, too much dosing yourself with anti-scurvy grass to make the crew follow your example. It is also, I believe, the result of too much stress and strain.'

'Is it serious?'

'Not yet, sir, but it could be.'

'Then we have no need to mention it, in your journal or mine. Or speak of it to anyone, do we Mr Patten?'

The Surgeon agreed. Cook was sure he'd make old bones yet.

At last, the fog lifted and they sailed east in cold and bitter weather. Cook had in mind to landfall at Van Diemen's Land, but the winds were contrary. The passage across the Tasman Sea was made and on the 26th of March 1773, The *Resolution* put in at Dusky Sound, New Zealand. No land had been seen for 117 days. There, in that safe anchorage, they picked up wood and fresh water. Only a few Maoris were seen in the tall, silent forests. They planted some European seeds and seven weeks later left for Queen Charlotte's Sound. Everyone hoped that Tobias Furneaux and the *Adventure* would be there.

At Queen Charlotte's Sound Furneaux strolled on the deck of the *Adventure* watching as his men rested. One played the fiddle, others fished in the glassy waters and the longboat lay on the shore. He felt quite pleased with himself, this would be the place to spend the winter. A cannon fired and echoed over the hills, then another. As Furneaux spun round, he saw a square-rigger approaching. The men laughed, shouted and cheered, the pipers played, the chains rattled, and the *Resolution* anchored a cable's length away.

They met in Cook's cabin. 'Scurvy?' the Captain said. 'How many?'

'Only four, sir. Not many.'

'One is too many. They must be forced, Mr Furneaux, to take lemon juice. To eat the celery grass and fresh meat and fish. If they refuse, flog them. Now tell me, why have you stripped down the rigging?'

'The crew are tired, Captain. I hoped to winter here.'

'You will re-rig your ship, sir, as quick as you are able. Some of my men will be sent to assist you. There are no winter quarters on this voyage, Lieutenant. We are sailing east.' Cook rose and indicated on the wall map. 'Out here, to prove to the world that Mr Dalrymple's south land does not exist. We shall run to latitude 46° and then north to Otaheite to take on stores and repair the ships. Winter, Mr Furneaux? We have no time for winter.'

June and July were angry months in the South Pacific. They reached longitude 133° with no sight of land and Cook decided to have Surgeon Patten examine the crew of the *Adventure*. He did not altogether trust Tobias Furneaux – his regimen was slack and the man lacked imagination. The Surgeon reported in Furneaux's cabin.

'How many sick?' Cook asked.

'Twenty, Sir.'

'My God. And how many with scurvy?'

'All of them.'

146

Cook stared at Furneaux. 'I told you in Queen Charlotte's Sound what was to be done, Mister. Do you not remember?

'I tried, sir.'

'Not hard enough. You run a slack ship, Mr Furneaux.'

'I resent that, sir.'

'You can resent it all you like. Enter it in your log, because I certainly shall, in mine.'

'I've done my best.'

Cook stood up. 'I'll be damned if you have. Had you obeyed my orders and fed your men ascorbics, there would have been no need for all this. Do you realise they will die unless we find land. No, Mr Furneaux, you have not done your best. Not at all.'

Cook turned north and by the 25th of August, they were he waters of Matavai Bay. Otahaeite seemed much the same: canoes welcomed them; the natives wore flowers and sang; the weather was warm and balmy; the surf thundered on the reef; and the women were beautiful. Cook recalled the theft of the quadrant and the taking of the hostages. He hoped to heaven there would not be that type of trouble again.

The Tahitians were met on the deck of the *Resolution* and Owhaa was there, he was greyhaired now but still dignified. The new ruler was an impressive young man called Tu. Corporal Gibson stood close by with Cook's officers and the native chiefs. Tu spoke briefly and Owhaa translated. 'King Tu welcomes you back, Great Friend to Otaheite.'

'My thanks and greetings to the King, and to you and

the chiefs,' Cook replied. 'What of Queen Oberea? Is she dead?'

Owhaa and King Tu talked, while Gibson listened. 'I think, sir,' the marine said, 'that she's been deposed.'

Then Owhaa spoke, 'Oberea is no more. A bad woman. The King commands. We must all enjoy ourselves.'

Cook and his men were treated with great enthusiasm: they were followed everywhere and many of the natives asked after Banks and Solander. Charlie Clerke was recognised and Corporal Gibson embraced his girl. Once more, the lutes and drums played, and that afternoon, the *marae* was packed with people who had come to feast and dance. As before, the men were delighted, here, it seemed, was paradise.

James Cook was the guest of honour, sitting alongside Tu with Pickersgill, Forster and his son. The smoke rose from the ovens and the women came close.

'Magnificent, sir.' Pickersgill said. 'An enchanted place.'

'Disgusting.'

'What is, Mr Reinhold Forster?' Cook asked as he watched the dancing.

'This lewd behaviour. It's quite disgusting.'

Cook sighed, and went on eating his roast pork. He watched Gibson walking past with his woman. Pickersgill was intrigued, but the botanist was outraged. 'I really cannot tolerate any more of this immorality, this licentiousness. I am amazed, Captain, that you cannot control your men.'

'My men, sir, have been at sea a long time.'

'That is hardly an excuse for this excess. My son and I wish to return to the ship.'

George reacted, but Cook shrugged, pleased to be rid

of Forster. 'If you must, try to do so tactfully.'

'What?'

'Try not to give offence to our hosts.'

'You astonish me, sir. Our hosts, as you call them, are nothing but ignorant savages.'

As Forster got up with his reluctant son, Cook's mind went back to Banks, Solander and Monkhouse, what was it that made a man civilised? Despite all Banks had done, he wished he were here now.

Fort Venus was re-opened and it was found to be in reasonable condition. The sick men from the *Adventure* were taken there, and, with a diet of fresh fruit and vegetables started to recover. There was no end to the food, fresh meat and coconut milk: Tu was most co-operative and the chiefs friendly, but, Cook wondered, what had happened to Oberea?

This time, the call at Otaheite was much more pleasant. The pilfering seemed to have abated and he did not have the transist of Venus to worry about. As the ships were revictualled, Forster and his son gathered specimens, and on the clear nights, Wales was busy with his telescopes. The health of the Furneaux's men improved and Cook became anxious to depart. If they overstayed, they would risk the next winter in the ice. It was not till the last week that Cook learned that Queen Oberea had been overthrown in a rebellion. It seemed the Polynesian natives had their politics, too. Some men from the *Adventure* treated the natives badly and Cook had them punished. On this occasion, more than last, he hoped that when he left the islands it would be with the reputation of humanity and fair-dealing. On the 17th of September 1773, in the company of a large fleet of native canoes, they left Otaheitie.

The course was now southwest: to Tonga and the Friendly Islands. After several landfalls, where the natives were honest and generous, they sailed for New Zealand. But the weather was turning foul with frequent storms and squalls, the winds were contrary and the going hard. The officers and men grew tired. Cook kept a weather eye out for the *Adventure* and Mr Tobias Furneaux. What, he wondered was the state of things on that vessel?

Both ships were standing off the coast of Poverty Bay when the storm came. The sky grew dark and greasy, the sea grey. Cook noticed that the fowls and pigs had left their food and were acting strangely. When the sky grew livid and green, the sails were closed-reefed and the decks cleared. The wind blew fitfully and lightning glimmered in the south, the clouds turned violet and then black. Cook watched all this and knowing what was to come, ordered all the civilians below decks. The *Adventure* was still astern and he hoped to God that Furneaux's seamanship would pass this test.

It was as dark as pitch by noon and the wind came up rapidly – a gale veering from south to east. The rain struck, as thunder echoed and lightning streaked the sky. The tempest was upon them. The inky seas grew as high as the decks and smashed over the forecastle, taking all before them; the pens disappeared and the animals with them. The stay-sails blew out and the ship pitched and rolled as the two helmsmen tried to keep her up. Down below, crockery smashed and lanterns fell, ruining paintings and smashing gear. The day and the night seemed endless and even Cook began to have his fears as the ship rose and plunged. Once or twice, the moon shone through the turbulence, but it was impossible to see.

The next morning, the wind was gone and the *Resolution* lay becalmed in a choppy sea. Cook and his officers stood in the forecastle with their telescopes and searched the horizon. The *Adventure* was gone.

'Nothing, no sign,' Cook said.

'When the wind's favourable, shall we search for them?' Clerke asked.

'I don't think so, Mr Clerke, I don't think we shall find them. I think from now on, we're alone.'

The *Resolution* wallowed and drifted as the carpenter and the sailmaker worked. A single albatross wheeled over the vast sea.

Chapter Ten

It was the beginning of November 1773 and the *Resolution* lay safely at her familiar anchorage in Queen Charlotte's Sound. Most of their supplies were unfit to eat and had to be thrown out, but thankfully there was a good supply of wild celery and some vegetables from the garden they had planted previously. The natives had become used to the Europeans now and Cook optimistically gave them some fowls and pigs to rear. There was still no sign of the *Adventure* and Cook was determined to set upon the next stage of his voyage of discovery as soon as possible. After three weeks they were ready.

Cook sat down and wrote a message for Furneaux.

. . . I am therefore, now that my ship is reconditioned and re-equipped, obliged to put to sea again, without further delay . . . I must head south to the polar regions again . . . I trust you are safe and you will find this message in the place we arranged. Proceed to England, if you are able, and be kind enough to give word of my good health to my wife.

The missive was buried in a bottle beneath a blazed tree in the vegetable garden. They departed on the 25th of

November leaving the safety of the Sound for the unknown seas between New Zealand and Cape Horn. The cannon was sounded in the last hope that the *Adventure* might be close at hand. There was no answering reply.

Although Cook's health seemed to have improved, the colic pains struck from time to time. The condition of the crew, however, was excellent. Not one man had reported to Patten, and their spirits were high. Reinhold Forster continued to grumble and complain, saying that there was nothing for him to collect and classify in such cold, inhospitable regions. The Captain reminded him that this was a voyage of geographical discovery, and as such the implications for Science and the Empire were considerable. The unwilling botanist had also acquired a small dog in Otaheite, and the barking of this animal caused everyone great annoyance. Cook still thought often of Banks, his black servants and the greyhounds. Why was it, he wondered, that men of learning were so eccentric? But most of all, his thoughts were of Elizabeth and the children. What were they doing? He had married the most patient and understanding woman in the whole of England.

At latitude 66°, the ice appeared. First, loose pack ice and then the mighty bergs, even bigger than those they had encountered in the previous southern summer. The airs were light and they drifted east, cruising off these leviathans where penguins, petrels and seals gathered and whales could be seen, surfacing and spouting. Some of the icebergs looked like great medieval castles and others like prehistoric monsters as they glided by. The silence was terrible and a dreadful sense of unease and dread fell upon the crew. Water became short and they had to carve off great chunks of ice and melt them down in the ship's coppers. In these latitudes, the sun never set and sleep became impossible as the sky was lit with an unearthly glow twenty-four hours a day. On Christmas day Wales counted more than one hundred bergs floating around the ship. The cold was so intense Cook ordered that the crew be given an extra dram of rum a day.

The fresh food began to run out and they were obliged to eat the salt beef and infested bread. Clerke knew that Cook's colic pains had returned as he looked pale and sickly, but still he persevered and latitude 71° was reached. This, Cook thought, was the most terrifying part of the world he would ever see.

The temperature sank to minus 37°; the sails became encrusted with ice as thick as armoured plating and the snow lay five feet thick on the decks. The *Resolution,* so heavily encumbered, became difficult to handle. At last they were stopped by a field of ice so thick and vast that they had to turn north. Cook concluded that if a southern continent did exist, it was far too cold to be of any use to man. He had proved that there was no great land in the southern oceans worthy of annexation. That would fix Mr Dalrymple and his learned friends.

There was still much to learn of the Pacific, it was possible that large islands existed. After conferring with Clerke, Pickersgill, Cooper and Wales, it was decided to venture north, fix the position of Easter Island, call once more at Otaheite, sail east to the Horn in November and explore the South Atlantic the following summer. This meant another year at sea, but everyone seemed in favour of it. The plan was a mighty one, but still quite possible. They would give shape to and chart the world's largest ocean to dispel all myths and to aid all those who may come after them.

154

As they sailed north, the ice on the decks and rigging melted, the winds became less bitter, but Cook's condition worsened. The pains grew so severe that the big Yorkshireman was confined to his cot. He lay there, sweating, his limbs shaking and his stomach gripping. Surgeon Patten examined him and pronounced the illness serious. Privately he thought Cook might die, but dared not voice his thoughts.

One cold morning, Clerke and Cooper bailed Patten up. 'Well, how is he?' the Lieutenant asked.

'Worse.'

'Pickersgill says,' Clerke broke in, 'he's close to dying.'

'It's possible. Anything's possible.'

'For God's sake, do something.'

Patten raised his hands. 'Damn you, what? His whole system has broken down. I have no treatment. We've no fresh food, no poultry, no meat and no vegetables. Salt rations will kill him, and without fresh food he *will* die. Don't tell me to do something.'

The news spread through the crew, they tried to catch fish without success. Prayers were said, and the men fretted when Cook became unconscious. Without fresh food to administer, all Patten could do was to wait and hope. Two nights later, Clerke and Patten stood by the rail talking, it seemed there was nothing that could be done.

'He's now bleeding internally,' Patten said.

'What else can you do?'

'Nothing further,' the Surgeon replied. 'I have neither the instruments, nor the skill.'

'They're praying for him,' Clerke said. 'This Godless, heathen crew are saying prayers.'

'I've said a few myself.'

Someone came up in the gloom, it was Forster with his dog. He greeted them. 'What is the news?'

'There's no change, Mr Forster,' Patten said as he looked at the dog sniffing around his feet. It was a most unattractive animal – why had the Captain allowed such a cur to be on board?

'I want to help,' Forster said.

'That's kind of you, sir, but there's nothing that can be done.'

'I disagree: I studied science, remember. He must be fed broth. Unless he takes nourishment, he will die.'

Patten could take no more. 'Don't you think I know? We've tried shooting seabirds and catching fish without luck. I am already too well aware of the Captain's needs and don't need to be told by you.'

'You must believe me, Mr Patten, I said I was trying to help.'

Clerke and the Surgeon watched Forster walk away, his wretched dog snapping at this heels.

The next morning Patten was attending Cook when Forster appeared at the cabin door, holding a steaming pot.

'Give the Captain this,' the botanist said.

'What is it?'

'Fresh broth.'

'*Fresh* broth? We have no meat, sir, save the salted pork.'

'We have now, Mr Patten.'

'How did you obtain it?'

'May I point out,' Forster said, 'that while you and I are talking this broth is getting cold?'

It was given to Cook for the next two days, and on the third, he was sitting up. Thereafter, to the relief of all, the Captain improved, a week later as they drew near to

156

Easter Island, he came on deck. The crew cheered and the south wind felt good on his cheeks.

'Good morning, Mr Clerke,' Cook said.

'Good morning, sir. You have improved, I see.'

'I have, indeed. What course do we have?'

'Latitude 29° south, longitude 95°, 20° west, barometer rising.'

Cook looked at the ship. 'Thank you, Mr Clerke. Carry on. I must say I feel somewhat unnecessary.' He walked slowly toward the stern and spied Forster standing alone at the taffrail.

'Good morning, sir,' Forster said. 'I'm glad it worked.'

'I hear I am indebted to you' Cook replied. And the broth, I am told, that you learned of as a student of science.'

'Yes.'

'It's remarkable how recovered I feel. The Surgeon gives you all the credit, but refuses to tell me the contents of the elixir.'

'It is of no account. Thick broth and fresh meat – that's what was essential to save you.'

As Forster turned to leave, Cook asked suddenly: 'Mr Reinhold Forster, where is your dog?'

Ten days later, the huge and mysterious statues of Easter Island were sighted. Wales fixed the position with great accuracy and the longboat was put out. The Islanders were welcoming, some wearing Spanish hats and kerchiefs, but it was a dreary, arid place. The wind-swept gardens lay unattended and the trees were stunted. The natives did not worship the statues and no one seemed to know where they had come from. Cook and Clerke wandered over the rough ground and stood before the monoliths.

'Well, Charlie,' Cook said, 'where do you think these came from?'

'Maybe they're from a lost city, sir.'

'Do you think so?' Cook thought of the Aborigines at Botany Bay and Endeavour River – their lack of dwellings and aloofness. The Pacific was a strange place, he could not see how the native races could be connected. Perhaps, long ago there were great voyages and migrations, even more ambitious than their own journey. Wales came over with his telescope, but he could offer no theory or explanation.

Easter Island was a sad and lonely place and water and wood were scarce. They would be glad to leave it. The island had inspired melancholy in the men and their thoughts were with home.

On 16 March, they left Easter Island and steered a northwest course for Otaheite by way of the Marquesas. There, they found the natives the most handsome of any in the south Seas. Water and fresh fruit were plentiful and by the 22nd of April, they were back in their familiar anchorage of Matavai Bay. They found that the place had prospered under Tu, but the thieving this time was worse than ever. One group of his men lost all their firearms and Pickersgill, Cooper and Clerke, their clothes. Cook seized hostages and eventually the objects were returned. While they were there, the Tahitians gathered a great war fleet of canoes together to attack the island of Moorea, and Cook was greatly impressed by their military organisation and seamanship. By this time, he was regarded by the Tahitians with much reverence and love. They had known no other explorer with his humanity and intelligence. He was asked to return, but he said this was his last visit; he longed for England, for Elizabeth and his children. Cook dared not tell any of the officers that he was very tired, tired with a weariness that was inexpressible.

The *Resolution* left Otaheite on the 14th of May, the voyage they had before them was still immense. On 20 June they called at Niue Island, then sailed northwest to the New Hebrides, south once more to New Caledonia and finally, on the 17th of October, back to Queen Charlotte's Sound in New Zealand. There was still the passage across the South Pacific and the rounding of the Horn to the Atlantic to come.

At the Sound, they found that the bottle left under the tree for Furneaux had been removed; the Maoris told them that the *Adventure* had arrived shortly after they had departed. Cook was relieved that Furneaux had made it to the Sound and only hoped to God that he would be as succcessful on his voyage back to England. The *Resolution* was refitted, and although the garden was overgrown, there was an adequate supply of scurvy grass and celery. Three weeks later, they left for South America, following latitude 55°. On the 17th of December, the Strait of Magellan was reached and they stood off the barren coast of Tierra del Fuego. By the 3rd of January 1775, they were in the South Atlantic and eleven days after Cook took possession of South Georgia – a most desolate place first thought to be a huge iceberg.

All the company thought the mountainous island the most terrible place on God's earth. Despite the bitter cold and the total lack of vegetation, wild life abounded, they saw all kinds of seabirds, geese, sea lions, seals and penguins. Killing these animals on the ice was easy, some of the sea lions weighing over 1000 pounds. Forster and Wales marvelled at such an abundance in this frozen place.

But the *Resolution* was now in bad shape: barnacles grew on her timbers, weed trailed from her hull and the rigging was rotten. Scurvy was close again and they sailed north for Capetown, where they anchored on the 21st of March 1775. The South African autumn was brilliant, the skies clear and the country smelt of wildflowers. After almost three years at sea, the men rambled over the fields, slept on the side of the roads in the sun, drank tea and ate freshly baked bread. There was news from home and they learnt that the *Adventure* had called in a year before.

After an easy sail to St Helena, Ascension and the Azores, they anchored at Spithead on the 29th of April. The second and the greatest voyage of the Pacific was over.

Chapter Eleven

> Father, Whose creating hand
> Made the ocean and the land;
> All Thy creatures are thy care,
> Thou art present everywhere.

The small congregation raised their voices to the heavens in the Church of St Michael at Stepney. Elizabeth stood with Nathaniel and James as the organ played.

> Christ, Who did of old appear
> On the waters, drawing near;
> Thou art still able to save,
> Calmly ruling wind and wave.

Outside, in the churchyard, Cook stood before the grave, knelt and placed the flowers at the foot of the small headstone. Then he walked up the gravel path, past the cypresses and yew trees into the church.

The sexton saw him first at the door, smiled, then bowed as Cook walked quietly down the aisle toward the altar, where the sun shone in shafts upon the gleaming cross. The vicar saw the sailor home from the sea, and sang with more voice as the congregation turned. Cook reached the pew and stood beside Elizabeth and his two sons. Elizabeth was overwhelmed, she smiled and took his hand offering up a small prayer in thanks for his safe return. The singing ended and the clergyman spoke, 'From the Book of *Ecclesiasticus*. "Those that were honoured in their generations, and were the glory of the times." Let us, with heartfelt pride and grateful minds, give thanks unto God . . ."

Elizabeth thought he was looking older now: his hair was turning grey, his face was lined and the veins stood out on his strong, rough hands. His eyes were deeper set and his mouth a little hard. She, too, was older, but her eyes were lively and her movements deft as she worked in the kitchen. Where should he start? 'I have explored the Pacific,' James Cook said, 'and there is little left to discover.'

But Elizabeth said: 'Three years and eighteen days. I have counted every one of them. Thank heaven, I'll never have to do that again.' They stood and held each other. 'You have done more than any man, and that's the end to it.'

Cook became the favourite of the learned and the great, indeed he was something of a celebrity. Lord Sandwich eulogised him at the Admiralty in the presence of his colleagues and Banks praised Cook before the members of the Royal Society – he was elected a Fellow and presented with the Copley Gold Medal, the highest honour that could be awarded. The King received James and Elizabeth at the palace and he was promoted to Post-Captain and there was talk of his being offered a senior shore position. Cook was, it was generally agreed, the greatest explorer the country had ever seen.

Joseph Banks was generous and fulsome in freely acknowledging his errors of judgement and his friendship with Cook remained steadfast. But Banks was concerned for the future: he would never forget his own days on the *Endeavour,* the grinding routine, the terrible burden of leadership and the diet of salted meat when the fresh food was gone. The members of the Royal Society, the Sea Lords and the King had not one inkling of the endless passages between the ports of call, the monotony of the voyage and the painstaking work of surveying unknown seas and treacherous landfalls. All the great and learned saw was the map of the Pacific filled and the myths dispelled. The Yorkshireman was as brilliant as any general, but all great commanders became tired. Banks knew that weary men, no matter how brilliant, made mistakes. But would the Sea Lords realise this, and what of Cook himself?

One morning the two men strolled in Kew Gardens which Banks now managed for the King. Like Elizabeth, he too had seen the changes in Cook, the signs of growing older. 'My dear James,' Banks said, as they stopped and looked at the prospect of plants and trees from the end of the earth, 'what's to become of you?'

'There's talk of a sinecure – a post at Greenwich Naval Hospital, a position ashore.' Cook thought of Elizabeth, her arms around him. *That would be the end to it.*

'Eliza will be pleased.'

'She will.'

'I believe she's still the same, outspoken woman?'

'Nothing will change that.'

They walked on toward the conservatories. 'My friend,' Joseph Banks said, 'you're forty-seven years old.'

Cook stared at him. 'What has that got to do with it?'

'You've spent six of the past seven years at sea. Two great voyages. Time to rest, perhaps?'

'You make me sound like a veteran ship of the line,' Cook growled, 'beached after a long service.'

'You have a lovely wife and two sons. Time to think of them.'

'I do, sir, I do.' They walked on the lawns where the peacocks strutted. 'I worry about Elizabeth's future, I've seen too many sailors' widows end up in the alms house.'

Banks was disturbed. 'Nonsense. You've years to live, and England would never allow it.'

'England has, in times past. I need to secure the future, the future for her – and for James and Nathaniel.'

'The best way for that, James, is to live in honourable retirement. That's the future she wants for you.'

Cook agreed. But Joseph Banks wondered what the Captain would do now that the ship did not move under his feet.

James and Elizabeth stood before the impressive building with its columns and porticoes where pigeons fluttered. Like Banks, Sir Hugh Palliser stood back watching and wondering.

'Captain of the Royal Greenwich Hospital,' Cook said.

'If you will take it,' Palliser replied. 'It's not retirement.'

'But hardly active service: you must agree on that.'

'Active service at present, James, is fighting the American colonists, and that, for you, is out of the question.'

'I was not referring to that.'

'James, we want you to be comfortable. Let me show you the accommodation.'

'*We?*'

'The Seas Lords, everybody.'

'James,' Elizabeth said, 'please stop arguing. You're as cranky as one of your ships.'

Cook did not reply and they entered the Naval Hospital.

The rooms in the suite were spacious, the ceilings high and the fireplaces ornate.

'I think it's all splendid,' Palliser said. 'Your own entrance, and a fine view of the river.'

Elizabeth stood next to her husband. 'I agree.'

'You've got servants,' Palliser went on, 'and light and fire all provided. Two hundred pounds a year salary and a shilling and tuppence a day table money.'

Elizabeth looked up. 'That's more money than we've ever known, Sir Hugh.'

'A serving Captain's full pay, ma'am. And light duties, James, while you prepare your journals of the voyage for publication,'

'I'm not sure I need light duties.' Cook said, but saw his wife looking at him and acquiesced. 'I'm grateful. This rather grand apartment, the right to publish my papers and receive the profits. No-one could have been treated more kindly.' He walked around the room, smiled and turned back. 'I expect Eliza and I will find it a trifle awe-inspiring to *live* here. We're used to simpler fare.'

'Our cottage at Mile End,' Elizabeth agreed, 'is certainly cosier.'

'Live in Stepney, by all means, Palliser replied. 'But at least occupy the rooms, James, and edit your papers here. That is, if you accept the post of Captain of the Royal Hospital?'

Cook was silent and they waited. 'I accept.'

Elizabeth took her husband's arm, she felt a sense of relief she had not had in years.

The dinners and social occasions became less frequent and the days started to drag by. Cook worked at his journals at Greenwich and found the King's English and syntax far more troublesome than charting and navigating. The *Resolution* was dry-docked and found to be in better shape than expected. So went the report of the contractors. Despite the war with the American colonists, she was to be refitted for another voyage. Ship repairing and building was booming because of the hostilities. The Admiralty asked Cook's advice from time to time, but he was mostly left to edit his journals. The days became leaden, and as he struggled with the words, he felt increasingly like a prisoner. A well-cared for one, but a prisoner nonetheless.

The *Resolution* was refloated in one of the quieter parts of the Thames estuary, and one afternoon Cook went down to look at the ship. As he rowed himself out in the skiff, he saw the bare masts and the stained, battered timbers of her hull. He secured the skiff and climbed aboard. The decks were bare and deserted, and his shoes echoed on the creaking teak. It was a dull day and he could almost imagine ghosts about. He went below into the great cabin. It too was bare, desolate and unpromising. Spiderwebs trailed from the beams and rats' droppings lay on the floor. Cook shrugged, why should he worry, it was nothing to do with him anymore. He heard a sound behind his back and turned.

'God damn, sir. It is!' In the doorway stood Corporal Samuel Gibson, a musket in his hand.

'It is, indeed.'

'Welcome aboard, sir.'

'Thank you Gibson. Picquet duty?'

'Yes sir. There's been some thieving.'

'The old ship looks a bit forlorn. When does she go for the refit?'

'There's talk sir, any day. But the yards are busy fitting out vessels for the American war. And making fat profits. Are you well, Captain?'

Yes, thank you.'

'No more of that stomach sickness that nearly did you in?'

'Nonsense. An exaggeration. I'd rather it wasn't mentioned, Gibson.'

'Yes, sir.'

'And I can assure you, I've never felt better.' Cook thought of the rooms at Greenwich and the journals waiting.

'That's good. Is there any likelihood of you taking the ship out again?'

'No, I don't believe so.'

'There's been talk sir, of an expedition to look for the Northwest Passage.'

'I've heard of it.' Cook remembered the peaks of South Georgia, his men hunting the seals and the whales rolling and spouting, the icebergs higher than St. Paul's, the uncharted coasts and the awful uncertainty. All was certain now.

'Do you reckon it exists, sir?'

'I don't know, Samuel, I truly don't.' It was the last great mystery.

'A seaway through the top of the Americas to China and the East.'

'Aye.' Cook became aware of Gibson studying him. 'I'm too old now, it's a job for a younger man.' He laughed. 'I have a handsome retirement and a splendid view of the river.'

'So you just came all this way to have a look around, for old time's sake?'

'That's it precisely, so don't you start any river talk.'

'I won't sir. I'll tell them you just wanted to see if the old hulk was still afloat.'

The marine saw Cook to the rail and watched his Captain slowly row to the docks. The tide was running hard, but the big man did it easily.

Over the years, Cook had read all the accounts of the voyages to discover the Northwest passage. The idea of an ice-free Arctic Sea had obsessed men for generations. The Italian, Cabot, had been the first to try and find the passage in 1497 and there had been over fifty voyages since. The Russians had searched but their way had been blocked by the great ice barrier and they had been defeated. A route did, in fact, exist – the problem was to find a way which was navigable. If it were found, the riches of the East would be open to all the trading nations of western Europe. The idea still prevailed that the ocean cannot freeze, that ice came from the rivers and formed ramparts on the coast. There was some evidence of this; were not the great glaciers of New Zealand and the Antarctic frozen rivers of ice? No man knew that part of the world better than James Cook.

Magellan had found a navigable passage in the south, linking the Atlantic and Pacific Oceans, so there must be a similar route in the north. John Davis had sailed as far north as latitude 72° and, although he was forced back by unfavourable winds and ice, had reported that a way through existed and was easy. But despite attempts by the English, French, Portuguese, the Spanish and the Russians, the way through remained elusive. The ice was the over-riding problem; it came from the great rivers, melted, reformed, appeared and disappeared with the seasons. The mighty fortress of the North Pole, with its stupendous embattlements of drifting ice, presented a puzzle that few navigators could resist. And if there were not a practical passage from the west, was there one from the east – north of the Kurile Islands and through the Bering Strait?

The rumours were correct, the British government had decided to make another attempt to find the Northwest Passage, and the choice of the leader had fallen to Lord Sandwich. This was, once again, an appointment of the greatest importance to the First Lord as he had to face the Parliament and the King. Whom better to assist him with the prosecution of this project than Joseph Banks? The place Sandwich chose was his London club.

'I need your influence with Cook.'

Banks was surprised. 'Why? Your own is considerable.'

'The King is insistent the Navy send two ships to

search for the Northwest Passage. It's not yet known, but twenty thousand pounds has been voted as the prize for finding it.'

Joseph Banks thought of Cook and his concern for the future of Elizabeth and their two sons but he also thought of the weariness of the sea Captain and the terrible navigational mistake Cook had made when he almost ran them aground off the coast of southern Africa. 'That's a fine, handsome sum, but Cook is retired. What's it got to do with him?'

'Dammit, sir, you know he's the logical man to command this voyage.'

'What I do know,' Banks replied as he leant forward in his chair, 'is that he's retired, and he's been ill. You can't ask him.'

'Of course I can't. Furthermore, I must not be seen to ask. That would be most unpopular with the Admiralty. But *you* can ask.'

'No, I will not do that.'

'Confound it, Joseph.'

'No, he's done enough, more than enough. Find another commander.'

'There's not one to match him.'

'It's not right, sir, and you know it. Damn your schemes. I will not help you.' Banks swallowed his wine and got to his feet.

Lord Sandwich shrugged. 'That's a pity. We are determined on that voyage, and I mean to have Cook command it.'

'Not with my connivance.'

'There are, sir, other ways.'

Chapter Twelve

Charles Clerke walked across the flagstones of the forecourt toward the impressive building. Swans glided by hardly bothered by river traffic; naval pensioners sat quietly in the watery sun. Somewhere beyond the walls, a squad of men were marching. He saw Cook coming out of the arched entrance and hurried to meet him, Cook smiled warmly as they shook hands.

In the big room the fire glowed while a servant dispensed drinks. When the old man had gone Cook said: 'I'm well looked after, Charlie.'

'I should hope so, sir. And now that you command a hospital, I trust you have had a full medical examination.'

'Utter nonsense. I'm fit. I've had no further trouble.'

'I'm glad to hear it.'

Cook moved toward the window and Clerke joined him. 'Command a hospital, indeed. It's a very far cry from Otaheite or Queen Charlotte's Sound. But as I watch the men-o'-war going down river to fight in the Americas, I'm happy to edit my papers – and my wife is content.' He looked back from the casements. 'They're sending two vessels, I hear?'

'And you'll command one?

Clerke smiled. 'Yes.'

'And a prize of £20,000 if you succeed.'

'Much depends on who leads us. Lord Sandwich says it is not resolved who will take the expedition out.'

'Have you read the journals of the previous voyages, Charlie?'

'I find reading hard, sir.'

'Well you had better try.' Cook knew that Clerke would never survive without direction. 'Do you hear me, sir? You had better try.'

'Aye, aye, sir.'

At the Deptford yard, work on the *Resolution* continued and a new vessel was procured, another Whitby-built collier of 250 tons. When Cook learned of this he had to smile, at least this time there was no argument about the type of vessel, or how she would be fitted out. From time to time, he went down to Deptford to inspect the refitting. Although it seemed satisfactory, the job was in the hands of private contractors – and that meant the task of supervision was even more important. All the yards in southern England were very busy as the war with the Americans was proving difficult.

The Parliament and the King were waiting to know who would lead the expedition. For this meeting, the Earl of Sandwich met Sir Hugh Palliser in the First Lord's room at the Admiralty. Once again, Sandwich wanted to discuss the question of leadership.

'Who else *is* there?' Sandwich grumbled. 'For God's sake, who else is there?'

Palliser knew of the First Lord's difficulties, but was not sympathetic. 'Charles Clerke himself? Lieutenant Furneaux? John Gore? bring Wallis back from America, he knows those seas well.'

'Don't talk rot.'

'They're all good men.'

'You know as well as I do,' Sandwich said, 'there's only one man.'

Palliser was reluctant. 'I don't like it.'

'Why not?' Sandwich knew and recalled his conversation with Joseph Banks.

'Cook gave his word to his wife.' Palliser ignored Sandwich as he was about to speak. 'And two long voyages are enough to ask of any man. He's no longer young, there's the strain of command, the diet, the responsibility.'

'It appears to me, sir, that you're determined to exhibit your conscience for us all to applaud.'

Palliser was angry. 'I care about him.'

'And I admire him.' The First Lord sat up straight now. 'Which would he respond to, do you think? Your concern or my admiration? Cook is an ambitious man, of humble birth, whose spirit cannot be contained in the entire southern hemisphere, put out to pasture in the confines of Greenwich Hospital. Which of us is his real friend, Palliser? You who want to leave him in dull retreat, or I who hand him his last chance of glory?'

'Those are fine words, my Lord. We both know that Cook's exploits have adorned your term of office.'

Sandwich would have nothing of that. 'We both know that the Passage is there. Cook is the man to find it. If he does not, he will bring his ships back safe and sound.

That, sir, is the nature of the man. He *has* to command.'

'Then you'll offer it?'

'My dear Palliser, nothing so obvious. I have my faults, I admit, but I do know how to handle men like James Cook.'

Early in February 1776, they met at Lord Sandwich's house for dinner – the four men, Sandwich, Mr Stephens, a man from the Admiralty, Sir Hugh Palliser and James Cook. The dinner had been a success; the venison was excellent, the wine refreshingly dry and palatable and the conversation engaging. The discussion had paid homage to the Captain's contribution to navigation, geography, the sea-faring diet and natural science. And after touching on the latest events with the troublesome American colonists, the subject of the Northwest Passage was raised. Although he knew most of the Admiralty's plans, Cook listened carefully: despite Elizabeth, James and Nathaniel, despite the comforts of Mile End and the familiar paths of the moors, his blood raced. This was the last great adventure.

'We know, of course,' the First Lord was saying, 'that you are contentedly retired, and two long voyages are enough to ask of any man.'

Palliser interrupted. 'Indeed it is.'

Sandwich frowned. 'It was I who said so. Which is why, my dear Cook. I thought that over a friendly meal together, you could give us the benefit of your vast experience.'

'By all means.'

Palliser and Stephens listened sipping their wine uneasily.

Sandwich pushed his chair back and crossed his legs. 'It seems to me that we don't meet socially enough, you

174

and I. And the enjoyment of dining with you is an added inducement to seek your counsel.' The First Lord gestured to a footman and a globe of the world was brought up. 'If an expedition to discover the Northwest Passage were to proceed, what plan would you recommend the commander of the voyage to adopt. Would there be two ships?'

'Certainly two ships.'

'Your Whitby coal cats?'

'With respect, my Lord,' Cook answered, 'it is not *if* such an expedition is to be mounted, it is *when*. And your Lordships have already acquired a second vessel – built in Whitby.'

Sandwich smiled. 'It is as you say, sir.'

'And if I may also say,' Cook continued, 'the *Resolution* is currently being refitted for such a voyage.'

'Yorkshiremen,' Sandwich observed,' are noted for their plain speaking, are they not?'

'So I have been told,' Cook said, and smiled.

'Good, now may we have your advice on the approach?'

'It is generally agreed, is it not,' Cook answered, 'that this time the approach is from the east: the route taken by Bering and Chirikov.'

Palliser had to contribute, despite his misgivings. 'But not with the same outcome.'

'No,' Cook said, 'not with the same outcome.'

Sandwich was getting impatient. 'We go by way of the Magellan Strait and Cape Horn?'

'No, sir, we do not. We water and refit in Capetown, winter base at Otaheite or the Friendly Islands, which will give us two arctic summers to search for the Passage. The most likely possibilities are here, here and here.' Cook ran his finger up the east coast of Califor-

175

nia, New Albion and to the sounds and rivers to the north. He then realised what he was doing. 'Forgive me. That is what *I* would do.'

'On the contrary,' Sandwich said, 'what you would do is exactly what we want to hear. Is it not, Palliser?'

Sir Hugh knew it was. 'Yes.'

Sandwich started to drive the nails home. 'Do you agree, Stephens?'

'Absolutely.'

Despite himself Palliser was becoming positive. 'The sailing strategy makes good sense.'

'It does,' the First Lord agreed. 'And no one knows those seas better than James Cook.'

'I would be pleased,' Cook said, 'to advise whomever you choose.'

The Earl of Sandwich pressed home. 'Which brings us to the heart of the matter.' He raised his hand; the servants came, removed the globe, refilled the glasses and the First Lord waved them away. 'Now just between the four of us, whom would you select?'

Cook looked at Sandwich. 'Whom would *I*.'

'Yes.'

'I would imagine your Lordship has someone in mind?'

Palliser thought and remembered. 'Charles Clerke perhaps?'

Sandwich turned to Cook. 'What about Clerke?'

'A fine sailor. A splendid companion. I'd trust him with my life.'

'But does he have the dignity?'

'That's not a quality I associate with Clerke.'

'Does Gore have it?' Sandwich went on. 'Or Mr Furneaux?'

'Certainly not Furneaux,' Cook said. 'I would not recommend him.'

'Gore is an American,' Palliser observed, 'and we're at war with them. He could sail, but not lead.'

'Then whom? Give me a name. Who has the stature and the judgement?' Sandwich raised his hands. No one answered and he turned to Cook. 'You, sir, know the weight of duties that face a great commander. The daily decisions, the state of the weather, the condition of the ship, the food and water supplies, the defaulters to be punished, the discipline to be preserved. You know better than I can tell you that a commander lives alone amid a hundred men, with all their lives in his hands. He has to be a diplomat, an astronomer, a navigator and surveyor. Who in the entire world is there with these qualities? Except you, of course.'

There was a silence. Cook stared at Sandwich; Stephens looked at Cook and Palliser averted his gaze.

Cook spoke: 'Are you asking me to nominate myself?'

Sandwich fiddled with his glass. 'That would be unfair.'

'Do you wish me to take the voyage?'

'We have no right to ask it. You're retired – and you have been ill.'

Cook kept his eyes up. 'Do you wish it, my Lord?'

'Naturally.'

'If so, if you mean it, then I'll go.'

'Now, sir,' the First Lord said, 'think carefully.'

'I have.'

'You must not be hasty.'

'If you need me, I accept command.'

Sandwich raised his glass. 'My dear fellow . . .'

'Bravo,' said Stephens.

But Palliser's misgivings returned. 'You're quite certain, James?'

'Yes, I'm certain.'

Sandwich drank his wine and said: 'The final voyage, finish the job?'

'Aye.'

'Then with great humility, we accept your offer. His Majesty will be delighted.' He rose to his feet. 'Gentlemen, I give you Captain James Cook.'

Later that night, the gentlemen stood in the courtyard as the carriages were brought up.

Sandwich knew he had done well. 'A remarkable evening, eh James, and an eventful one.'

Palliser stared into the gloom. 'When will you sail?'

'Next April. That should be time enough.'

'Whatever you wish will be done,' Sandwich said. 'Your choice of ships – and men.'

Cook thought of what he had done. 'My post at Greenwich, when I return. And a secured future for my family.'

'I guarantee that.' The First Lord put out his hand and they shook. 'The news will thrill all London.'

'Not quite all. Oblige me, sir, and keep the matter private for the present.'

'Until when?'

'Until I can find the courage to break the news to my wife.'

Chapter Thirteen

Cook strolled through Kew Gardens. Now that he was known ladies and gentlemen looked his way and the gardeners touched their caps. As he walked down the path toward the main greenhouse he could hear a tapping on the glass and could see Joseph Banks peering out and grinning. Cook saluted and went inside to join him.

Inside, the air was hot and moist, the foliage thick and the atmosphere heavy with perfume. Banks was taking cuttings from a bottle brush, growing in a large tub. 'Observe our humble brush tree,' Banks said, 'transported from Botany Bay. It thrives so vigorously, I've decided to honour it with a change of name. It will be known henceforth as *Banksia serrata*.' As Cook smiled, Banks looked at him carefully. 'Is what I hear true?'

'And what do you hear?'

'You know damned well, James Cook. That you've accepted command of a new voyage. Two ships and a purse of £20,000 to find the Northwest Passage.' Banks paused for Cook to respond and then said: 'Lord Sandwich boasts he achieved what no one else in the

179

United Kingdom could do: he persuaded you.'

'His Lordship gossips too readily.'

'I, for one,' said Banks, 'hoped it was not true.'

'Why?'

'You've done enough. It's time to enjoy the rest of your life ashore.' He dared not mention Cook's health and the possibility of making errors. Again, Cook did not respond. 'What does Elizabeth say?' Banks asked.

'Like you, she will no doubt disapprove.'

'*Will?* She doesn't yet know?'

Cook was becoming defensive now and started to sweat in the heat. 'Any announcement is to wait until I acquaint her with my decision.'

'Then I shouldn't delay. I doubt such news can be kept a secret. Not for long.'

'No, no. I'm merely awaiting the right moment.'

'Rather you, dear fellow, than me.'

'I daresay you've got no advice on how to impart such a matter?'

'None,' Banks answered. 'None, whatsoever.'

'No, I thought not.'

'I wish you good fortune, James, and if the Northwest Passage is not a figment of man's imagination, then I'm sure you'll find it.' Banks wondered how far he could go; he thought of Otaheite, the stealing of the quadrant and the hostage-taking. 'You'll winter at Matavai Bay, of course?'

'Naturally.'

'I sometimes think our Polynesian friends are not always what they seem. But far more than that, I wish you would listen to those of us who admire and care for you. And I wish to God you would not undertake this voyage.' Banks ended his little speech quickly and turned towards his shrubs. Cook was taken aback.

At Deptford, the *Resolution* was in dry dock once

more, and Cook went down to inspect. He walked about the decks for a moment and then went below. The vessel was a shambles. The timbers were rotten and cracked; the decking needed replacing; what work had been attempted had not been completed and the whole aspect was slipshod and dispiriting. As he poked and probed around, Cook estimated that the work needed would take three months or more. He would come every day and oversee the shipwrights. He must also ascertain the name of the builders and their reputation.

When Cook came up on deck, Gore was standing there. 'Good morning, sir.'

'There's a great deal to be done,' Cook said. 'Extensive repairs, and not many months before we sail.'

'I'm honoured you asked for me, sir.'

'It won't be easy to have the ship made ready,' Cook went on. 'The navy yards are full, all making fat profits out of the war.'

'Captain . . .'

'I heard what you said.'

'It's not been easy, being an American in the King's Navy, these past few years.'

Cook looked toward the forecastle. 'I imagine.'

'So I'm grateful you chose me.'

'I choose my officers, Mr Gore, on their seamanship, not their politics, their theories of natural history, or any other reason. Kindly understand that.'

'Yes, sir.'

'You can start to raise a crew, Mister. In the meantime, I am commanded to other duties.'

'What duties would they be, sir?'

'You can mind your damned business.' Then Cook saw Gore's face and said: 'I'm ordered to have my portrait painted.'

The Lieutenant raised a laugh. 'Indeed, sir.'

'The renowned Nathaniel Dance wishes my attendance in the apartments of the Royal Hospital at Greenwich. If you require me, I shall be sitting – and suffering there.'

'My good luck, sir.'

Cook did not acknowledge him, but went over to the rail and climbed down the ladder. He was pleased to have his portrait painted.

John Gore walked over the decks of the *Resolution*: the ship wasn't in quite the condition the Captain had described. He put Cook's ill humour down to his wanting to be at sea.

'Please do not turn your head, sir.' Nathaniel Dance had his brush poised. Captain Cook may be the best navigator the kingdom had ever seen but he was also bad-tempered. Dance had never cared for Yorkshiremen. The big man moved again, and the painter sighed, 'Kindly remain still.'

'I am trying to remain still, but I need to know what Mr Cadell thinks of my journal.'

'You need to hold your head in the required position, sir,' Dance said. 'This portrait is commissioned by His Majesty the King and Mr Banks.'

'I am well aware of that, Mr Dance, otherwise I should not be here, should I? Is it too much to ask Mr Cadell to comment on my journal?'

Dance sniffed. 'If it does not turn your head.'

'Indeed it may,' Cadell said. 'I'm very much impressed. We are delighted to publish this work, Captain. The interest in natural science and exploration has never been higher, and your journal is a fine example of the genre, if I may say so.'

'You mean you will publish it as it stands?' Cook remembered his indifferent education.

'Certainly, sir, as it stands.'

Dance was frustrated now. 'Please don't alter your expression, Captain.'

'Mr Dance, did you hear what Mr Cadell said?'

'That he intends to publish.'

Cook was delighted and proud: the men of learning would not treat him lightly now. He thought of Banks and Reinhold Forster. 'As it stands. You know,' he said to Cadell, 'that after my first voyage, my logs and journals were handed over to a scholar to be edited.'

'And what a mess he made of them. No, sir, we will have no tame writer wreak havoc on this.'

'But the style,' Cook answered, 'I'm not an educated man, Mr Cadell.'

'The style, sir, is rough and honest – and exactly how the style for such a book should be.'

Cook glowed and shifted in his seat. 'I'm pleased to learn that.'

'Your head, sir.'

'I beg your pardon, Mr Dance.'

Cadell collected the journals and got himself ready to depart.

'We shall have a number of meetings before your departure, Captain, if that suits you.'

'It does. I'm greatly obliged to you Mr Cadell.' Cook sat quite still as Dance worked; first, the portrait and now the journal: he had come a long way since that evening with Hawke in the library at Revesby Abbey. It was worth all the work and hardship, and the North-west Passage would be the crowning piece. It was said

183

that the ice in the north did not pose the same threat as that in the south. The room was becoming stuffy and he drowsed a little.

'Your head, Captain.'

Suddenly Cook became aware of Elizabeth swathed in her cloak to conceal her pregnancy. She was pale and stony. Surprised, he half rose. 'My dear,' he said, 'I believe you know the celebrated painter, Mr Dance.'

'Indeed.'

'Madame.' The painter bowed.

'Please forgive this interruption, Mr Dance, but my husband is so busily occupied of late that I rarely see him.'

Cook realised that something was amiss, and he knew what it was.

'What is it, my dear?' He hoped to God to avoid an embarrassment.

'Tell me, James,' his wife said, 'and please don't lie. Am I the last, the very last in all London to know?'

Cook rose from his chair. 'I regret, Mr Dance, we shall have to continue at a later time.'

Stricken with guilt and anger, he followed Elizabeth from the room.

He lit the lamp in the darkening room; the house seemed small and gloomy as she sat in her usual chair and faced him. Elizabeth had stopped weeping, but her face was stained with tears. Cook couldn't bear to look at her and wished to God he were at sea. Why had he not told her the night of the dinner? His courage had failed him. 'If you won't forgive me,' he said, 'I can hardly blame you. But I did try to tell you.' But he had not: he had put off the evil day. 'I tried a number of times, and each day and each week it became more difficult.'

Elizabeth was not to be placated. 'I dare say it amused

184

the Admiralty, and your powerful friends. Cook is going on another of his three year voyages, and he hasn't yet remembered to tell his wife.'

He got up and walked to the windows; in the dark a horse and cart clattered by and there was the sound of revelry in the nearby tavern. 'Whatever you say is justified.'

'You are incorrect, James: whatever I say is wasted. We talked this over – you and I. Do you remember? We agreed that two long absences were enough. You gave me a promise there would be no more.'

'I did. I regret that.'

'Do you think,' Elizabeth went on, 'that I would have welcomed this child if I'd known. The truth is that family life is not enough for you. It never has been, has it?'

'That is not so.'

She was bitter and her anger rose once more. I'm thirty-two years old, and have been married to you for fourteen of them. How many *months* have we lived together? How many nights have we slept apart? Clearly, my presence in your life has never been enough to keep you from the sea.'

Cook still stood at the window. 'You have every right to feel angry.'

'I feel betrayed, I feel used, deceived and humiliated. And frightened because you're often ill and quite unfit for another voyage. This could be your last, I mean your very last. Do you realise that? And where does that leave me – and the children – not the least the one you might not see.'

He was apprehensive now, and a strange fear began to steal over him. 'I'm well enough. Just a few years older, that's all.'

'If you say so, James.'

He left the window and tried to console her. 'Believe me, I'm sorry.'

Elizabeth threw his arm off and faced him. 'In God's name, if you profess to love me, what worm of ambition drives you? What makes you unable to rest, when you've achieved twice what most men would be proud of in one lifetime?'

Cook felt powerless before her questions; he didn't want to know about himself. What had Cadell said about his journal? Was it, rough and honest? The irony of it.

Elizabeth continued. 'Or is it my inadequacy to keep you ashore. Am I weak?'

'You must never believe that.'

'Then give me something else *to* believe.' Once more he was unable to explain and sat with his shoulders hunched. 'Why do you turn your back on me?' she asked. 'And your sons, and all the things you've wanted, all your life. Being secure, and known, and recognised wherever you go. You did want those things, James.'

'Yes. Always.'

'And now you've got them, but it seems they're not enough.'

Elizabeth considered her silent husband. 'If I'm to have any peace, I have to know why. You must tell me.'

This time he must try and explain. 'I'm afraid.'

'You're what?'

'Afraid that nothing will last, that fame is just an illusion, that history will find me lacking. Can you understand that?'

'No.'

'I don't want to be derided in the years to come as the man who made great voyages, but accomplished nothing.'

186

'Dear God, you've spent your life accomplishing things.'

'On the contrary, I've spent my time proving things do *not* exist. The great South Land. I disprove, I tear things down, I destroy beliefs. I do nothing positive.'

'You've mapped the Pacific Ocean, you've charted New Zealand and New South Wales.'

'Which Tasman discovered, which Dampier discovered – I have done nothing. And the government shows no interest in New South Wales, except that they may send convicts there if they lose the American colonies.' Cook took her hands now and tried to make her understand. 'I want to be remembered for something positive, for some discovery. I know I'm a good mariner, but that's not enough. If I can discover the Northwest Passage, that would set the seal. It would finish the task, it would be my epitaph.' He held her hands tightly. 'That, my dear Elizabeth, is what I'm about.'

Had had said it now and hoped she understood. She pulled his arms about her.

Work on the *Resolution* proceeded slowly and without enthusiasm. This was the penalty always paid for an excess of demand and the young ship's master fretted. The carpenters and painters were slovenly, they did not seem to care.

'Good God, man,' the master said. 'Strip that timber before you paint it. You want the ship to last, don't you? Have some pride in your work.'

'Bastard, young bastard, who does he think he is?' The painters slapped their brushes and grumbled.

187

The master was convinced the yard was corrupt and that the supervisors were skimping on materials. By heaven, he would set that to rights. Then he saw Cook, Gore and Clerke approaching and came to attention. 'I am Bligh, sir, ship's master, William Bligh. And very proud to serve under your command.'

Cook inspected the young man, then put out his hand. 'Welcome aboard. This is my executive officer, Lieutenant Gore.'

Gore also offered his hand. 'You come highly recommended, Mr Bligh.'

'Thank you, Lieutenant.'

'And,' Cook said, 'you already know Commander Clerke, who will captain our escort, the *Discovery*.'

'Indeed I do, sir,' said Bligh. 'I was pleased to congratulate the Commander on his recent promotion. May I have permission to inspect the ship?'

'By all means.'

'Thank you, sir.'

'Carry on, Mr Bligh.'

Cook watched the young man stride off. 'I have the feeling there's something special about the master,' he said. 'He may not be popular, but he may be indispensable. And he's younger than I expected.'

'Twenty-one, sir,' Clerke said. "He's come highly recommended by Sir Hugh Palliser and Lord Sandwich.'

'A good navigator, I understand,' Gore observed.

Cook shrugged. 'Well, we shall see. Let me say just one thing before our young Drake returns. And that is how pleased I am that we three sail together. It's just like old times. I couldn't be happier.'

Cook's temper had improved, Gore thought. 'That goes for us, too, sir.'

Then Bligh came back. 'Beg your pardon, sir, but

there's someone here who demands to see you.'

'Who?'

'A constable from the King's Bench, sir.'

Cook was puzzled. 'Bring him up.'

A constable came forward with an armed guard, carrying manacles. 'Sir,' the constable said, 'I hold a warrant which I am commanded to execute for the arrest of Commander Charles Clerke.'

The men looked on appalled as the manacles were locked on. 'In God's name,' Cook said, 'on whose authority are you acting?'

'By the order of the Justices of the King's Bench: Mr Clerke is to be apprehended and taken into custody.'

Chapter Fourteen

Unknown to Cook, the easy-going Charlie Clerke had gone guarantor for his brother's debts. Sir John Clerke, a Captain in the Royal Navy, had sailed for the West Indies, leaving a string of unpaid debts to money-lenders; and when word got out that Charlie was leaving too, the gentlemen of finance pounced. A warrant was easily obtained, and Clerke found himself thrown into the depths of the King's Bench Prison. Everyone was appalled from the first Lord down, but rules were rules. Sandwich, Banks, Palliser and Cook met to scheme for Charlie's release, but it all seemed hopeless.

Although Cook now had many powerful friends at court, this third voyage seemed hobbled by delay: there were Elizabeth's remonstrations, the contractors at the yards, the continuing round of social obligations and now Clerke. In his darker moments, Cook wondered if they would ever get away.

'God damn the Israelites,' Sandwich said.

'I've got no views about them,' Cook replied. 'I just want Charlie out.'

'I've come from the prison,' Banks said. 'James, have

you seen that place?'

'Aye.'

'Damn, it's a disgrace. Clerke's incarcerated with common thieves and murderers.'

The First Lord spoke loudly: 'I'm using my influence to have him moved.'

'Use it,' Banks replied, 'to have him set free.'

'Unfortunately, even *my* influence does not extend that far. These rules are *not* made to be broken – even the King would find it hard to intervene. And it seems that there's a case to answer.'

'What case?' Banks asked.

'This is one area where you are not experienced,' Cook said.

'Charlie guaranteed his brother's debts, and Sir John has sailed for the West Indies, leaving Charlie beholden.'

'That's not a crime.'

'I think not, but it is, by God. And the Justices have convicted him. That's our system.'

'And sentenced him,' Palliser broke in. 'It will take time to free Clerke from that dreadful place.'

Sandwich placed his hands on the desk. 'It's unfortunate, but you'll have to sail without him.'

'No.'

'What?'

'I said, no, my Lord. I shall wait.'

'For how long?'

'For as long as I am able.'

They were all surprised, not the least, Palliser. 'James, I sympathise, but you could miss the Arctic summer.'

'I said I shall wait. Unless you would prefer someone else to take out the voyage?'

'My dear fellow,' the First Lord said, 'don't be ridiculous.'

'Then, sir, I shall wait. The *Resolution* needs more time in the yards. The work so far leaves much to be desired.'

'What do you mean?' Sandwich asked. 'Is there anything I can do.'

'No, my Lord, you may leave it to me. I'm experienced in such matters.'

'You are, indeed.' Cook's preparation for the first two voyages had been impeccable.

Cook got up. 'I must take my leave – I have a full agenda.'

'My felicitations to Elizabeth,' Banks said.

Cook look blankly at him. 'Thank you.'

The door shut and Banks was worried. 'I'm concerned about him. He looks tired and, if I may say so, his temper has become somewhat short.'

'Nonsense,' Sandwich said. 'It's the worry of this matter. Commander Clerke is a close friend.'

'Granted,' Banks replied, 'but the James Cook I remember would not have waited for any man, even a friend like Clerke. I just hope to God, in tempting him to take this voyage, you know what you're doing.'

'Of course I know what I'm doing, and the man volunteered.'

'Volunteered?' Banks stood up to leave. 'That's not quite what I heard. He was seduced, sir, and you know all about that. If anything goes amiss, it will be on your head, my Lord Sandwich.' 'Blast you, sir, I am not responsible for the exigencies of seafaring.'

'Ah, but you are responsible for inveigling men into positions of responsibility, are you not? Good day to you, gentlemen.'

Banks closed the door loudly.

'Blast the man,' Sandwich said.

'Banks?'

'Yes, Palliser, Banks. Whom else would I mean? I find him less agreeable each time we meet.'

'And yet,' Palliser said, 'there's some sense in what Banks says, and you and I both know it.'

Sandwich only stared out the window at the river.

Cook and Palliser sat at the table with the charts and the complement of the ships' crews.

'Is there any news of Charles Clerke?'

'No, Hugh, there is not.' Cook sighed. It's a damnable system: we throw good men into gaol with riffraff for not paying their bills, and in Charlie's case, they weren't even his. And the prisons are disgraceful – Newgate, the Fleet and the King's Bench – I've never seen such degradation in my life. The conditions are dreadful. I only hope young Charlie will survive it.'

'Charles Clerke is the most cheerful man I know,' Palliser said. He took up the list. 'Have you met young Bligh?'

'Briefly. A tough fellow, I thought, but he could grow up to be a martinet. However, one or two men like William Bligh are needed on every voyage.'

'Whom else do you not know?'

'James King,' Cook replied.

'Ah, your Second Lieutenant.' Palliser was surprised. Why had he not bothered to make the man's acquaintance?

'Well?' Cook waited while Palliser thought.

'King is the son of a Lancashire parson, a young man with respect for learning. The family has connection with the Burkes. After he served under me, he went to Paris to study science. King has a good knowledge of astronomy – a person of sensibilities, not your usual naval man.'

'A respect for learning, eh?' Cook cleared his throat. 'I don't give a damn about learning, it's his seamanship that concerns me.'

'You will find,' Palliser replied, 'that his seamanship wants for nothing. And I think you do care about learning.'

'With respect, sir, I have had the pleasure of men of learning on two voyages around the world, and you have not. I've had a ship which looked like the main greenhouse at Kew, two men frozen to death because the men of learning did not have the wit to learn bad weather signs, greyhounds and a botanist with a yapping dog who did nothing but complain for three long years.'

'A dog which saved your life.'

'How did you know that.'

'These stories get around.'

'I would have survived nevertheless. Who else is there?'

'I fear that Mr King and Master Bligh may not get along,' Palliser said.

'That's their business, as long as they keep their differences to themselves.' Cook peered at the copperplate writing. 'Who is Molesworth Phillips, Lieutenant of the Marines?'

'A well connected Irish family I am told.'

'The marines are the most pestiferous mob in the navy. I hope our Mr Phillips can keep them in order. If he cannot, my friend, Samuel Gibson, will.'

'And,' Palliser said, 'there is Mr Williamson.'

'What do we know about him?'

'Nothing much.'

'Why,' Cook complained 'do I know nothing about my third Lieutenant?'

'He was recommended by someone in the First Lord's office,' Palliser replied. 'I suppose that's enough.' He unrolled the charts. 'May we look at the sailing plan once more?'

'With luck,' Cook said, we can set sail in June, but all depends on this damned Clerke business. I repeat, I do not intend to leave without him. First, the Cape of Good Hope; then south to search for the islands of Marion and Kerguelen; then east to Queen Charlotte's Sound. After that, the Friendly Islands, Otaheite and then north to New Albion and as high as latitude 65° to explore all the rivers and sounds for the Passage. We can winter at Petropavlovsk in Kamchatka – it's ice-free, I believe. We can spend two Arctic summers looking.'

'Are you confident?'

'If the Passage is there, sir, I will find it.'

'James Cook,' Hugh Palliser said, 'I believe you will.'

They raised their glasses and drank and Sir Hugh Palliser found himself feeling much more at ease about the voyage.

For one so young, William Bligh had most definite opinions and the highest of standards. Every day, he went down to the yard to oversee the refitting of the

Resolution. He often wondered about the Captain, whom he rarely encountered. Gore was also absent, raising the crew and undertaking other administrative duties. Cook's name was still to be seen in the daily journals, but Bligh privately thought he should have been giving more time to the practical aspects of the voyage. As he walked around the yards, it seemed to Bligh that the most experienced shipwrights were working on the ships needed for the war in America. This was simply not good enough. Were they not to embark on a voyage of discovery of benefit to all mankind? The American ambassador in Paris, Benjamin Franklin, had guaranteed complete immunity to the expedition for the duration of the hostilities. Surely that was positive proof of its importance. The work that was being carried out on the *Resolution* was appalling.

One morning, Bligh strode around complaining and threatening as usual. He bailed up the supervisor of the yard and took him over the vessel. 'Look at this,' Bligh said, 'and this, and this. Rotting timber, bad caulking, loose tar, second hand material. The hull is unsound and dangerous. Are you aware, sir, of the importance of this voyage? It has the support of the King and the blessing of the Parliament, and it's being commanded by the greatest navigator in the kingdom.'

The supervisor was not impressed. 'There's nought wrong with the hull. If Captain Cook is satisfied with it, that's good enough for me.'

The man finished filling his pipe and made as if to leave, but Bligh kept at him. 'You know the Captain has not been here for weeks. He's busy in London, and you, sir, are taking advantage of his absence.'

'You're too high and mighty, Mr Bligh, when you've been around ships as long as I, you'll know about standards. Your Captain trusts me.'

'Then he's unwise.'

'Have a care, young sir. I could pass that on and you could find yourself ashore when the day comes for sailing.' The supervisor tapped Bligh on the chest. 'And I don't like your tone.'

'And I don't like the corruption that flourishes in this shipyard.'

'The what?' The man's eyes narrowed.

'Corruption.'

'Those are serious allegations, my boy. I could have the law on to you.'

Bligh stuck to his guns. 'I insist you survey the ship and re-do the work.'

'You young pup.' The man snorted and blew his nose on the deck. 'You *insist*?'

'The vessel is unsound, a disgrace to your trade, repairs must be made.' Bligh stuck his chin out and stood over the man.

'Listen, I've got surveyors' certificates that says this ship is as good as any one afloat. You best pipe down, boy, or maybe you'll find yourself floating upside down in the river one of these dark nights.' The man stared straight back. 'We're a reputable shipyard, and I don't take kindly to the likes of you coming here and throwing your weight around. You watch yourself . . . Mister Bligh.

The supervisor turned on his heel and disappeared behind the scaffolding and piles of timber. William Bligh watched the men lounging around and was appalled. He despaired of what could happen at sea.

While Bligh was doing battle at the Deptford yard, Cook was horse-riding with Joseph Banks and King George. The Captain had already had an audience with the King, but this occasion was different. Cook felt he was more than up to it, despite the King's obvious decline. It was said that he spent more time on his farm than on the affairs of state. They rode for an hour, when at last they stopped and the horses were led away. The King stood large and regarded Cook with his pale blue eyes. 'Nothing like it to circulate the blood, gentlemen?' What say you, Joseph? You ride well for a sailor, Captain.'

'I was born and bred in the country, sire.'

'So you were,' the King replied, 'so you were. Raised yourself up from a farm labourer's tied cottage. Damned fine. What say you, Joseph?'

Banks smiled. 'Indeed, sire.'

'You'll take some horses with you, sir.'

Cook gaped. 'Horses, Your Majesty?'

'That's what I said, sir. Horses, damned wonderful animals, don't you think? Practically human. You'll take them as gifts to foreign rulers. Gifts from farmer George. Ha ha.'

Cook was about to explain to the King that there were no foreign rulers whom he would recognise in the South Pacific or the north, when he saw Banks looking at him. 'Yes, Sire.'

'I must have a word with the head groom,' the King said. 'I wish you luck with the foreign potentates, sir, and when you present the horses, tell them you offer them the protection of His Britannic Majesty.'

As the King walked away, Cook and Banks sighed and regarded each other. 'Horses,' Cook said. 'Do I have to take them?'

'He's often confused of late. He may forget.'

'I don't think so. Not in matters of livestock. I'm already bound to take a flock of sheep and a herd of cattle.'

They strolled off, through the stables. 'No good news of Clerke?' Banks asked.

'No. I'll have to sail without him, and pray he can find us at Capetown.'

'But you said you would not leave before Clerke was released. You were adamant.'

'Needs must when the devil drives, Joseph, and it seems he is driving very hard at present.'

'And Elizabeth?'

'Her time's close.'

'Are you forgiven?'

'I doubt if I'll ever be.' Cook stopped and turned to Banks. 'If anything ever happens to me . . .'

'Don't be foolish.'

'If it does,' Cook continued, 'I trust you and Hugh Palliser above everyone else to see that she's cared for – and the children.'

Cook followed the turnkey down the underground corridor. Water seeped through the mildewed stinking walls. No man, thought Cook, whatever his crime, should have to live in a place like this, let alone men as innocent as Charles Clerke. He thought of the King, his horses and the royal estate. At length, they reached the cell. Clerke saw them, struggled to his feet and put his hand out through the bars. He looked pale, filthy and half-starved.

'Charlie,' Cook said, 'my God, what have they done to you?'

'I'll survive. But it's wet, sir, wet and cold. I've not been dry and warm for months.'

Cook was horrified. 'We've done all we can to get

you out.' It seems that the law of imprisonment is beyond the power of the influential. I'll have to sail without you, Charlie.'

'I understand, sir. You should have long gone. I'll find a way.'

'Your ship,' Cook said, 'will wait in Plymouth until you're free. Then you'll follow us to the Cape.'

'You can't take the risk.'

'The *Discovery*, Charles Clerke, will wait until you board her. Now you get out of here. You join me. Do you hear?'

'I hear.'

The refitting of the Resolution was completed; Cook made his peace with Elizabeth; the horses, cattle and sheep, together with the fowls, were taken on board. Cook bade farewell to Joseph Banks and Hugh Palliser and to the tune of a military band, they sailed on 12 July 1776. The wind was fair and from the north, but young Master Bligh uttered a curse as he heard the timbers creak and strain. He could only hope his fears would not be justified.

THE
THIRD
V·O·Y·A·G·E

THE THREE VOYAGES

Resolution 1776-1780

ICELAND

BRITISH ISLES

EUROPE

ASIA

AFRICA

Tropic of Cancer

ATLANTIC OCEAN

Ascension

St. Helena

Bouvet I.

Sandwich (Group) Is.

Cape of Good Hope

Table Bay

P. Edward Is.

Crozet Is. Kerguelen I.

Marion I.

INDIAN OCEAN

Mauritius

Tropic of Capricorn

Macao

JAPAN

Kamchatka

Kuril Is.

Petropavlovsk

Bering Strait

ALASKA

Aleutian Is.

Umnak I.

Unalaska

Nootka Sound

NORTH AMERICA

PACIFIC OCEAN

Equator

Hawaii (Sandwich Is.)

Christmas I.

Marquesas Is.

Tuamotu Is.

Tahiti

Friendly Is.

Marianne Is. Marshall Is.

Caroline Is. Ellice Is.

Solomon Fiji Is.

NEW GUINEA

New Hebrides

New Caledonia

Norfolk I.

Botany Bay

AUSTRALIA

TASMANIA

Stewart I. Chatham Is.

NEW ZEALAND

Chatham Is.

SOUTH AMERICA

ATLANTIC

Strait of Magellan

Juan Fernandez

Cape Horn

Strait of Le Maire

South Georgia

Graham Land

OCEAN

WILKES LAND

K. Wilhelm Land

Enderby Land

Chapter Fifteen

For a time, Cook stood at the rail and looked at the cliffs of the Cornish coast. As he raised his telescope and spied the windswept trees and pebbled beaches, he thought of Elizabeth and the boys. This time, he intended to sail west and call at Tenerife for water and fresh provisions. He calculated on reaching the Cape of Good hope on the third week of October. What, he wondered, was happening to Charlie Clerke? He prayed to God that Sandwich and Palliser were still working for his release.

The sealed orders from the First Lord confirmed all that had been discussed about the route, and Cook was satisfied. But he read the last page twice to get the full import of what Sandwich had said:

. . . in conclusion, if by any illness or accident, you are unable to continue the voyage and carry out these instructions, you will assign them to the officer in command, who is required to execute them in the best way he can. Given under our hands, the Sixth Day of July, 1776.

Coldness gripped him as he heard the run of the sea and the working of the timbers. What in God's name was the First Lord thinking of? *If by any illness or accident.*

That night, Cook met Gore at the taffrail. 'Did you read it?'

'Yes, sir.'

" 'If by any illness or accident, you are unable to continue . . .".'

Gore thought. 'It does seem unusual.'

The moon was watery and the night dark as Cook answered:

'Extremely.'

'But surely, sir, a formality.'

'One they didn't need on either of my two previous voyages. Why the formality, this time, Mr Gore?'

'I would not attach much to it.'

Cook thought of Banks' admonition in the greenhouse at Kew: *I wish to God you would not undertake this voyage.* 'My friends, Sir Hugh Palliser and Lord Sandwich, are showing a sudden lack of confidence in my health. It seems that is something they preferred not to discuss ashore, so they wrote about it in my instructions.'

'It does seem insensitive.'

'It seems that they're apprehensive, that they're nervous. And that makes me uneasy.'

Bligh was behind them. 'We're losing the breeze, sir. Will you give the order to alter sail?'

'God Almighty, Mr Bligh, why do you always interrupt in such a confoundedly rude manner?'

Bligh saw Cook's face, dark with anger in the moonlight. 'Beg pardon, sir, but we've too much canvas aloft.'

'Are you aware, Master Bligh, that your executive officer is having a private conversation with me. What

206

do you think you're about?'

'But sir . . .'

'You have a great deal to learn, Mr Bligh.'

'I'm sorry, Captain.' Bligh melted away into the darkness, and Gore tried to placate Cook.

'You must not allow it to upset you, sir. Forget it.'

'I doubt if I can do that,' Cook replied. 'It's a poor start, old friend. Clerke still in prison, and God knows if he will be freed in time to join us. The King's tame zoo on board, taking up precious cargo space, and now this portent from Sandwich and Palliser.' He remembered the master. 'Mr Bligh?'

'Captain?'

'You may give the order to alter sail.' Cook moved away, and for once, Bligh stood there.

'You heard the Captain, Mister,' Gore said. 'Get on with it.'

'Aye, aye, sir.' Bligh went forward, aggrieved.

Next day when Cook did his rounds, it became obvious there were other problems. It was clear that Molesworth Phillips was totally without experience. It was his first time at sea, his commission had been purchased by his father and it was certain that the marines would have little respect for him. Cook thanked heaven for Gibson and cursed the system of acquiring commissions. The ruling class still had its way.

The horses, cattle and sheep were going to take up inordinate care and time. They were in the care of Phillip's marines, most of whom were from the slums of Manchester and Glasgow and who had never been close to a cow in their lives. The animal holds were foul with manure and the beasts whinneyed, bellowed and bleated in their misery. Farmer George's gifts to the

Polynesian potentates were an act of madness. If any of them died, at least they would have fresh meat but his sense of duty reasserted itself; he had to keep them alive as long as possible.

However, worse was to come. Bligh took Cook below and showed him the water already inches deep in the hold. The ship was leaking in many places; this was the legacy of the indolent workers at the Deptford yard. And that afternoon when it poured with rain, water dripped from the ceiling of the great cabin. There, Cook found the artist, Webber, trying to keep the cabin dry. Bligh then inspected the Captain's cabin to find it drenched with water from the deck above. Cook stood there, his boots in the water, and said: 'I'm afraid, Mr Bligh, our British shipyards have been less than honest.'

But the young master did not reply.

By the end of the afternoon, the rain had stopped and the sails were dragged up on deck to dry. Many of them were already mouldy, and as he watched them being spread out, Cook thought of the voyage to come: the heat and humidity of the Pacific.

'I blame myself for this,' Cook said to Gore.

'Sir, if there was corruption in the shipyards, why should you shoulder the guilt?'

'Because I should have been there, Mr Gore. I was too busy being lionised – sitting for my portrait, meeting with the King, lunching with the scholars and scientists and attending to my literary endeavours.'

'I'm equally to blame.'

'You know, sir, and I know that the Captain is responsible. And we both know that this vessel is unfit for what lies ahead.'

Bligh watched as Cook and Gore talked. This was

Cook's first mistake, he thought and he hoped there would be no more.

Ten days after Tenerife, the *Resolution* reached Buena Vista in Cape Verdes. The weather was warming up and the evenings were becoming longer. The leaks had become so obvious that is was necessary for the pumps to be manned all the time. After dining with Gore, King and Webber, Cook felt weary and retired to his cabin to write up his journal. The course was set and he looked forward to a quiet night. On the quarter deck, Bligh paced back and forth while Williamson kept the watch.

'It's a hot night,' said Bligh.

'Aye.'

Bligh thought privately that Williamson was a surly, lazy devil.

'What course did the Captain set?'

'South, eighteen east.'

'East?'

'That's what he set.'

'Thank you, Mr Williamson.' Bligh moved away but stopped at the rail and stared out at the moonlit sea. He thought he heard a sound, but couldn't be sure. He listened once more, turned and saw someone near him. 'Who is it?' For some reason, Bligh felt anxious.

'Phillips, old man. Molesworth Phillips.'

That idiot, Bligh thought, and listened once more. 'Can you hear anything, Lieutenant Phillips?'

'Don't believe I can.'

Bligh knew what it was now. 'Listen,' he said. 'Over

there. God almighty.' he saw the breakers. 'Can you see it now?'

'Surf?'

'Surf and reefs. Get the Captain.' Bligh screamed at the young officer. 'Don't stand there. Get him.'

'Right you are.'

Bligh turned and bellowed. 'Helmsman, hard astarboard.'

'What's happening, Mr Bligh?' It was Williamson.

'Breakers ahead. Brace the yards. Spring to it. Sound the alarm, Mr Williamson.

Cook had almost finished the entry in his journal when he heard the noise and the alarm. And when he emerged into the great cabin, he found Gore, King and Phillips.

'Breakers, sir,' the officer said, his face white and body shaking. 'Half a league away.'

As Cook burst up the companionway, the others following they found Bligh shouting orders, very much in command.

'Breakers port side, sir. I ordered hard astarboard.' But the Captain was silent and immobile. 'There was no lookout posted,' Bligh went on, 'I've taken soundings – six fathoms. Sir?'

Gore pushed past Cook. 'Right, Mr Bligh, brace the yards sharp up.'

'Aye, aye, sir. Bligh shouted. 'All yards, brace sharp up. All hands stand by to secure lines.'

The lines were hauled, the ship came up and the course was altered. The noise of the reef receded and Bligh turned to the Captain. 'I think we're safe now, sir. Should we shorten sail? Sir?'

At last, Cook spoke. 'Aye, shorten sail. All crew to stand by emergency posts until daylight.'

210

In the calm morning, Cook stood on the quarter deck. Bligh watched him, then moved over to Gore. 'I don't understand it.'

'What?' But Gore knew.

'Since I was ten years old, I was brought up to believe he was the greatest of all navigators.'

'He was? Mister, you mean he is.'

'He set a course that almost put the ship on a reef. In a calm sea. In clear moonlight. They must have been talking of someone else.'

Gore made no answer.

Cook saw Bligh and raised his arm. 'Master, if you please.'

'Sir?'

'You did well, Mr Bligh. I shall note in the log that your action may well have saved the ship.'

'Thank you, sir, but I'm not sure of that.'

'What?'

'That it's true. And worth recording.'

Cook stared at him. 'Allow me to decide what is worth recording in my own log. That is all, Mr Bligh.'

It seemed now that the *Resolution* was coming apart at the seams, and the entire company was relieved when on 18 October they saw Table Mountain come into view. They anchored in the Bay and saluted the garrison with thirteen guns. The cattle were taken ashore to graze and the carpenter and the men set about the business of caulking the ship. King and Webber set up a small observatory to observe the equal altitudes of the sun and Bligh arranged for quantities of fresh bread and vegetables. The southern spring weather was mild and balmy and the perfume of fresh-cut grass and wild flowers drifted over the waters. Regularly, Cook scanned the entrance to the Bay with his telescope, but there was no sign of the *Discovery*. Cook joined King and Webber from time to time and enjoyed their company, but he could not relax for thinking about Charles Clerke.

In the three weeks that passed, the ship was made as water-tight as possible, more cattle were purchased and the compass variations were checked. Time hung heavily on all of them as they waited for the escort ship. By the first days in November, Cook was losing heart. When the *Discovery* arrived, *if* the *Discovery* arrived, it too would need re-caulking and loading with provisions for the long voyage ahead. What had happened to Clerke? It was possible that Lieutenant Burnley, Clerke's deputy, had taken the ship out, but Cook doubted it. At last on Sunday the 10th of November, a cannon sounded: it was the *Discovery*. A delighted Cook stood on the quarter deck with his officers. He lowered his telescope for a moment, smiled and said: 'Make a signal, Mr Bligh. To Captain Charles Clerke, HMS *Discovery*. Welcome and well done.'

That evening, the officers of both ships gathered in the great cabin of the *Resolution*. Cook broke open his best wine and the dinner of fresh beef, mutton and vegetables was excellent.

Lieutenant Burnley turned out to be a most engaging young man of charm and wit. As Cook listened to him speaking he was reminded of the good days with Joseph Banks.

'So there we were in Plymouth Sound,' Burnley was saying, 'sail up and standing by, when out of the mist hove this carriage, and out of this carriage hove Commander Clerke. And out of his mouth, he bellowed; "Weigh anchor for Capetown and the South Seas." I swear they heard it on Plymouth Hoe, where the ghost of Francis Drake was finishing his game of bowls . . . .'

Cook laughed with the others but drew Clerke aside while they all chatted and drank. 'Is young Burnley a good officer?' he asked.

'Bright, sir, and a constant source of amusement. How are Mr King and Mr Bligh?'

'King is very able and Bligh is efficient.' He thought of the miscalculation and the sound of the seas on the reef. 'Which is more than I can say for some others.' Cook looked at the ships' companies as they talked and drank. 'Let us go to my cabin, Charlie.'

Under the light of the lantern, Clerke looked pale and thin.

'It's good to see you, sir.'

'No ill effects from the prison, I hope, Charlie?'

'Just nightmares. The memory of the damp and the smell, and never being warm. That's the last time, believe me, I ever stand guarantor for my brother's debts.'

'Thank God, he arranged to have them paid, or you could still be in that dreadful place.'

Clerke spoke quietly. 'I doubt I could have endured it for much longer.'

'How was the passage?' Cook asked.

'The weather was foul, sir, and I lost a man overboard.'

'Did you?'

'A corporal of the marines.'

'Why is it always the damned marines?' Cook said.

'I think you know, sir.'

'This ship, Charlie, is in a deplorable state. It leaks like the proverbial sieve – the work done at Deptford was disgraceful. Young Master Bligh was right.'

'Right, sir?'

'He complained to the owners of the yard, but alas got nowhere.'

'Will it make the voyage? sir.'

'Yes, Charlie, it will make it, but by God it's good to have you as escort.' He put his hand on Clerke's shoulder and felt the bones beneath. 'You eat plenty of fresh meat and vegetables to build yourself up. Do you hear me, Mister?'

Clerke grinned. 'Yes, Captain, I hear you.'

'We should leave by the end of this month, I think. Can you can get the *Discovery* provisioned in that time?'

'Easily, sir.'

'Good, and we've done our best with the repairs.' Cook paused and went on. 'We'll sail south to try and pick up those islands reported by Marion and Kerguelen, then use the trade winds for Van Diemen's Land, then Queen Charlotte's Sound. After that, it's the Friendly Islands and Otaheite when the adventure really begins.' He stopped once more. 'You brought letters from Lord Sandwich and Mr Banks. Was there nothing from my wife?'

'No, sir,' Clerke replied, 'I am afraid there was not.'

Chapter Sixteen

 The *Resolution* and the *Discovery* left Cape-town on the 30th of November and sailed southeast for the islands supposed to have been discovered by the French. After several days the weather turned foul; the *Resolution* lost one of her topmasts and the sheep and goats began to die. Conditions worsened and once again Fearnoughts were issued. For Cook, Gore and Clerke, this was plain sailing, but not for the newcomers, who grumbled and froze. Of these, only King and Bligh performed their duties without complaint. Williamson did as little as possible, and this did not escape Cook's sharp eye. He was the veteran and knew troublemakers from the moment they came on board. Williamson was not only lazy, he could be dangerous.

At latitude 47°, they sighted the islands where Cook made a running survey and continued southeast. It was bitterly cold and great fog banks made visibility poor. Unused to such a determined captain, King began to worry for fear of losing the *Discovery*: he kept packing the deck with his telescope. Cook watched the young officer and said: 'You are not happy, Mr King?'

'These waters are new to me, sir.'

215

'They were to me, once. I have been as far south as latitude 67°. Have no fear.'

Nevertheless, Cook found the navigation both tedious and dangerous: he kept lookouts posted for ice day and night, but there was no sign of those fearsome leviathans as yet. On Christmas eve, they picked up Kerguelen island, with its rocky hills, inlets and sounds where the gargantuan seaweed washed over the reefs where the seals and penguins lived in numbers much reduced now; since Cook's second voyage, the sealers and whalers had done their bloodthirsty work. Another running survey was made, and they left this desolate region on 30 December for Van Diemen's Land. As much sail as possible was carried, for they were a month behind schedule. The animals in 'Farmer George's zoo' continued to die. The holds became foul and the men laboured at the pumps to keep the water at bay.

Bligh's work was exemplary, but Molesworth Phillips was having trouble with his marines and Williamson continued to do as little as possible. Cook was concerned about this disaffected man: the contagion could spread. One morning in the Tasman Sea, he bailed up Phillips and the two of them went below to the animal hold, where Williamson and his men were working.

'Come on, you bastards,' Williamson was shouting over the noise of the sheep, cattle and horses, 'hurry on and don't complain to me about the stink of this floating farmyard. I've said it often and I'll say it again, bloody lunacy, that's what it is, taking a bloody zoo to sea.'

'Mr Williamson?'

The officer turned and saw the Captain. 'Sir?'

'A moment, if you please.' They moved to one side while the men mucked out the straw and manure. 'This zoo, Mr Williamson,' Cook said, 'this floating farmyard comprises animals sent by His Majesty the King to be presented to the Chiefs of the Polynesian Islands.'

'It's just the smell, sir. It's foul down here.'

Cook considered this unattractive man. 'I'm aware of it. We're all aware of it. We'll all be glad when the animals reach their destination. In the meantime, Mister, I expect loyalty from all my officers, and I find it singularly lacking in you.'

'Sir?'

'Do you hear that, Mister?'

'Aye, aye, sir.'

As Williamson turned away, Cook faced Phillips. 'Come with me, Mr Phillips, I wish to talk with you.'

'Really, sir?'

'Aye, really.' Cook mounted the companion way and the young officer followed. On the deck where the breeze was fresh, he continued. He gazed steadily at the young finely bred face and the clear blue eyes: such a different background from his own. 'I have sailed with some shoddy marines in my time: some slack, unwashed, ill-disciplined marines; but yours, sir, are the worst I have ever sailed with. I had thought, Mr Phillips, that as the months passed, there might be some trace, some evidence of an attempt to smarten these gentlemen, but, on the contrary, they decline daily. In short, sir, they are rabble, barely worthy of the animal hold. If they do not improve immediately, immeasurably, I shall promote Sergeant Gibson to have you replaced.'

'But Captain, my commission was legally purchased.'

'Not from me, sir. Not from me.'

By the 10th of February 1777, they were at their old
anchorage in Queen Charlotte's Sound. Clerke came
aboard and Cook learned he had lost another man
overboard – otherwise all the crew were well. Clerke
had put on some weight, which made him look less
fragile, and his spirits were high. Cook recalled the
slack Furneaux and once again blessed his good fortune
in having Clerke whose seamanship was beyond
criticism.

Cook went ashore with Gore, Clerke, King and
Webber. Although the gardens were overgrown with
weeds and creepers, they gave up some potatoes and
pumpkins. As usual the supply of wild celery and
scurvy grass was plentiful. They climbed the hill and
looked out over the strait. Cook recalled the days of
Banks and Solander with their incessant collecting and
the disputes over going ashore at the most unlikely
places. Those were good times, he missed Banks more
than he thought. His thoughts turned to Elizabeth, had
the baby been born yet? The journals must be published
now. He hoped Mr Cadell was enjoying some success.
On the previous voyage Furneaux had lost some men to
the Maori cannibals: no doubt they would be expecting
revenge, but he would have no part in that. What was
down, was done, and they had to keep the friendship of
the natives, wherever they journeyed.

The ships were re-provisioned with all the fresh
vegetables they could get. The leaks on the *Resolution*
caulked once more, and they left the Sound on the 25th

of February for Tonga and the Society Islands.

This time, it was the winds that were against them. When they expected westerlies, they got easterlies, and on many days the gales and squalls blew from all points of the compass. The sailing was tedious and the going slow. Cook thought he knew the winds in this part of the world, but it seemed the year 1777 was different. They were well behind schedule now and, to cap it off, he felt liverish and rheumaticky; for all the vicissitudes of the first two ventures, this seemed to be the most unpleasant voyage yet. As they laboured north, Cook became anxious, time was out of joint. The cattle were starving and the rain squalls seemed endless. At last on the 28th of April, the day dawned fine and they sighted the reefs and palm-lined beaches of Tonga. The men lined the rails and gave a cheer as the canoes came out and the sound of singing drifted towards them. Gore and Clerke were delighted: this was more like it.

There was plenty of feed and the cattle were taken ashore. Gore and Bligh made successful arrangements for trading as the islands were rich in fish, coconuts and all kinds of vegetables. King and Webber set up observatory tents while Cook paid his respects to Finau, King of Tonga and 153 islands. The natives were making arrangements for a series of festivities. Cook had been here twice before and he was pleased to be remembered so cordially. It was good to stretch one's legs on the beaches, eat ashore and lie in the sun. The monotonous days of tacking and beating against the foul winds were quickly forgotten. Even Cook relaxed, but despite the warmth of the weather, his rheumatic pains persisted.

It was obvious right from the start that the pilfering and thievery was on a scale that made even the Tahitians appear honest. The carpenter lost some of his tools, clothing disappeared and cutlery was filched; it seemed nothing was safe. Phillips even had the buttons cut from his uniform. The Tongans made the pickpockets of East London look like novices.

On the other hand, there were large presents of food, continuous entertainment and great friendliness. The Tongans took great pride in boxing and wrestling. The native men and women were big and strong, and the ships' companies were treated nightly to exciting contests, while the men cheered and layed wagers. In return, Cook arranged fireworks displays and Phillips took his marines and the band through their uncertain paces. But the thieving continued and after the third week, Cook held a meeting.

'How much was stolen this time?' the Captain asked.

'I've compiled a list, sir,' Gore said. 'Mr Bligh has it.'

'I have indeed, sir. Almost everyone has lost something.' He passed the list over to Cook who read carefully. Something over fifty items had been taken.

'Do these people always steal?' Phillips asked.

Bligh looked heavenward as Gore answered: 'It's a game they play – all over Polynesia.'

Clerke spoke: 'Those wretches have been on board my ship. They've stolen all four of our cats and left the rats.'

The men laughed, but Cook, frowning, pored over the list.

'It's childish and irritating, I know,' Gore said, 'but we'll never stamp it out.'

'I disagree, Mr Gore,' Cook said as he looked up. 'I also take issue with your use of the word, "game".'

'I think you know what I mean, sir.'

'It, sir, is not a game, and I will not tolerate it any

longer. These devils have been at it three weeks now.'

'But the natives are generous, sir. You can't deny that.'

'If they are generous, that's their affair. All I know is that we are losing our inventory. May I remind you all that we are on the King's business, not some holiday. And stealing is a crime in anyone's book.' He turned to Bligh. 'Is it true that a thief was caught on board?'

'Yes, sir. He tried to steal some chickens, and when they clucked too loudly he grabbed them. And we grabbed him.'

The officers grinned this time, until they realised that Cook was not amused. 'Tomorrow he will be taken ashore and be publicly flogged.'

John Gore could not believe it, after Otaheite. 'Flogged, sir?'

'That is what I said, Mr Gore. Flogged. One dozen lashes. May I remind you that our own crew would get more.'

'But, sir – these people – we've never flogged natives before.'

'Which is why these thefts go on.'

'But they won't understand.'

'I intend to make them, to further their education. I intend to keep order. Twelve lashes, Mr Bligh.'

'Aye, aye, sir.'

The next morning, a huge crowd gathered on the white sand of the beach. The marines stood in line; the kettle drums rolled and the officers and men stood to attention. The sun was hot and sweat dripped down their threadbare uniforms. Gore could not believe what was happening; it was like some ghastly nightmare. The Tongan was tied to a punishment block and the Master at Arms took up the cat. The drum roll ended and Cook spoke: 'Inform them of the sentence, Sergeant Gibson. Tell them the reason, and tell them that all thieves and miscreants will be severely punished from now on.'

Gibson translated to the impassive crowd. The Master stepped forward and commenced to flog. As the cat bit into his back, the Tongan screamed with pain. Gore and Cook were startled; not so much by the man's screams but by the laughter of the crowd. These people were not like the Tahitians.

The thieving continued: the punishment had had no effect whatsoever. Although King Finau and his chiefs had promised the officers protection wherever they went, goods and equipment went missing. Muskets were now being stolen and two of Cook's men were attacked and robbed. Even William Bligh had his firearm taken, despite the fact that Cook had warned all his officers to take extreme care. When the thieving involved the ships' furnishings, tools and equipment, Cook became desperate to find an effective punishment. What should he do? He knew that John Gore was correct when he said it seemed to be the habit of all Polynesians. The King and his chiefs had been presented with their horses and cattle, but still the robbery – for that is what it was – went on. Although he detested violence, Cook was being driven to it. Clerke had hit on the idea of shaving the culprits' heads, but this strategy was only partly successful. By the end of the second month, Cook found himself ordering more floggings: ears were cropped, natives put in irons and men's arms slashed with knives. All to little avail. When several of the chiefs were siezed as hostages, Cook thought it may have the same effect as it had in Otaheite. But it did not. All it succeeded in doing was corroding the goodwill which had been built up over the years.

Another attack and robbery occurred, this time two of the men from the *Resolution* were badly hurt. Bligh was the first on the scene with Gibson who questioned the villagers; they said nothing. The attackers could not be found. By the time Cook and Gore arrived the natives were sullen. Phillips and the marines were standing around helplessly, Gore was apologetic and Bligh, for once, was no help. The late afternoon was muggy, the sky thundery as the Europeans and Polynesians faced each other. Cook made up his mind.

'Right,' he said, 'I will not allow these attacks on my men. They have been warned. Tell them, Gibson, I am having the entire village burnt to the ground.' Gibson hesitated. 'Tell them, Sergeant.'

Gore stepped forward but stopped when Cook stared at him. Flaming torches were thrown into the grass huts, the roofs fell in as the huts were razed to the ground. The natives screamed and the children cried, the heat was so intense that the native dogs slunk down into the undergrowth. As he walked away, Cook said over his shoulder: 'Sergeant Gibson and you, Mr Gore, will stay and supervise this punishment. I do not want a stick left standing.'

Chapter Seventeen

John Gore was worried. He had known Cook for over six years, and thought he was as close to him as any man – apart from Charles Clerke. Unlike most naval captains, Cook had avoided using the cat and, while he was a disciplinarian, he rarely resorted to violence. Gore recalled Cook's treatment of Gibson when he had deserted in Otaheite and his humane attitude toward the blacks at Botany Bay. He had also been more than understanding of the men when they first called at Matavai Bay. Gore knew that Joseph Banks admired and loved Cook, as did Sir Hugh Palliser. What would they have thought of Cook's conduct now? Something was happening to the Captain, but Gore could not explain it.

William Bligh was not so concerned about the burning of the native village; he was thinking about efficiency. He could not forget the episode off Cape Verdes, the work on the ship at the Deptford yard and the ineptitude of Lieutenant Phillips and the marines. Bligh had always considered the Captain as a hero among navigators, an efficient seaman, but this was obviously not so. There were two Arctic winters to come, and those in dangerous, unknown seas. Thanks to Cook's oversights the *Resolution* was in a perilous condition. Clerke was manifestly unwell and the Captain had failed to cope with the depredations of the savages. Of two things, Bligh was sure: discipline and efficiency, Captain Cook had failed on both counts. It was an unhappy group of officers who sailed for Otaheite on the 17th of July 1777. All Gore could hope for was that the familiar shore and climes of those islands would improve his Captain's disposition.

During this westerly passage, the winds were less unkind and they reached Matavai Bay on the 23rd of August. As they anchored, Cook and Gore gazed at the shoreline and the canoes racing out to greet them. As the men hung from the rigging the enticing smells wafted across the clear, blue waters of the lagoon; and the smoke spiralled from fires high in the mountains. Cook and Gore took this in and their spirits lifted.

'Signal to *Discovery*, Mr Gore,' Cook said. 'Select a safe anchorage. I intend to winter here.' Gore stood still, a smile on his face. 'Send it, Mr Gore.'

'Aye, aye, sir.' Despite his joy at being back, Gore was apprehensive; he hoped to God the thievery had abated but he knew that was most unlikely.

An observatory was set up at Fort Venus, a garden dug and vegetables planted. The *Resolution's* damaged mast was repaired and the inevitable re-caulking commenced. The last of the animals were landed – not the least of these were horses. Clerke came over to the *Resolution* and he and Cook watched the operation from the rail.

'How's your health, Charlie?' Cook asked.

'I am much improved, sir.'

'Would you care for a spot of horse-riding?'

Clerke grinned: 'I most certainly would.'

'Right you are, then. But first, we have to present them to the King.'

The crowd on the beach was vast, headed by King Tu and his chiefs. The Tahitian girls were as beautiful as ever: old friendships were re-established and new ones made. Gore had already seen Parita and Gibson had found his girl. Bligh watched all this and it seemed to him it would not be long before desertion would be in the air. He wondered how the Captain would cope with that. Cook stood on the foreshore, pleased by the welcome. He turned to Gore saying:

'Tell the King and chiefs that the horses are presents from King George of the United Kingdom.'

Gore translated and Tu and the chiefs were delighted. When the cattle and sheep had been presented, Clerke spoke up:

'Would you also tell the King that the Captain and I will demonstrate the generosity of the King of England, by galloping these fine animals up and down. In other words, stage a race. Is that right, sir?'

Cook smiled. 'That is correct, Mr Clerke.'

They each cantered off to a distant point up the beach, where the surf broke on the reef. Gibson dropped a handkerchief and they rode as hard as they could. The salt air was clean and bracing and Cook remembered his riding on the moors and the King's estate. Clerke rode strongly ahead, the crowd yelled as they pulled up in a shower of sand. The Captain laughed as he dismounted but he turned to see Clerke double up in a terrible spasm of coughing. Gore and King dashed forward and the young Commander was taken to the *Resolution* in the longboat. As the men rowed over the bay, Cook prayed it was not serious, for if Charlie Clerke were to die he would be losing his best friend.

Clerke was stripped to the waist and examined by Surgeon Anderson. Cook stood close by: Anderson had been with him on the previous voyage, and he had every faith in the man.

'When did you first start to cough like that?' Anderson asked.

'Months ago. Before we left New Zealand.'

'Any blood?'

'On occasions.'

'You can dress, Captain,' the Surgeon said. 'It's consumption. But I expect you guessed.'

'Yes.'

'From the prison?' Cook asked.

'Very likely,' Anderson replied.

'Don't be upset,' Clerke said as he tried to smile. 'I'll survive.'

Cook did not share his confidence. 'I wish to God we could send you home. But it's not possible. I fear for what might happen when we sail north, to the Arctic cold.'

'It could be fatal,' Anderson said.

'What nonsense,' Charles Clerke broke in. 'Don't be gloomy. I intend to reach a ripe and venerable old age.'

Cook turned away. *A ripe and venerable old age.* He wondered about that, and his own prospects, too.

Bligh watched the sailors and the Tahitian women with interest. It seemed to him that discipline was totally lacking: almost every man, including Lieutenant Gore, seemed to have his girl, and that, Bligh considered, was totally reprehensible. No officer should consort with a female savage. He was dismayed that Cook should permit such a situation. Only Molesworth Phillips seemed unable to make a liaison, and this gave Bligh some comfort. As for the young Master, he would spend his time usefully – collecting botanical specimens. There would be no fleshly indulgences for him.

Bligh searched along the beach while the sailors fished and ogled the girls. He carried several shrubs and put them by the longboat. He saw Williamson approaching and wondered if he could avoid him, but there was nowhere to go.

'I didn't know you were a naturalist.'

'I've developed an interest.'

Williamson sat on the gunwale of the longboat and ran his hands through his untidy hair. Bligh noticed this his uniform was unkempt and grimy. 'One needs something to pass the days. How much longer do you think we shall remain in these waters?' Bligh stood tall and erect. 'Like you, Mr Williamson, I do as I'm told. I think you should ask the Captain.'

The officer pursued the subject. 'I'm asking you as navigator. Is it not too late to foray north this year to the Arctic?'

Bligh became evasive. 'The Captain must know best.'

'Do you believe that.'

Bligh wished the man would go away. 'In truth, I don't know what to believe. It's clear we've long since lost our passage and the trade winds.'

'Ah,' Williamson replied. 'And Cook is apparently unconcerned. Like you, I'm disappointed in the man.'

Bligh stared. 'I didn't say that, sir, nor will I ever say it. So have a care what you ascribe to me.' He walked off down the beach, whatever mistakes the Captain had made, he would have no part in such disaffection.

That night Cook studied the charts in his cabin. He had before him Muller's map of the Russian discoveries and the routes taken by Bering and Chirikov. He studied the bays, sounds and rivers carefully. There were many islands, far more than in the southern ocean. Although navigation in the north would be far more difficult, it was thought that the ice did not drift as far as it did in the Antarctic. His finger traced latitude 66°: was there a passage? This time, would there be a positive outcome? His epitaph. Then there was Charlie. Jem Burnley was obviously capable, but to lose Clerke was unthinkable. His thoughts turned to the Tongans, the pilfering and the assaults. The Tahitians had not given up their old habits – Clerke had again adopted the method of shaving heads in an attempt to use ridicule. Cook rolled up the charts and lay in his cot. For the first time he found himself wondering whether he should have taken Banks' advice. And what of Elizabeth? Was she right? His cabin was stuffy, he rose, opened the window and listened to the sounds from the *marae*. He thought of the jolly evenings in the great cabin of *Endeavour*, the heaps of specimens and Banks holding forth. For all his faults, that man was excellent company. Cook went back to his cot again, listened to the waters but he could not sleep. For all his faults . . . and what of his own?

Next day when Cook went down to inspect the hold, he found Bligh, Phillips, Williamson and a marine involved in a heated argument.

'I don't care what excuses you give,' Bligh was saying, 'I've sent for the Captain.'

'Which was not necessary,' Williamson replied, 'you take too much on yourself, Mister.'

Good God, Cook thought, what was it now? Could

not one day proceed without trouble? 'What is it?' he asked.

'There's no trouble, sir,' Phillips said, but he was unconvincing.

'Just a minor theft.' Williamson was equally untrustworthy.

It was Bligh now: 'I don't think so.'

Cook was getting sick of the prevarication. 'Will you tell me what has happened?' Only Bligh was worth talking to. 'You tell me, Mister.'

Phillips had hold of the marine's arm. 'It's nothing, sir.'

Cook felt his blood rising. 'I, sir, shall determine what is nothing. Mr Bligh?'

'The ship's goat, sir.'

'Where is it, Mr Bligh?'

'Precisely, sir. It's been stolen.'

'Been what?'

'Some natives last night,' Phillips said.

'Stole the goat?' Cook ground his teeth. 'After the sheep and the cattle and the horses we've given them, they came aboard and stole it?'

Bligh nodded. 'Yes, sir.'

'And this is what you call a minor theft, Mr Williamson. Who was on watch?'

Phillips pushed the bedraggled marine forward. 'This man, sir.'

'He was asleep,' said Bligh.

Cook considered the little man from the slums with his bad teeth, his torn uniform and his vacant eyes. 'Clap him in irons, Mr Phillips.'

'What sir?'

Cook stepped up close. 'Are you hard of hearing, Lieutenant? I said, clap him in irons. He will have a

230

dozen lashes a day for the next three days.'

The marine started to shake, and Phillips tried to protest. 'But sir . . .'

Cook was shouting now. 'God's truth, man, you heard me.' He swung around and faced Williamson. 'You were the duty officer, and you, sir, will help me rectify this. Get both ship's cutters alongside.'

Williamson tried one last throw. 'But sir.'

'I said, get the ship's cutters. Move. Move.'

They were on deck now and Cook was angry.

'I want three parties of marines, Mr Bligh, all to be armed. Lieutenant Gore and Sergeant Gibson are to act as interpreters.'

'Neither is aboard, sir. I think they're off somewhere with their lady friends.'

'You know the answer to that, Mr Bligh. Find them.' Cook walked away, his fists clenched and face white.

Lieutenant Phillips and his squad of armed marines were in the longboat with Cook, who carried his double barrelled shotgun; and the cutter followed with Williamson and armed sailors. The Captain said nothing and Phillips was apprehensive. But Williamson was excited: some action at last. When they reached the beach, Bligh, Gore and Gibson were waiting for them. Cook stepped out and said: 'Make it known that I intend to recover the goat. I want it back by noon. If not, I am going to burn their canoes.'

'Sir, Gore argued, 'the canoes are their livelihood. Without them . . .'

Gibson also tried to reason: 'Could we take a hostage instead, sir?'

'Neither of you will argue with me. I said the canoes will be burnt. After that, their villages if necessary. I'll put the whole island to the torch if the stolen animal is

not returned.' Gore and Gibson turned away and began
to pass the message on. The Lieutenant's heart was
heavy as he spoke to his innocent friends. It seemed to
him they were going down a path that had only one
end.

The goat was not returned by noon and the destruc-
tion of the canoes began. Williamson and his men
swung their axes, smashed the ornately carved prows
and stove in the timbers. The craft were destroyed
where they lay – in the villages or on the beach. The
men from the slums and villages of England found the
work enjoyable. As the day wore on, huts were put to
the torch and, by evening, the shoreline glowed with
fire and the women and children had fled into the hills.
Cook was waiting by the longboat when Williamson
and his sweating, grimy men returned.

'Twenty houses burnt, sir.' Williamson said. 'And
more than a dozen canoes. Do you want us to go on.'
Cook considered what he had done: there was no
health in it. 'Sir,' Williamson asked, 'what are your
orders?'

'We'll return to the ship, Mr Williamson.'

It was Lieutenant King's watch and he paced the
quarter deck. The fires still smouldered and the smoke
drifted north to the mountains. King wondered how
many innocent people had lost their canoes and
houses. Cook had not turned out to be the man he
expected, nor had the voyage, it was now a sad, dour
affair. Where was the man whom Mr Banks had told him
about? The compassionate sea captain, who understood
the ways of natives and who was curious about natural
history. It now seemed to King that Cook was like any
other officer in the Royal Navy. He heard a footstep and
turned, it was Cook.

'All quiet, sir.'

'Go below, Mr King, and have your supper. I'll take the watch.'

'Aye, aye, sir. Thank you, sir.'

Cook gazed toward the shore; what else could he have done? He became aware of Gore. 'Yes, Lieutenant?'

'What are your orders for the morning, sir.' Gore's voice was as cold as ice.

'You think the action is too severe, don't you?' Cook said. 'You think this is over a trifle?' When Gore gave no answer, Cook went on: 'It's refusal to recognise my authority. If I back down on this, there will be no end to it.'

'That goat does not even give milk, sir.'

'I thought, Mr Gore, that you might understand. It's not about the goat. Do you think what happened today gave me pleasure?'

'I hope not, Captain.'

Cook looked very hard at his officer. 'Do not presume too far on our friendship, Mr Gore.'

When Cook had gone Gore regretted what he had said, he stood looking blankly at Matavai Bay. Then he heard a sound – the bleat of a goat. He looked down at the water to see a canoe with the animal in the prow.

Clerke entered Cook's cabin and shut the door.

'Well, we won,' the Captain said. 'I know even you think I was wrong, and I regret the losses they suffered, but it was a matter of respect and authority.'

Clerke was not convinced. 'They'll respect us now, sir, but they won't love us.'

'Perhaps, Charlie, you can heal things.'

'How?'

'It's time to venture north: we've already missed one

Arctic summer. I'm afraid of what the ice and the cold might do to you. You could stay here.' Clerke was surprised as Cook came to the point. 'Resign your command and rest here until I come back for you.'

Clerke thought and was tempted. 'I could say here in the sun.'

'And Gore could take your ship.'

'It would create too much trouble.'

'Damn the trouble, Charlie, I'll handle that.'

'No, sir. You'd have wholesale desertions – it's in the air. Half the crews ache to spend their lives here, and who can blame them? I'm grateful, sir, but I'll sail.'

Cook knew he had no choice. 'As usual Charlie, you are quite correct.'

On the 7th of December 1777, the two ships weighed anchor and left Otaheite for the north, and the most perilous part of the voyage.

Chapter Eighteen

By the 7th of March, the ships were cruising off the coast of New Albion in North America. Because the winter was late that year, the weather was foul with gales, squalls and fogs. The wooded coast appeared formidable and Cook was hard pressed to find a safe place to refit and obtain wood and water. Day after day, they were obliged to stand off the coast in the westerlies. Hail and sleet drove in, the vegetables rotted, the work was hard and the men became irritable. Despite the maps of the Russians, these were unknown waters and the fogs made navigation a nightmare for Bligh and Cook. The Captain's bones cracked in the cold and his legs and back ached – he found himself envying the younger man who seemed unaffected by the weather and the uncertainty. One day, Cook thought, William Bligh will be a great navigator. Then at the end of March, they discovered a large sound west of a large island. Cook called this sound Nootka, and they made plans to stay in the harbour for a month.

The trees were immense: talls, barkless and growing to the water's edge. The supplies of firewood and water were good, but the wind and rain kept the men cold and uncomfortable. The Indians put off in their canoes as soon as the two ships were sighted. These indigenes were flat-faced, swarthy and filthy. Cook was reminded of the natives of Tierra del Fuego seven years ago. Were they of the same race? But these people were aggressive, expert at fishing and cutting timber. They hunted whales and were obsessed with anything made of metal. It was obvious that the Indians of Nootka had encountered Europeans before. The Spanish perhaps? Anything moveable was stolen with great dexterity.

Two days after they left Nootka Sound, a hurricane blew up. The *Resolution* sprang a leak and for several days they were unable to observe the coastline. Bligh issued Fearnoughts and an extra tot of rum. As they inched north, they saw huge mountains and ice-capped peaks but there was no sign of an inlet. In all his voyages, Cook could not remember being so tired: even the simplest of tasks was an effort, he was losing concentration and felt the cold so badly he slept fully clothed under the grimy blankets. Each day, he watched the *Discovery* astern and worried about Clerke. What was this damp and cold doing to him? This was indeed, a most terrible place, there was a sense of evil here not present in the Antarctic.

When yet another fog came down, the *Discovery* lost sight of the *Resolution*. Clerke and Burnley stood on the forecastle and listened to the muffled sound of a cannon. By now, Clerke was coughing continually, his handkerchief stained with blood. 'As soon as the fog clears, sir,' Burnley said, 'I'll send a signal to the Captain.'

'Saying what, Mr Burnley?'

'Saying that you cannot continue, sir?'

'Don't talk daft, Jem. We have to go on. Around the next headland, behind the next bay, may be the

Northwest Passage. That's worth £20,000 and fame. Do you not realise that?'

'The money's no good if you aren't alive to enjoy it.'

Clerke drew himself up. 'I have no intention in dying yet awhile, Mister. We'll send no signals, but I will, if you insist, go below and try to get warm.'

In his bed, Clerke found himself counting the days. He could only count them out from the Sandwich Islands, not back, as this time there seemed no end to the passage.

On board the *Resolution,* the leaks grew worse and the hold was now half full of freezing water. Cook and Bligh looked over the dismal scene as the men worked the pumps.

'The hull must be riddled, sir,' Bligh said. 'The water's coming in faster than we can pump it out.'

'There are no more pumps,' the Captain replied. 'We need the others amidships.'

Gore came down and looked. 'I'll send the *Discovery* a signal asking for theirs.'

'You do that, Mr Gore.' Cook turned back to Bligh who was helping with the pumps now. 'When I get home, Mr Bligh, there are certain people in a certain shipyard I intend to see indicted.'

'Yes, sir. I hope so.'

'Do you believe there is a Northwest Passage, Mr Bligh?'

'I'm sure we would all like to believe it, sir.'

'I said, Mister, do *you* believe it?'

Bligh took a chance – he would speak his mind. 'Through the ice, across seventy thousand degrees of longitude to the Atlantic? My heart wants me to believe it, sir, but my mind won't let me.'

Cook made no reply.

For once luck was with them, and they were able to

put into another sound. The Indians, dirty and smelly, came out in droves and climbed up on to the ships, with drawn knives. The men unsheathed their cutlasses and drove them off. The natives here were more like Eskimos than the people of Nootka. The *Resolution* was careened on the icy beach and they found that the oakum had gone from most of her seams. Cook spent some time with Clerke and was relieved to find him in good spirits but, still, very thin. They decided to go as far north as latitude 65°, and then west to the coast of Asia. Clerke said he was more than willing to venture into these high latitudes and that his crew was in excellent shape. The Captain took fresh heart in all of this and they left the sound on 17 May in uncertain, threatening weather.

It was several days later when a large inlet opened before them. The mountains climbed high and the forests were silent and impenetrable. The two ships anchored and Cook consulted with his officers. The waterway was huge – their best hope yet. Even though Cook had told Clerke he must stay in the estuary, the young commander was all for exploring it.

'Who knows, sir?' Clerke said. 'It may go through to Baffin Bay. It may be navigable. And if it is, we shall have achieved what no other men have done.'

Cook then asked Gore, Bligh, King and Williamson, who were all in favour. Although the weather was freezing, there was still no sign of ice.

After the days of sailing, the inlet became too narrow to enable the *Resolution* to put about. They anchored and Cook and Gore considered the situation. There was no sign of any settlement and it looked as though a glacier or ice pack lay ahead. Once again, Cook conferred with his officers in the great cabin. 'Two hundred leagues, and now a field of pack ice,' Cook said. 'Is it the Northwest Passage?'

'What else could it be?' Gore asked.

'A river,' Bligh replied. 'It could simply be a river.'

But King was hopeful. 'Surely not.'

'Already the water tastes less of salt,' Bligh said.

'Mr Bligh,' Williamson observed, 'always manages to look on the gloomy side.'

'Mr Bligh is entitled to his doubts.' Cook answered. 'I think before we go further, it's time to find out.'

A week later, Bligh sat in the longboat with the pinnace close behind. The cold and the silence were terrible; the trees were smaller now and the ice cliffs rose around them. He took up a drinking mug, leaned over the gunwale and drank; the water cut his lips like a razor and tasted brackish. The men rested on their oars. 'Come on, you lot,' Bligh said. 'There's still a long way to go.' But he now knew that the chances of this being a passage were slim.

Two days on, the way was narrower and a fog was down. A film of ice lay on the water and several of the men were complaining of frostbite. Bligh knew this was most unlikely, but he understood their weariness and exhaustion: they had served him well. Once more, he dipped the mug into the freezing water and tasted. It was fresh. Then the fog cleared to reveal a glacier and snow capped mountains.

'Ship oars,' Bligh said. 'Ship oars.' The men rested a moment, then the boat was turned around for the long trip back.

Doubt and uncertainty now began to plague Cook. How far north should he go? What of the condition of his ship? And what of Clerke? he sat down at his desk and wrote in his journal:

The gulf of hope has turned into a river of disappointment. Now we must turn back, head south, before we are hemmed in by the frozen ice and the Arctic winter. If there is a Northwest Passage, we shall not find it this year . . . The ship leaks constantly. The masts and sails are in poor condition. Certain fat profiteers in England have set our lives at risk, and by God, if they were here, I would have them aloft on their worm-ridden timber. It is becoming urgent to find a safe anchorage to repair and rest, for this ship is as exhausted and discouraged as we are.

Cook knew he would have to pull himself together. He made a decision to survey the coast of the Alaskan peninsula and the Aleutian Islands. At least, he would fill in the gaps of the Russians and the Spanish. He continued north along the coast to latitude 65°, turned east and landed on the coast of Asia. Here, the country was treeless and desolate and the prospects unpromising. They went north once more to latitude 70°, and here the first pack ice was seen. There was no choice now but to abandon the search, turn south and return to the Sandwich Islands.

The course was set for Unalaska in the Aleutian Islands and they groped south through a labyrinth of reefs, shoals and islands of this sprawling archipelago. At Unalaska, they found a safe harbour, beached the *Resolution* and once again set about the tedious task of re-caulking. The rotten vegetables were replenished with wild berries and the fishing was good on those barren shores. Russian traders were about – big, fearsome men clad in furs, who lived off and on with the Aleuts. Although they were generous with their drink and food, nothing of any consequence was learnt from them concerning a passage in the north. They let Cook take copies of their charts and he gave them a letter for Lord Sandwich to be sent on from Siberia. Nothing but the most basic of conversation was possible, and as he watched the Russian, Ismailov, grin and stuff the letter into his purse, Cook wondered if the message would ever reach London. He doubted it.

Charles Clerke's cough was no better but at least it was no worse and Lieutenant Burnley was more than capable. After a discussion with the officers of the two ships it was decided not to winter in Kamchatka on the Asiatic coast, but return to the Sandwich Islands. All of them longed for the tropics, the native girls and the fine food. Cook also thought of the generous reception the islanders had given him. Hawaii was the place to recuperate and refit for the next foray to the north.

On the 26th of November 1777, the *Resolution* and the *Discovery* were off the palm-fringed coast of the island of Maui in the Sandwich Island Group.

Chapter Nineteen

 After enduring six months of sleet, foul winds, fogs, uncertain landfalls and cliffs of ice, the Hawaiian Islands were paradise. As they stood off Maui, they saw steep volcanic mountains, ravines and waterfalls, surf beaches and the thatched huts of the villages. The canoes came out to greet them but Cook was not to be hurried in going ashore. He issued two sets of orders: one was that there was to be no unauthorised trading with the natives; and the other concerned women. No female was to be admitted to either ship and any man found to be suffering from venereal disease would suffer the direst of consequences.

To the frustration and despair of the men, Cook spent the next seven weeks cruising off the coasts of the islands. All the trading was done from the canoes, and the women were kept away as the Captain searched for a suitable anchorage. However, the *Resolution* was again leaking badly and the *Discovery* was also in need of urgent repairs. The ships lost sight of each other for thirteen days and it became obvious that Cook could not stay at sea for much longer. Finally, a safe anchorage was found at Kealakekua Bay. As Cook and his men gazed from the rail, they saw that this was a big settlement with large huts, extensive gardens, temples and totems. The canoes were so many and the natives so pressing that Cook ordered muskets and cannon to be fired to keep them off. Curiously, the natives did not seem to be very frightened.

In the afternoon, Cook, Gore, Clerke and Gibson went ashore to pay their respects to the King and the priests. Cook was well aware that the Hawaiians had their gods and that theirs was the most highly organised religion in the Pacific. The men hung from the rigging whistling and cheering at the Hawaiian women as they waved and flaunted themselves in the canoes. It seemed to Gore that they were far more licentious than the Tahitians and he foresaw great problems with thievery and desertion. But Cook stepped into the longboat, unsmiling in his best uniform and oblivious of the laughing and beckoning sirens of the South Seas.

As the boat drew near the beach, they saw that the crowd was vast – bigger than any at Otaheite. Then as they heard the strange chanting, Cook felt the men's unease. The chanting grew louder and the echoes drifted through the mountains where, it was said, the Gods lived. What was about to happen? Clerke put his hand on the butt of his pistol, but Cook sat in the prow, impassive, neither looking right nor left. There seemed to be a tumult on the beach now, and Clerke admired his Captain's courage. The oars creaked in the rowlocks and the boat grounded on the beach. When Captain Cook stepped on to the beach, the great crowd prostrated on the ground, echoing the chant: *'Lono . . . Lono . . . Lono . . .'*

Cook stood on the beach, uncertain of what to do. Then he saw an old priest who was carrying a large red cloth; with the priest was a proud, old man, whom Cook guessed was the King. He made up his mind; gesturing to Clerke, Gore and Gibson, he advanced up the beach.

They learned that the King was called, Kalaniopu, and the priest, Koa. The totems were the most fearsome and elaborate the men had ever seen and the natives were extremely devout. Everywhere Cook went he was followed by the same chant. It seemed to him that he was being treated like some god, and this unnerved him.

It seemed it was impossible to keep the women off the ships. They were everywhere: in the canoes, in the seas, hanging off the cables and anchor chains; climbing aboard, sneaking below and enticing the men. Young men and children boarded the ships and the thievery began, it was chaos. Despite all this, King managed to put up an observatory, Gibson established a trading post, a stockade was built and the ships careened. In the village, preparations were being made for a great ceremony.

Before the chanting crowd, Koa presented Cook with a pig and coconuts. Then after he had draped the Captain with a large red cloth, he conducted him to a ceremonial place of human skulls and hideous images. Clerke, Gore and Gibson watched with fascination, as the crowd lay on the ground. What was the purpose of this? The ceremony was long and Cook found it embarrassing. The pig was slaughtered and prayers and incantations were droned. He was asked to sit between two large totems; then he was given baked hog and fruit and was rubbed with coconut. All the while, the crowd were chanting the word, *Lono*. Suddenly the ceremony was at an end, Cook responded by giving the King and the priest mirrors and other presents.

All of them found the afternoon exhausting: Cook was given more pig and kava and the crowd showed something close to adoration. Koa and King Kalaniopu kept bowing deeply and another priest who seemed to be attending Cook personally, accompanied him to the longboat. When they were a reasonable distance from the shore, Cook removed his three-cornered hat and, wiping his forehead, looked at his officers, but said nothing. This was something none of them had counted on. When they got to the *Resolution,* Cook took aside Clerke, Gore and Gibson. 'If you have the time,' he said, 'I would like to see you in my cabin.'

'Well, Gibson,' Cook said, 'What do you make of all that?'

The marine rubbed his chin. 'The King is the frail, old man, Kalaniopu, and the priest is Koa.'

'Samuel, I'm aware of that. Who or what is *Lono?*'

'I think it's you, sir.'

'Me?'

'Yes, sir. From what I can understand of the lingo, I think they've been waiting for someone like you.'

'What do you mean, waiting?'

'I don't know, sir.'

'You must mean something,' Cook insisted. 'You must have a reason for saying it.'

Gibson hesitated. 'I don't want to sound stupid, sir.'

'Tell me what the devil you mean.'

'Not the devil, sir,' Gibson answered. 'Certainly not him. Maybe the opposite.'

245

'What, then?'

'Like a God, sir.'

'A God?' The men were silent.

'I told you it would make me sound stupid, sir.'

'Let me think,' Cook said.

The marine got up. 'Will that be all sir?'

'Yes, Samuel you may go. But I don't want this mentioned, do you understand?'

'Aye, aye, sir.'

When Gibson had gone, Cook said: 'It's nonsense, of course.'

'Maybe,' Gore replied. 'But we've not encountered this behaviour in any other island group.'

Clerke was still worried. 'It makes me uneasy.'

'Nonsense,' But Cook, too was apprehensive.

'I think we should be careful,' Gore said.

Clerke tried to persuade his Captain. 'Why not find somewhere else?'

'That would be absurd. This is the only safe anchorage in the whole island of Hawaii. I want the ships repaired. I want fresh stores and water. When that is done, we'll think about leaving.'

Samuel Gibson had half-guessed the truth. Cook had arrived at the time of the Hawaiian year when all warfare was forbidden: this was a time of sport and relaxation – the time of *Lono*, the God of light and peace. The natives believed that *Lono* would return from the sea, bearing gifts, and that he was divine and should be revered. Cook had been deified: he could do no wrong.

Work proceeded, and although the chief and the priest

kept the women away, the stealing continued. *Lono* was among them: the priests offered Cook every assistance, they oversaw the exploring parties and made it possible for the ships to be repaired. Whenever the girls did manage to slip aboard, the King's warriors threw them into the sea. The flow of pigs, yams, breadfruit and fish was endless. Each time Cook set foot on shore, the people threw themselves on the ground at his feet. Trees were felled for firewood, the fields dug for sweet potatoes and each day the King and the priest visited the *Resolution*. Cook responded by arranging displays of fireworks. Despite the thievery, they had never been treated so generously by any island tribes.

It became clear to John Gore that the priests were instructing their people to make offerings. King was also intrigued by the generosity: soon, he thought there would be an embarrassment of riches. He, too, learnt about the God, *Lono,* and discussed it with Clerke and Burnley. King was an observant man: he looked at the stripped gardens and bare potato fields. How would the natives survive the coming winter? They had given up most of their produce. What would happen if it were realised that the Captain was not a God? All four men agreed that the situation could become dangerous, but it seemed little could be done while they stayed in Kealakekua Bay. Charles Clerke found himself thinking about the warlike Maoris at Poverty Bay: at least that situation was clear cut. What did the Captain think about when the natives threw themselves on the ground? He consoled himself. Cook was consummate in dealing with native peoples. In all the voyages to the South Seas, they had never become involved in great bloodshed – and that was a credit to the character of the man.

At the end of January, a great feast was held. Inevitably, Cook was given pride of place with King Kalaniopu and the High Priest, Koa. All the dancing and festivities seemed to be directed toward Cook. When the singing and feasting was over, the time came for the Captain to address the King.

'Tell him' Cook said to Gore, 'that this island of Hawaii is a happy and fertile place. That his people are the fairest and most honest of all the Polynesian islands, and we have never been so welcomed.' Gore translated and the old King listened. 'They are the most generous and well mannered of their race,' Cook went on. 'You could say, but you had better not, that not in all the world are there ladies so eager to please and so determined to share their charms.'

Gore smiled and the men cheered. 'I will not put it in quite that way, sir.'

Then the King rubbed his stomach and spoke. Cook leant forward and asked: 'What is he saying, Mr Gore?'

'He is saying, sir, that his people have been generous to *Lono,* that we have spent weeks here and eaten well.'

'That we have.'

'That we have taken much from here,' Gore continued, 'the priests have demanded sacrifices for *Lono,* that the people have obeyed and are now hungry. Their farms are empty.'

King, Clerke and Bligh listened carefully, and Cook asked again 'What is he saying now?'

'The King says, sir, how soon will we leave?'

Cook was silent.

'I think our time is up,' Clerke said.

Gore bowed to the King and sat down. 'Unless I've mistaken him, sir, and I don't think I have, it's an invitation to go.'

The camps were broken up, the last of the provisions taken on board and on the 4th of February 1779, the ships departed Kealakekua Bay. To the end, the natives displayed their friendship and they were accompanied by an armada of canoes. The women wept as they waved farewell and the crowd roared. But the priests and the King watched, impassive.

Relieved to be at sea and away from the festivities of Kealakekua Bay, James Cook again sat down to write in his journal:

10th of February, 1779. We are now six days out of Hawaii. The ship is laden with fresh food and water. I intend to map the island of Maui and the remaining Sandwich Islands, then forage northward to prepare for another search for the Northwest Passage. It is hard to realise we are in our third year at sea, and the voyage perhaps only half done . . .'

There was a knock on the cabin and Bligh entered. 'The wind is rising, sir. I've close reefed the topsail.'

'Thank you, Mr Bligh. I'll be topsides presently.' Cook resumed his journal:

. . . perhaps only half done. I dare not think when I shall see England or my family again . . .'

That night, a sudden gale blew up and the sails were split; the next day it was found that the foremast was sprung. As the storm grew worse, Cook summoned his officers to the great cabin.

'Is there no way we can make the repairs at sea, sir?'; Williamson asked.

'That appears to be impossible. The foremast is next to useless. Tell him, Mr Bligh.'

The Master enjoyed lecturing Williamson. 'We have

to take down the topsails and all canvas on the topgallants. That means six sails instead of the normal twelve. All the lower masts and the foremast will have to be taken out.'

'And that,' Cook added, 'can only be done on an even keel, in a safe harbour.'

'That is correct.' Bligh knew they had no option.

Then the door opened: it was Clerke and Burnley. 'I meant you to stand off, sir,' Cook said, 'not heave to and row over in this sea.'

'I saw the masts, Captain.' Clerke was breathless and shaking.

'Then you know we have no choice, Mr Clerke. I'm putting about for Hawaii.'

Gore protested. 'Not Kealakekua Bay, sir. Not the same anchorage.'

But Cook was calm. 'It's the only safe one we know on the island.'

This time, it was Bligh. 'But is it wise, sir?'

'Wise? Who knows if it's wise, Mr Bligh? We both know it's essential.'

'The people were glad to see us go, sir. They may not welcome this.'

'You can go, Mr Bligh.'

'Bye, aye, sir.'

Cook looked around. 'You may all go, except Mr Clerke and Mr Gore.'

'Bligh means well,' Clerke said when they were alone.

'Mr Bligh will know better, when he's older, not to question orders.'

'He's concerned about Kealakekua Bay. As we all are.'

'I, too, am concerned about it,' Cook answered. 'I

have no wish to return and disadvantage their generosity. But what else is there?'

'I would rather search to leeward, sir,' said Gore, 'for some other place.'

'On half sail? In the stormy season? Please don't make me say it again. We're going back.'

The bay was empty. As Cook and his officers looked from the rail, Gore thought it possible that King Kalaniopu may have put a *tapu* on it; that would account for the silence. The foremast was taken out and floated ashore: the work was easy with no one to disturb them. King went to the land and put up his observatory; then the priests appeared and offered a house for the carpenters and sailmakers to work in. When Cook learned of this, he was much relieved.

The next morning, the King, accompanied by a fleet of canoes came out to the *Resolution*. Kalaniopu was most affable when Cook explained why he had returned. But Gore and Gibson thought his mood had changed, and the natives in the canoes were silent. Gone was the laughing and cheering; gone also was the reverence toward Cook. It was all most odd. Gore thought about trying to convince the Captain to leave, but the mast was out and it was too late now. Where were the priests and what were they doing?

In the afternoon, Cook, Gore and the marines went ashore. As they walked along the beach to inspect the work on the mast, a few groups of natives followed them. This time, no one even bowed to Cook. The day was hot and the weather thundery.

'There's been a change, sir, don't you think? Gibson was sweating in his worn uniform.

'Change?'

'For the worst, sir.'

'That may be, Samuel,' Cook said, 'it's natural enough. We did outstay our welcome.' Cook seemed calm as they walked over the sand.

Suddenly, stones were hurled, one striking a marine and Gibson swung round with his musket. 'Careful, Samuel,' he heard the Captain say. 'Stand your ground.'

The natives retreated and Cook heard the sound of laughter in the long grass. He was uncertain now and dared not risk going on. By the time they got to the boat, the crowd had come back, this time jeering and shaking their fists. More stones were thrown as they rowed back to ship. Gore and Gibson looked at the Captian, but his face was set.

In the evening, Cook and Gore stood on the quarter deck. The sunset was brilliant, the thunder clouds had gone and lights flickered on the beach. All was quiet and they looked toward the tents where the mast was being repaired. Some marines were with the carpenter, and Gore hoped they would see the night through safely.

'We want just three days,' Cook said, 'and then we can put to sea.'

Gore took a chance. 'I'm afraid for something I cannot put a name to, sir. Will you listen?'

'If I must.'

'It's what Gibson once said – the way they treated you – perhaps not as a God, but it was idolatry. Now it's derision and anger. It's as though they've decided that you are not – whatever they thought you were. I looked at those priests today and I saw more than anger, I saw hatred.'

'What is your point, Mr Gore?'

'My point, sir, is that *Lono* has had to return with a damaged ship, and in their legends I don't think *Lono* would do that. And the priests, who forced the people to give their pigs and their sweet potatoes as an offering, have been made to look foolish.'

'By me?'

'By circumstances, by their own legend and their own fervour. I think now they may want to harm you.'

'Nonsense,' Cook replied. 'Fanciful theories.'

'Then why the stones today? Returning here was a mistake.'

'Perhaps. See that the marines guard all shore parties, and take all possible precautions.' Cook left Gore alone on the quarter deck.

Cook's first act next day was to call in his officers.

'I am determined to end these attacks, and the thievery,' he said. 'The picquets will be doubled, Mr Gore.'

'Aye, aye, sir.'

'Lieutenant Phillips?'

'Yes, sir?'

'From now on,' Cook said, 'your men will load their muskets with ball, not shot.'

The young officer looked worried. 'If we shoot at them with ball, Captain, people will be killed.'

'If, sir, they attack, your duty is to kill as many as it takes to calm the situation.'

'Aye, aye, sir.'

When the officers had gone, Cook sat down to think.

This time he would exert his authority.

The carpenters and the sailmakers worked that quiet, tense day; and toward the evening, the armourer's fire tongs were stolen. There was a chase through the bush, more stone-throwing and an affray on the beach. Where was the God, *Lono,* now?

In the morning, it was discovered that the cutter had been stolen. Clerke, Gore and Bligh watched Cook as he held the frayed and cut rope in his hands.

'Why would they take the clutter? They've got their canoes.' Clerke looked ill.

'They want it for the nails, but that's not the point. Whatever reasons they have are immaterial.'

'I expect they've hidden it ashore,' Gore said. 'We'll search the villages.'

Cook did not reply and twisted the rope around his fist.

'Might I suggest, sir,' Bligh said quietly, 'that this is the gauntlet.'

'Please explain, Mr Bligh.'

'The final humiliation. We can't sail without the cutter.'

'I don't intend to sail without it.'

'It's time we taught the natives a lesson.' Bligh was hard-faced.

'I think we should remain calm, Captain,' Gore said.

'I intend to, Mr Gore. But I agree with Mr Bligh. This is a deliberate provocation – an open attempt to show their contempt. I will not have that.'

'Sir, I don't think it's provocation, that's not in their nature.'

'I don't give a tinker's cuss about their nature.' Cook turned to Bligh. 'Mr Bligh, you will take the launch and blockage the bay. No canoe goes in or out. Shoot if necessary. Get to it, Mister.'

'Aye, aye, sir.'

Cook then spoke to Gore: 'Have Mr Phillips prepare his marines. Williamson will take the skiff and stand off shore in support. You, sir, will be in charge on board. Prime the guns and have the crew standing by.'

'Where are you going, sir?'

'Ashore. I intend to take the King as hostage.'

Clerke got up. 'Sir, is that wise?'

'Look, Charlie, we've done it before. We three know this way is best. We've done it before.' He rose and touched Clerke on the shoulder. 'Come and rest. We want to get you home to England safe and sound.'

Cook walked into the village with Phillips, Gibson and the marines; and Williamson and his men lay a few yards offshore in the skiff. They heard the sound of conch shells being blown in the still morning air. Few people seemed to be about. Where were the women? Cooked glanced at Gibson.

'Walk with me, Samuel.'

'Sir, I've heard the women have been sent away, and that warriors are coming from other villages.'

'I need you to interpret my wishes to the King.' Cook wondered about Phillips. How would he acquit himself?

The village was crowded, mainly with men. Cook and his party stopped outside the King's hut, and Phillips went inside to bring Kalaniopu out. The crowd watched: they were armed now, with spears and clubs, and some of the men were wearing protective mats. There was a feeling of unease. The King appeared and Cook spoke to Phillps.

'Tell the King that I respect him and know he is innocent of the theft of the cutter. However, I must ask him to accompany me on board my ship.

To their relief, the King smiled, nodded and agreed. The crowd was huge now and Cook and the marines pushed through back to Williamson in the skiff. Gibson was wary and fell in behind Cook.

'Move ahead,' Phillips said, 'and see to the boat.'

'Sir, let me guard from behind.'

'Do as you're told, Sergeant.'

As the old King stumbled, Cook took his arm; then Kalaniopu's wife appeared with two priests. They pushed through; wrenched the King away from Cook and forced him to sit on the ground. Then the shouting rose; the crowd moved in, brandishing their spears and clubs. Cook changed his mind and called out to Phillips:

'Get your marines aboard the boat, sir. Leave the King – we cannot compel him – not without bloodshed.'

Shaking and white-faced, the young Lieutenant tried to bundle his men into the skiff where Williamson was waiting, but it seemed the crowd was out of control now. As the shouting became a roar, a man ran toward Cook with an iron spike. Stones began flying; Cook raised his musket, fired a charge of shot. A man went for Phillips who struck him down; Cook fired the second barrel and the warrior fell. Now Phillips screamed at his men who fired point blank into the mob. William-son saw all this, his men were ready with their oars in the water. He raised his gun, fired and saw the Captain raise his hand. The marines broke and ran into the sea, their boots filling as they struggled through the water.

'Put about, put about,' Williamson shouted. 'Make for the ship.'

Cook was surrounded now. Gibson fought two men off in the bloodied water; Phillips was wounded, plunged for Gibson when he fell and made for the skiff. Both were blinded by blood and water – where was Cook? In the skiff, the men dropped their oars, dragged the wounded men aboard, heard the roar and saw their Captain go down. Gibson lay speechless as the skiff was rowed out. On the lava edge, Cook fought for his life, but he was overpowered. He was stabbed in the neck, clubbed on the head, his skull split. Bloodied and beaten, he rose from the water, cried out, fell and was bludgeoned to death in the shallow waters of Kealakekua Bay.

Gore and Clerke watched the dreadful scene through their telescopes, powerless. Gore saw the skiff dragging through the water and ordered the cannons to fire; water spouted, but there was no point to it. Clerke took command, the firing stopped and awful silence fell. His grief could not be measured.

Two nights later, a priest came aboard with the Captain's bones. Cook had been given the honour of all paramount chiefs: his flesh had been scraped away, his bones burnt and preserved as sacred relics.

The yards were crossed and the flags flew at half-mast. The drums rolled and the coffin wrapped in the Union Jack. Charles Clerke read the service:

We therefore commit his body to the deep, to be turned into corruption, looking for the resurrection of the body, and the life of the world to come, through our Lord Jesus Christ.

The weighted coffin sank into the waters of the bay: the Pacific had claimed its greatest navigator.

Epilogue

Charles Clerke assumed command of the expedition and took the two ships north. He failed to find the Northwest Passage, and died of consumption on the 22nd of August, 1779.

John Gore became commander and took the ships home to the United Kingdom, arriving on the 4th of October, 1780.

Samuel Gibson died at sea, off the coast of Scotland on the 22nd of September, 1780.

William Bligh became Captain of HMS *Bounty*, and later the Governor of New South Wales.

Joseph Banks became President of the Royal Society, and one of the most eminent scientists of his century.

Elizabeth Cook outlived all her family. She burnt all the papers left by her husband and died a widow at the age of ninety-three.